T0209307

ALSO BY DOUG ZIPES

Nonfiction
Into Africa
Taking Ban on Ephedra
I Was a Target of the KGB

Fiction
Stolen Hearts (short story with Joan Zipes)
The Black Widows (a novel)
Ripples in Opperman's Pond (a novel)
Not Just a Game (a novel)
Bear's Promise (a novel)

Memoir
Damn the Naysayers

Medical Textbooks (coeditor, coauthor)
Comprehensive Cardiac Care (seven editions)
The Slow Inward Current and Cardiac Arrhythmias
Cardiac Electrophysiology and Arrhythmias
Nonpharmacologic Therapy of Tachyarrhythmias
Treatment of Heart Diseases
Catheter Ablation of Cardiac Arrhythmias
Antiarrhythmic Therapy: A Pathophysiologic Approach
Arrhythmias and Sudden Death in Athletes
Electrophysiology of the Thoracic Veins
Catheter Ablation of Cardiac Arrhythmias
Sudden Death: A Handbook for Clinical Practice
Heart Disease: A Textbook of Cardiovascular Medicine (seven editions)
Cardiovascular Therapeutics
Cardiac Electrophysiology: From Cell to Bedside (seven editions)
Clinical Arrhythmology and Electrophysiology (four editions)
Electrocardiography of Arrhythmias (two editions)
Case Studies in Electrophysiology (two editions)

Medical Articles
More than nine hundred authored/coauthored

ARI'S SPOON

DOUG ZIPES

ARI'S SPOON

Copyright © 2021 Doug Zipes.

All rights reserved. No part of this book may be used or reproduced by any means, graphic, electronic, or mechanical, including photocopying, recording, taping or by any information storage retrieval system without the written permission of the author except in the case of brief quotations embodied in critical articles and reviews.

Certain characters in this work are historical figures, and certain events portrayed did take place. However, this is a work of fiction. All of the other characters, names, and events as well as all places, incidents, organizations, and dialogue in this novel are either the products of the author's imagination or are used fictitiously.

iUniverse books may be ordered through booksellers or by contacting:

iUniverse
1663 Liberty Drive
Bloomington, IN 47403
www.iuniverse.com
844-349-9409

Because of the dynamic nature of the Internet, any web addresses or links contained in this book may have changed since publication and may no longer be valid. The views expressed in this work are solely those of the author and do not necessarily reflect the views of the publisher, and the publisher hereby disclaims any responsibility for them.

Any people depicted in stock imagery provided by Getty Images are models, and such images are being used for illustrative purposes only. Certain stock imagery © Getty Images.

ISBN: 978-1-6632-2572-6 (sc)
ISBN: 978-1-6632-2574-0 (hc)
ISBN: 978-1-6632-2573-3 (e)

Library of Congress Control Number: 2021923380

Print information available on the last page.

iUniverse rev. date: 04/14/2022

CONTENTS

PART III

Dedicated to the six million Jews and five million
non-Jews the Nazis killed during the Holocaust
and to those fortunate survivors and their
offspring who carry the torch to never forget

ACKNOWLEDGMENTS

Many people have helped by reading and commenting on early drafts, finding errors, and making important suggestions that contributed to *Ari's Spoon*. I am indebted to Clair Lamb, Michael Rosen, Marilyn Wallace, Peter Jacobus, Steven Yussen, and David Zipes. Hani Najm advised on the surgical repair of the dissected aorta. My editors at iUniverse did a great job helping perfect the story. The biggest shout-out, as usual, goes to my wife, Joan, without whose constant editorial suggestions and emotional support, as well as her love, this novel would not have been completed. She has been my everything through sixty-plus years of marriage!

PART I

PROLOGUE

Indianapolis, 2017

Life is filled with *what-ifs* that determine your future. *What if* I had done this? *What if* I hadn't done that?

What if we hadn't had that first date? *What if* we hadn't baptized Zoey in my baptism gown? *What if* I hadn't flown to Warsaw to search for the missing pieces of who I was? I wouldn't have had to face the most agonizing decision of my life.

CHAPTER 1

With her stunning blue-green eyes, blonde ponytail, and long, graceful Audrey Hepburn neck, Cassie could have strutted a designer's runway in Paris or New York, rather than standing, dog-tired, for hours in an operating room in Indianapolis, as we learned how to repair broken hearts. I loved the lopsided dimple on her right cheek and found myself trying to make my new wife smile for it to appear.

Whoever finished operating by 6:00 p.m. became cook for the night. The other did the dishes. On this night, I was home first and made an awesome arrabbiata spaghetti sauce with red onions, green olives, garlic, and capers. I opened my favorite Rombauer and waited for Cassie to come home.

We sat down for dinner, and I poured her a glass of red.

She smiled at me. "No thanks." She pushed her glass away, and her smile grew bigger.

"You're not going to drink white wine with this fabulous Italian dinner, are you?" I asked, shaking my head.

"I'm not going to drink *any* wine with this fabulous Italian dinner, thank you very much."

Click!

I reached for her hand and brought it to my lips, went around the table, and kissed her.

⌘

Zoey Rachel Goerner was born almost eight and one-half months later, May 16, 2018. She was a gorgeous seven-pound, six-ounce re-creation of her mom, with the same bluish-green eyes, blonde hair, and button nose. No dimple, though.

When she was three months old, we scheduled her baptism at the Saint Luke Catholic Church in Indianapolis. My folks flew in for the weekend and brought along the family's cedar chest, my grandfather's most prized possession from Poland.

CHAPTER 2

That afternoon, Mom and I unpacked the cedar chest. My baptism gown was on top, carefully preserved in a clear plastic bag. I took it out and held it up for Cassie to see. She spread it out on the kitchen table and smoothed the wrinkles.

"Oh, my goodness. It's gorgeous." She caressed the material with her hand, gently, like stroking the fur of a puppy. "The workmanship is spectacular. The silk lace coat and the undergown are gorgeous. And a matching silk cap and lace booties. Gabe, where did you ever find it?"

I turned to my mother. "Mom, do you know where Dad got this?"

She shook her head. "I don't. Before we came, I took it out to be sure it was clean. I showed it to your father and asked him. He didn't remember." My dad was in the early throes of Alzheimer's and even forgot who I was some of the time.

"Maybe from Grandpa?" I asked. Grandpa Josef had come to the United States with my dad after World War II. He raised my father and then lived with our family until he died last year at ninety-three, never remarrying after Grandma Rachel died. Growing up, I was close to him and had inherited his straight nose, square jaw, and blue eyes. Before he died, his blond hair had thinned to dandelion fuzz, while mine always needed cutting and combing.

"Probably, but we'll never know. Grandpa just said it was from the old country. Just enjoy it for what it is—a beautiful piece of material. See how the hem is made of doubled-over heavy silk that matches the silk sash tied in the back and the lace booties. Lovely. And enjoy it for Zoey Rachel, beginning her voyage into Catholicism. We need to keep this in the family forever."

I folded the plastic bag and replaced it in the chest. As I did, my fingers touched something furry near the bottom of the chest. It was a blue bonnet with rabbit ears.

"Mom, what's this?"

She studied it, turning it over and over in her hands. "I don't know. It still has little blond hairs sticking to it. Perhaps it was your dad's. Just put it back into the chest."

⁓

Sunday dawned as a lovely spring morning, bright and warm with a sunny and cloudless sky. Pink tulips, yellow irises, purple lilacs, and white hyacinths in harlequin designs transformed the garden around our building into an Impressionist painting.

We ate a hurried breakfast and dressed for church in a chaotic state of four adults sharing two bedrooms with one bathroom. Cassie outfitted Zoey in her new baptism gown, and she looked adorable.

My parents, Cassie, and I posed with Zoey for a family picture. Cassie's father, Jim McManning, head of surgery at the medical center, had been called away for an emergency heart bypass operation. Cassie's mom had died several years ago from breast cancer.

⁓

Saint Luke was a large church that sat at the corner of Seventy-Fifth and Illinois Streets in the Meridian Hills section of Indianapolis. The pastor, Reverend Monsignor James H. Sparkle, was an elderly gray-haired man with a round, kindly face and gray-green eyes framed by wire-rimmed glasses.

The baptism was planned to follow the 11:30 a.m. Sunday mass. We arrived around 11:00 a.m. to leave plenty of time for parking, walking to the church, and finding seats.

To enter the church, we had to pass through a security screening metal detector. Dad and I went through the usual routine of emptying pockets while the ladies placed their handbags on the belt for screening. My parents, who would be godparents to Zoey, breezed through first, followed by Cassie. I went last, carrying Zoey.

We triggered the metal detector.

I checked my pockets to be sure they were empty; I removed my belt and watch and sent them in separately.

The metal detector beeped again.

Rather than walk through a third time, the security guard—a slim African American lady named Jess—waved me over and fanned her wand over me—no beep—and then over Zoey—*beep*.

Zoey triggered the metal detector. Impossible!

Jess repeated the action more slowly with the same result. She focused the search inch by inch until the wand beeped over a barely noticeable bulge in the hem of Zoey's gown. The double-layered silk made feeling that small area difficult, but I sensed an irregularity in the smoothness of the hem.

I checked my watch—11:20. Zoey was getting fussy with all the attention.

"Jess, I don't know what's in the hem of the gown, but we're certainly not going to take it apart now. We've got just a few minutes before mass begins. I'm sure you'd agree whatever's there poses no security threat. So can we go in and sit down?"

She waved us through, and we walked to a pew near the front of the church. After we sat down, Cassie reached for Zoey and held her on her lap. I felt the hem of the gown as carefully as I could through the thick material. I could make out an object that had some sort of a flat shaft leading to a rounded top on one side but concave on the other. It felt like … like … a spoon?

Incredible. Why in God's name would someone sew a spoon into the lining of Zoey's baptism gown? I laughed to myself; "in God's name" was fitting.

We all walked forward when Monsignor Sparkle called Zoey's name. Sparkle was a good name for him since his eyes really did sparkle over this event that was clearly as blessed for him as it was for us.

"What name do you give to your child?" he asked. He'd told us our answer established that Zoey would become a child of God by name, with Jesus as her brother.

"Zoey Rachel Goerner."

He explained that she was dressed in this beautiful white gown to symbolize her purity of faith and cleansing and that Jesus also wore white when he was placed in the tomb after his death on Good Friday. White was the promise that Jesus would raise her some day from the dead.

"What do you ask of God's church for this child?"

Cassie and I answered, "Baptism."

"Are you willing to fulfill your duties to bring up this child in the Christian faith?"

"We are."

He made the sign of the cross with his thumb gently on Zoey's forehead and then on each of us.

He prayed for her future and smeared a little Oil of Catechumens, blessed olive oil, on her neck to symbolize her anointing.

"Do you renounce Satan? And all his works? And all his empty promises?"

"We do."

"Do you believe in God, the Father Almighty, Creator of heaven and earth?"

"We do."

"And in Jesus Christ and the Holy Spirit?"

"We do."

Cassie held Zoey over a basin, and the priest poured droplets of water on her forehead three times, repeating her name each time, and concluded, "I baptize you in the name of the Father and of the Son and of the Holy Spirit. Amen."

He anointed the top of Zoey's head with chrism oil.

We lit a baptismal candle and recited the Lord's Prayer together.

Our darling daughter slept soundly through the entire ritual, even after receiving the cold water on her forehead.

It was all so beautiful. I wished Grandpa Josef were here to share the splendor and significance with us, but I couldn't wait to get home to open the hem of this white gown that signified faith and cleansing.

CHAPTER 3

As soon as we returned to our apartment, I took a small pair of sharp scissors from a suture removal kit to nip the thread binding a seam over the tiny section of the hem where I felt the irregularity.

I teased out a baby's spoon that had been sewn into the hem of my—now Zoey's—baptism gown. The spoon was delicate, sterling silver, with a deep bowl and thin neck that expanded to a wide, flat surface, embossed on the sides with a scrollwork of leaves. There was writing on the spoon, but the engraving was so small, I needed a magnifying glass to read it.

On the back of the spoon was etched, *"Ari Holmberg,"* while the bowl had the engraving, *"Warsaw, 27-2-43."* The manufacturer looked to be a silversmith company named Piotr Latkowski. A Google search revealed they were a well-known silver manufacturer at the time.

I showed the spoon to Cassie. "What do you think?" I read her the inscriptions.

"It's lovely, but what does it mean? Who's Ari Holmberg?"

"I don't have the foggiest idea. I searched Google and Facebook but came up blank. Maybe Mom knows."

We sat at the kitchen table on Sunday afternoon for coffee and a snack before my folks caught the 5:30 flight back to White Plains,

New York, near their home in Pleasantville. I served sandwiches of smoked ham and Swiss cheese on rye.

"I wish I could be more helpful, Gabe," Mom said, turning the spoon over in her hand and studying it with the magnifying glass. "It really is lovely. Whoever bought this and had it engraved, particularly in the middle of the war, must've been someone with money and connections."

"I agree, but why hide it in my baptism gown?"

"It must be important for our family," she said. "If only Grandpa Josef was alive …" Her eyes misted.

"Or Dad could remember."

We looked at my father, but he sat with a blank expression, staring at his coffee cup. Mom held the sandwich to his lips, and he took a bite. He reminded me of a mechanical doll, where you push a button, and the mouth opens.

"I was just thinking—we call it my baptism gown, but could Dad have been baptized in it?"

"I've wondered the same thing," Mom said, after giving him a sip of coffee. "Do you think there's anything to the similarity of the name Ari on the spoon to Alex?"

"Unless Ari is short for something, like Alex is short for Alexander, I doubt it. Assuming Ari was born February 27, 1943, he'd be about Dad's age."

"Two months older. Your dad was born April 27."

"Maybe they were friends, and maybe Dad's baptism gown belonged to Ari."

"Possible, I guess. Ari would have been baptized first. Your grandfather Josef came to the US with Dad in 1945, right after the war ended. Ari and Dad would have been just two years old. I guess they could have known each other if their parents were friends. There's so much we'll never know," Mom said with a long sigh.

"Especially as the world war survivors die."

"Any clue from the gown?" Cassie asked. "A manufacturer's label or a name sewn in?"

"I already checked," I said. "The label is Jablkowski Brothers but no other name. I googled them. They were a high-end department store in Warsaw. Seems we're at a dead end."

Cassie poured more coffee. Dad stared into space. He only ate and drank when Mom fed him. I wasn't sure how much longer she'd be able to do this. He seemed to have deteriorated in just the few days of their visit. Perhaps the plane ride, new surroundings, and stress were too much. His health appeared very fragile, especially with his memory gone.

We finished eating, and Mom and Dad prepared to leave.

"Thank you so much for inviting us to stay with you and sharing Zoey's baptism. It was a beautiful ceremony, and we've had a lovely visit," Mom said.

"We loved having you," Cassie said.

I checked my watch and stood. "Mom, sad to see you go, but I think it's time I take you to the airport. You're all packed?"

"Packed and ready. I'm leaving the cedar chest. Your grandfather stored lots of stuff in it so maybe it has some clues to help solve your mystery. I'm sorry Dad couldn't contribute anything. Good luck."

CHAPTER 4

I couldn't wait to explore the cedar chest. In addition to the blue bonnet, I found another plastic bag that contained a green jacket and a pink blouse, faded as if it'd been washed many times. The blouse still bore a faint unpleasant smell I couldn't identify but that reminded me of rotten eggs. I wondered whether they belonged to my grandmother.

In a small box, I found Rachel's wedding ring that Grandpa used to wear on his pinky. With a magnifying glass, I read the name on the inside of the ring, expecting it to say Rachel. The engraving was *Irena Sendler*. That was a total shock. I had no idea who she was.

At the very bottom of the chest were two sets of identification papers, called *Kennkarten* in German. They were folded into thirds—with a picture in the middle section, and personal information on the first and third leaves—and stamped "approved."

The first *Kennkarte* showed Grandpa as a young man, Josef Goerner, born December 13, 1923. Curious, however, as his address was the Boduen's Children's Home, 75 Nowogrodzka, Warsaw, Poland. Google indicated Boduen's Home had been used to save many children during World War II who were often brought in by Irena Sendler.

That name again. My mind whirled. Did Grandpa have an affair with Irena Sendler?

The second Kennkarte was my father's, Aleksander Goerner—his picture as an infant and birthdate, April 27, 1943. His address was not Boduen's but the Franciscan Sisters of the Family of Mary in Pludy, Poland.

According to Google, the Franciscan Sisters was a "Polish female religious institute" established to "help Polish children stricken by hunger in the Russian Empire" located in Pludy, a town about seventy miles east of Warsaw.

None of this made any sense.

At dinner that night, Cassie and I tried to piece it together.

"For some reason, Grandpa and Dad were living in different places."

"Maybe after your grandmother was killed, he could no longer take care of your father and placed him with the Sisters."

"That could be, but why was his own address at an orphanage?"

"Maybe he worked there. What was his training, his education?"

"I don't know. The war started when he was only sixteen, so I doubt he'd had much schooling. Perhaps he worked as a manual laborer. Whatever, it doesn't explain why my dad wasn't with him and was living at some sort of a female institute."

"And who was Irena Sendler? And why was her name engraved in your grandmother's wedding ring?" Cassie laughed and reached for my hand. "I think your grandfather had a mistress."

"Maybe after Rachel died. I wish I knew. Maybe she was the one who owned that smelly blouse."

The following morning, I tracked down phone numbers and called the Boduen's Children's Home and the Franciscan Sisters. I struck out at both places. I was told that records going back seventy-five years had been either lost or destroyed during the war. Neither place had information on a Goerner, father or son.

"What will you do?" Cassie asked as we sipped our coffees.

"I have two choices. The first is to forget all of this, decide it no longer has any relevance for us, and go on living without knowing the past."

"I'm fine with that. Are you?"

"No, Cassie. I couldn't sleep last night, trying to piece it all together. It's like attempting to solve a giant family jigsaw puzzle but with missing pieces. They must be somewhere in Poland. I need to find them to know where I came from, to really know who I am. For the first time in my life, I feel incomplete, half a person."

"Will finding those pieces change you?"

"I don't know. Depends on what they are."

"And what if all traces have been lost or destroyed, like people at the home and the convent told you?"

"At least I will have looked for them, and I'll have to be satisfied with that. But there may be human survivors, someone with answers who might've known Grandpa or Grandma."

"They must be very old."

"Yes, which is why I need to do something now or forget it. Soon, there'll be no witnesses, no one left to tell me about Ari Holmberg and his spoon. I have a sense of urgency, Cassie. I know it sounds crazy, but this spoon is sending me a message that I have to search for to find the part of me that's missing."

CHAPTER 5

"No. You can't take time off," Jim McManning said, his eyes drilling holes in me when I asked for vacation days to go to Poland. "The hospital's too busy, and you're still in training. You have to fulfill your educational requirements to pass the surgical board, and that includes more time in the OR."

Cassie's father was a workhorse, a hard-ass who lived by the doctrine that great surgeons would rather operate than eat. Surgery was his life, and he expected the same total dedication from everyone else. His only diversion was opera. Once, a reporter writing a story quoted him as saying, "My lawfully wedded wife is surgery, and opera is my mistress. When I tire of one, I spend the night with the other."

Iron Balls was a demon in the operating room. When handed a wrong instrument, he'd fling it across the room, pitch-black eyes shooting daggers over his mask. "Goddamn it, can't you tell the difference between a hemostat and a fucking clamp? Get out of my OR." He seemed especially hard on the youngest doctors and—sad to say—those of color. One young doctor named Shapiro couldn't seem to do anything that pleased Iron Balls. Despite his temper, however, he was a superb surgeon, took on the most difficult cases, and always put his patients' interests first.

He was angry that I'd gotten Cassie pregnant in the middle of our training. He was certain she'd never come back to finish the program.

Though she'd proven him wrong, he hadn't changed his feelings. I didn't know what it would take to get him over his funk—maybe he was afraid she'd become pregnant again—but whatever it was, he wasn't going to give me time off until that happened.

"Dr. McManning"—although he was my father-in-law, in the hospital I maintained a deferential student/teacher attitude—"despite being in training, I'm still entitled to a two-week vacation."

"Doesn't matter. I said no."

"Sir, this is very important to me and to my family—your daughter and granddaughter. I need to get to Poland."

"No."

"But—"

"What part of this answer don't you understand, Goerner? I'm chief of surgery, and I said no. Keep this up and I'll fire your fucking ass, and that'll be the end of your surgical training. Then you can go to Poland—and stay there, for all I care."

"Yes, sir," was the only response I could give. Poland would have to wait.

∽

I worked alongside him and other senior surgeons over the next two months—often ten- to twelve-hour days—without a day off. My professional relationship with McManning was cordial, despite our personal differences, and we meshed well together in the OR.

During a difficult operation to repair a congenital heart defect in an infant, McManning's hand slipped and tore an artery. Blood shot out in a mini geyser as the free end of the vessel flipped about, spewing blood like water from an untended garden hose. I grabbed a hemostat, chased and caught the spurting end, and clamped off the spigot. Then I used rat-tooth forceps to pinch together the hole in the aorta so McManning could oversew the opening. The entire episode lasted less than a minute or two, and the patient did fine.

After the surgery, I found McManning in the surgical lounge, wolfing down a sandwich followed by a gulp of coffee—I guess even the greats got hungry. Maybe there was hope for me after all. He drained his coffee cup and nodded an acknowledgment.

"You're a talented surgeon, Goerner. I'm glad for your help." He looked about, making sure we were alone. "Don't tell anyone—I hate to admit it—but at age sixty-eight, I'm starting to slow down; my moves are not quite as precise as I'd like them. The change reminds me of a comment by Jascha Heifetz, the famous violinist. He said that if he didn't practice for one day, he could tell the difference; two days, the critics would notice; and three days, the public could. I'm at one day, surgically."

"Thank you, sir. I've still got a lot to learn from you."

"You do, but you're going to be a good surgeon. You showed that today."

McManning had mellowed. This was my chance. I had to get to Poland before it was too late.

CHAPTER 6

"Okay, I owe you," McManning said. "But be sure you're back within a week."

I traded with a colleague and moved one week of my vacation to start immediately. I booked a KLM flight from Indianapolis to the Frederic Chopin Airport in Warsaw. The flight took thirteen hours, with stops in Detroit and Amsterdam.

∽

Over the internet, I found a hotel room in Warsaw and an English-speaking tour guide who was knowledgeable about World War II, particularly the Boduen's Children's Home. Ludwik Grobelny agreed to meet me at the airport and spend the following week driving and translating.

The flight was long but uneventful, and I slept six hours. I breezed through customs and passport control and spotted a man waiting at the exit, holding a sign with my name.

Wik—*Veek*—as he asked me to call him, was fiftyish, average height, slim, and wearing a shiny blue suit that'd seen better days and a white shirt with a frayed collar. He had a sharp, pointed nose, almost like a knife edge; deep-set brown eyes; and brown hair flecked with gray.

"Welcome to Warsaw, Dr. Goerner," he said, extending his hand and taking the handle of my wheelie.

"Thanks, Wik. I'm Gabe."

His English had only a trace of an accent. "We'll drive straight to your hotel. You can freshen up, have a nap, or go for lunch—whatever you want."

We drove north from Chopin Airport on Route 634 through a landscape so studded with pine trees sprouting summer needles that they scented the air with fresh resin. We passed beneath tree branches that shaded the road like a church roof.

In twenty minutes, we arrived at the five-star Hotel Warszawa at 9 Plac Powstancow, an upscale tourist hotel with lots of marble, a fitness center, pool, spa, and restaurant. For only two hundred bucks a night, my room bulged with a king-size bed, dresser, flat-screen TV, desk, and stuffed easy chair. Historic downtown was a ten-minute walk.

We sat at a booth in the restaurant. Over a lunch of soup, herring, dumplings called *pierogi*, and a breaded pork cutlet—enough food to last me many hours—Wik asked, "May I ask why you're interested in the Boduen's Children's Home?"

I gave him all my background information and showed him the engraved spoon. He studied it at great length.

Finally, he said, "Fascinating. This spoon would have been virtually impossible to obtain in 1943 Warsaw—same for the baptism gown—unless you had pull with the Nazis or were extremely wealthy."

"No for both, as far as I know. I suppose they could have been purchased at a later date for my baptism in 1987, but that wouldn't explain the name Ari and the 27-2-43 date."

"I agree. Let's see what we can find out at the Children's Home first and then maybe drive to the Franciscan Sisters in Pludy."

⁊

Boduen's Children's Home at 75 Nowogrodzka Street was a two-story light tan building with a red-brick cathedral-like entrance, protected by an iron fence and set behind a red-brick wall. I'd read that a French missionary priest named Gabriel Baudouin established the home in 1736 as the Child Jesus Hospital for Foundlings.

A woman in a maid's uniform answered our knock and shepherded us to an administrative office in the back of the building. Director Jan Wolski was an elderly gentleman, dressed in a brown tweed jacket and tie. A short gray goatee and tiny mustache lent gravitas to his presence.

"I spoke with you on the phone several weeks ago, Dr. Goerner," he said with some impatience, hands waving like an accordion player. "I could have saved you a trip. I have no further information. We are a Catholic orphanage with barely enough funding for heating, water, and food for our forty children. We have no records of an Ari Holmberg, who sounds Jewish. I suggest you inquire at the Polin Museum of the History of Polish Jews at 6 Anielewicz Street. They have records on many Jews from the war, some of whom were smuggled out of the ghetto and may have been placed with us temporarily. During the war, we took in needy children of all religions."

The museum was our next stop. It was a modern building of concrete, copper, and glass, opened just a few years ago on the site of the old Jewish quarter. It housed the history of Polish Jews, from their arrival a thousand years ago through their decimation by the Holocaust and post-war control by the Soviets. The museum had multiple historical galleries but nothing on Ari Holmberg.

Frustrated and tired, we stopped for a coffee in the old city.

"The Nazis destroyed over 95 percent of the buildings here," Wik said, waving his hand in front of him. "All of this has been rebuilt on top of and using the rubble of the past. Little remains of the ghetto where they herded four hundred thousand Jews into a tiny living space and then deported most of them to the gas chambers in Treblinka."

"Did you lose family members?"

His eyes clouded, and he knuckled away tears. "All of us did. You don't kill hundreds of thousands without affecting every family lucky enough to survive. My father was one of the leaders of Zegota."

"I don't know what that is."

"An international relief organization set up during the war to help the Jews." He sipped his coffee and made rings on the table, seeming deep in thought.

"Is he still alive?" Under the table, I crossed my fingers.

Wik shook his head. "No, but Marek Edelman is. He's ninety-six and not in very good health, though his memory is still sharp."

"Who's he?"

"Marek and a friend named Mordechai Anielewicz were the leaders in the Warsaw Ghetto Uprising in April 1943. Marek was twenty or twenty-one and survived to fight the Germans as a partisan in the forests outside Warsaw. Anielewicz died in the war. There's a memorial in his name, and the street where we just visited the museum is named after him. Marek later helped the Poles fight the Nazis, lived in Warsaw after the war, and became a prominent heart doctor."

My ears perked up. "I'm a heart doctor—a surgeon. Do you think he'd talk to me?"

Wik pulled out a cell phone. "Let's find out."

CHAPTER 7

"Sorry, Gabe, his daughter said his health's too brittle to speak to anyone outside the family."

"Can I talk with her to change her mind?"

"She doesn't want him to relive anything about the war. It just upsets him. Then he can't sleep, gets even more stressed, stops eating, and his health deteriorates. How about we drive to Pludy first?"

As with the Boduen's Children's Home, I got nothing out of a road trip to the Franciscan Sisters of the Family of Mary in the tiny town of Pludy in eastern Poland, except burning up two more days of my week. During the war, the organization, originally established in Saint Petersburg to help starving Polish children in the Russian empire, took in orphans of all religions, focusing on the poor and disadvantaged. The supervisor listened politely to my story and searched her files but could find no record of an Ari Holmberg.

This was not going well. The mystery of Ari's spoon was destined to end unresolved. I'd always have a blank chapter in my past.

"Wik, I have three days left." McManning's warning hovered like a dark cloud. "Marek Edelman's my last chance. Drive to his home, and I'll talk with his daughter."

∽

"No. I told this man"—she tipped her head at Wik—"over the phone. You may not speak with my father." Elzbieta Edelman planted her foot firmly at the base of the front door. "He's old, frail, and should not be reminded of the war."

"Actually, I wanted to talk to him about cardiology and his practice here in Warsaw. He performed some remarkable research years ago that's helped save thousands of lives." I'd done a Google search and found that Edelman was one of the first to recommend using veins to bypass clogged arteries to the heart.

The door opened a few more inches as she looked out with an interested, unblinking gaze. I un-blinked back.

Elzbieta Edelman was short, with sandy-blonde hair wrapped in a tight coil. She assessed me with hooded but alert eyes. "You're sure you'll discuss nothing about the war?"

Before I could answer, an old man leaning on a cane hobbled to the door. He was bent like a comma, bald, with rheumy eyes staring at me from a wrinkled face. His baggy black knit sweater hung in loose folds over faded black pants. "Who wants to talk about cardiology?"

"Good afternoon, Dr. Edelman," I said, extending my hand. "I'm Gabe Goerner, a cardiovascular surgeon from the Indiana University Medical Center in the US. I'm researching the origins of coronary bypass surgery and your early work."

The comma straightened, the rheumy eyes cleared, and a smile ironed out many wrinkles. "Come in, young man, come in. Bieta, coffee, please, for our guests. I'd love to talk about cardiology."

I introduced Wik, and Dr. Edelman led us into a tiny living room filled by a couch of worn red velvet, a matching overstuffed chair with shiny arms, and two straight-back wooden chairs. A small glass coffee table in front of the couch held a red vase with a wilting rose, perhaps needing water. Wik and I sat on the couch and faced Edelman, who sat in the overstuffed chair. His eyes were lively and engaged, and his expression conveyed that he was happy to talk to us. I liked him before he even spoke. He seemed to be a good man.

Bieta set a tray of small cakes on the coffee table. "Coffee will take a few minutes," she said.

"Why did you become a doctor, sir?" I asked, convinced my first impression was right.

"It was a continuation of what I'd done in the ghetto during the war."

I felt a spurt of adrenaline. "What was that?"

"I was assigned to the entrance of the *Umschlagplatz* as the Nazis deported Jews from the ghetto."

"*Umschlagplatz?*"

"The train-loading station. I removed those too sick to enter the trains to Treblinka and saved their lives, lots of lives. I liked that feeling—that people counted on me, needed me. If the most important thing you did happened when you were just twenty years old, you had to find something equally important to do after that. So I became a doctor to continue to be responsible for human lives. My entire life's work has been a race with death."

I took a chance. "Does the name Ari Holmberg mean anything to you?"

"Not Ari, but I knew a man named Solomon Holmberg and his son Jakob. The Nazis killed Solomon—shot him in the head. Jakob married a woman named Rachel, who also died in the war. Jakob disappeared and probably died as well, but I lost track at the end."

Rachel! Of course, it was a common name, but still ...

"Would you know if Jakob and Rachel had a son?"

"Yes, they did. I suppose he could've been Ari, but I didn't know his name."

I showed him the spoon and told him what I knew.

"One of the only people in the ghetto who could've gotten a sterling silver spoon engraved and a baptism gown like you describe was the head of a band of thieves."

Bieta arrived with the coffee. This gave me a moment to digest what I'd just heard. A thief! How the hell could a thief have been linked to one of the most sacred rituals in Catholicism?

She poured coffee, and we sipped and snacked and chatted about summer coming and the weather getting warm.

Edelman spoke with his mouth full, and crumbs bounced off his chin. "Shmuel Asher was a thief, a big, fat fellow who controlled most of the crime in Warsaw before the war. He or his men could've pulled that off from the ghetto."

Asher was the man I needed to talk to. "Is he still alive?" I asked, again crossing my fingers.

"No. The Nazis gassed him along with all the others."

That knocked the air out of me. I drew in a sharp breath.

Bieta reentered the room, face grim with displeasure. "I said no war stories. Interview's over. My father needs to rest."

We chatted for another fifteen minutes about cardiology and his contributions. I thanked Dr. Edelman and Bieta for their hospitality, and we departed.

I had only one hope left, one last lead to pursue. We drove to the Piotr Latkowski silversmith warehouse, showed the spoon to the director, and asked if he had any records of 1943 sales.

He laughed in my face. "From the war? You've got to be kidding. Before the war ended, this place was bombed to rubble, to nothing, to no records, to no inventory, to no people. Sorry, but if you'd like to sell the spoon, I'd be happy to buy it back from you. Give you a good price too."

I was defeated. Done. I'd struck out.

ↂ

I flew home two days early with more questions than answers, little to show for a trip that cost me almost a week and about five thousand dollars.

I'd found out there'd been a family named Holmberg but not how a spoon with a Jewish boy's name got sewn into my Catholic baptism gown.

If Ari survived the war, who took care of him, and where was he now?

CHAPTER 8

Cassie and Zoey met me at the Indy airport. Gurgles and smiles from my little girl were uplifting after a wasted trip. Failing was not part of my DNA, and I was not happy.

"Sorry, Gabe, I know how much you wanted an answer, and you gave it a good try. Tell me about Warsaw. And Dr. Edelman. I looked him up after you messaged me. He was a leader during the war."

"The city's lovely, especially the historic center. It's been totally rebuilt using the rubble from the bombings to capture as much of a prewar look as possible."

"And Edelman?"

"Very impressive man, a real humanitarian. And the fact that he knew a Holmberg family was helpful. I think I'm on the right track, but I may be too late. There are so few remaining survivors. I need information about what went on in Warsaw during the war from someone who was there. And that may no longer be possible."

∽

I spent the next two days researching but found nothing to help solve my mystery. I returned to the hospital not much wiser. McManning welcomed me back to his OR but not to his personal space. It was hard to realize he was the father of my wife, grandfather of my daughter.

I was grabbing a quick lunch in between surgeries when the head OR nurse, Virginia Strozky, walked into the surgical lounge, prepared a sandwich, and sat down across from me. A nice lady, middle-aged and attractive, with soft, feminine features; I liked her. Rumor had it that she and McManning barely tolerated each other over some past conflict but maintained a truce in the OR for the patients' benefit. I never found out why. The whispers were that they'd had an affair after his wife died, and she'd jilted him.

"I heard you traveled to Warsaw, Dr. Goerner. Enjoy the visit?" She bit into her sandwich.

"Hi, Virginia. A lovely city. I wish I'd had more time to explore."

"My parents were born in Warsaw and lost a lot of family to the Nazis. We weren't Jewish but were called gypsies. Hitler didn't like us either. My folks came to the States in 1960, and I was born here."

"Have you visited?"

She sipped her Diet Coke. "Several times. We still have some family left. Do you? Is that why you went?"

I told her about the silver spoon and what I'd found out—or *not* found out was more accurate.

"Intriguing. Have you checked the Ringelblum Archive? That might be helpful."

I felt the same surge of adrenaline as when Edelman started talking about the war. "No, what are they?" I'd stopped crossing my fingers, though. That was a jinx.

"The discovery was all over the news years ago." She pulled out her cell phone and clicked on Google. Her thumbs flashed, and she handed me the screen.

It was a BBC story by a Monica Whitlock, dated January 27, 2013, and titled "Warsaw Ghetto: The Story of Its Secret Archive." It described how a group of Jews living in the Warsaw ghetto, led by Emanuel Ringelblum, collected over six thousand documents that detailed every aspect of life and death in the ghetto, for the world to see after the war. Code named *Oyneg Shabbes,* or "Joy of the Sabbath," thirty-five thousand pages in Yiddish and Polish were sealed into three large, watertight milk canisters and ten metal boxes and buried in three different locations in and around the brick foundations of an old school building at 68 Nowolipki Street.

Even though the building was blown to smithereens, two of the three milk canisters were unearthed on September 18, 1946, and the ten boxes were discovered by chance on December 1, 1950. The materials, mostly well preserved, were stored in the Jewish Historical Institute in Warsaw—not the museum I'd visited. They'd been collected into a book called *The Ringelblum Archive*, which detailed the contents and was published in 2009.

I needed to get my hands on that book. I didn't know why no one in Warsaw had clued me in on this resource.

I returned Virginia's cell phone.

"Did that help?"

"Oh, my goodness, yes, a lot." I was so excited I wanted to give her a hug but held back. "Thank you so much. I have a bit of archiving to do."

My heart did its usual quick dance. This could be my answer. I felt it in my bones. I was too excited to finish my lunch and dropped the remainder in the trash.

I called Cassie. She became as revved as I was and said she'd search the internet for the volume as well. We agreed I'd examine the first half of the book, and she'd start with the second half.

I couldn't wait to finish assisting in the next two surgeries—a triple coronary artery bypass and an implantation of an aortic valve—and run to the hospital's library for a quiet place to use the internet. I was certain I'd find answers.

Three hours later, I gave up in frustration. The English summaries of *The Ringelblum Archive* contained personal diaries and stories, essays, poems, drawings, pictures—the list went on and on, documenting everything concerning life in the ghetto—but nothing about an Ari Holmberg or even Jakob or Rachel. A list of members of the *Judenrat*, some sort of a Jewish council, contained the name Solomon Holmberg, but that was all I could find.

Dejected and defeated again, I called Cassie. The tone of her voice told me she'd struck out also. Maybe that's why no one in Warsaw had told me about these archives, even at the Polin Museum, where they had a Ringelblum display. They'd probably searched for the name Ari Holmberg and had come up as empty as I.

∾

"Show me the article Virginia pulled up," Cassie said as we drank our second glass of pinot noir. I needed at least two, or I'd never calm down enough to fall asleep.

I googled the article and showed it to her. I watched her face, eyes downcast, while she read what'd gotten me so excited hours ago. As she reached the end of the article, her features changed—her eyebrows rose, eyes got big, and a tiny smile bloomed.

"Did you read the entire article?" she asked.

"I thought I did."

"Even the last few sentences?"

I nodded.

She read aloud. "'Around 35,000 documents were recovered in total. All efforts to find the last cache—the biggest—have failed. Most recently, archaeologists looked under the garden of the Chinese embassy on what was Nowolipki Street but found nothing but the burnt scraps of a diary. The rest of the archives may still be under Warsaw.' Burnt scraps of a diary! Are you listening? The rest of the archives may be under Warsaw. You're still in the ballgame. Ninth inning, down one run, but you're still at bat."

"Great, but what do I do? Dig up the Chinese embassy garden?"

"That could be a start." Cassie grinned.

"I'd have to return to Warsaw, at least to talk to the people at the museum to find out firsthand about the last failed attempt. I doubt your dad would allow me to take the rest of my two-week vacation."

"You could call the Chinese embassy."

I thought about the garden. "I've read about ground-penetrating radar. It's a variation of the echo machine we use on the heart. I could use it to search for the third milk canister."

"You don't know anything about that. And besides, do you think the Chinese would let you mess with their garden?" Cassie asked.

"I have no idea."

⚬⚬⚬

The following day, I contacted the Emanuel Ringelblum Jewish Historical Institute in Warsaw to find out about the third milk canister. I spoke with a staff member, a man named Michael Wasserberger.

"Yes, the third milk canister still has not been found. My father, Hersh Wasserberger, was the staff member who searched for it after the metal boxes and two milk canisters were found, years ago."

"Will the Chinese embassy allow more exploration of their garden?"

"They did in 2005, which was the last search, but not now. Several historians have tried since then and have been refused access. One person sneaked into the garden and was caught, arrested, and deported to Beijing as a spy. I don't know what happened to him after that."

"Would it help if I flew to Warsaw and tried to talk with the Chinese?"

"Waste of time. They won't give permission. The milk canister has historical value to us but not to them and no monetary worth, so there's no incentive to find it. They don't want anyone digging up their garden. Plus, they're paranoid as hell about someone hiding cameras or microphones to spy on them. Not worth your time, talking to them."

⚬⚬⚬

At dinner that night, I fed Zoey a puree of a vegetables that were only recognizable by the picture on the jar. The mush was green and smelled sour, but she liked it; at six months old, she'd begun her transition to solid food. I grilled Faroe Island salmon steaks for Cassie and me, along with grilled zucchini and red peppers, sweet potatoes, and a fresh salad of mixed greens, carrots, celery, onion, and cucumbers.

I'd become obsessed with Ari's spoon and researched it whenever I could. I had to try to find the third milk canister, as all other sources had tapped dry. But that meant another trip to Warsaw.

"Hmm, you grill a superb salmon, but I still think you're nuts," Cassie said when I broached the idea at dinner. "Let it go. The spoon isn't that important."

"You may be right, but I can't. Something's driving me and won't stop. I think it *is* important—for me, for our family. The spoon was hidden in Zoey's gown for a reason. I need to find out that reason."

"Someone's sending you a message? From outer space or maybe the grave?"

"You can joke all you want, but whatever it is has grabbed me. It has to be tied to ghetto stuff, and that is somehow tied to my family. My problem is, there's nobody left to talk to."

"And even if you did find the milk canister, you have no certainty that what you're looking for will be in it."

"True, but it's my last lead. I'll stop if I strike out."

"You're going to waltz into the Chinese embassy garden, wheeling a ground-penetrating radar machine—you don't even know what one looks like, where to get it, or how to operate it—and find the milk canister?"

"Sounds crazy, but I have an idea."

CHAPTER 9

A week later, I was on Delta Flight 9278, flying from Indianapolis to the Chopin Airport in Warsaw, Poland. I'd contacted an engineer who worked in a geology office in Warsaw to rent a ground-penetrating radar machine. He agreed to help me explore the Chinese embassy garden.

On the flight over, I dialed up the garden on my laptop, courtesy of Google Maps.

My computer screen displayed two large stone lions flanking the entrance path to the garden. The path led beneath trees and past two pagodas with typical glossy, vermilion columns that supported curved, ribbed roofs with pointy corners. They looked more Japanese than Chinese. The path coiled around a lily-padded pond and over an arched white-stone bridge that spanned a stream filling the pond. A rectangular eight-columned pagoda stood at the water's edge. It was painted in the same bright vermilion, with an ornately sculptured pink roof, from which hung red lanterns.

It was lovely. I could understand why Chinese officials had refused further exploration. However, I'd be digging a tiny hole if the GPR did its job.

I thought about where someone might bury a treasure. The two metal milk canisters were found on Nowolipie Street, near the garden. That might be a good place to start.

I closed my computer to get some sleep before we landed. I dreamed about finding the cannister, just as the Chinese police found me and hauled me off in handcuffs. Not a good beginning.

I landed about noon the following day and checked into Hotel Warszawa. After a bite of lunch, I cabbed to find Jurek Zagorsk at the Red Copper Mining Company on Myslakowskiego Street in downtown Warsaw. Jurek already had the GPR—about the size of a backyard power lawn mower—loaded into a small truck, along with a pickax and two shovels.

"How big were the canisters?" he asked.

"Maybe four or five feet tall and as big around as a fat man's belly."

"I'd recommend we start close to Nowolipie and run a crosshatched pattern into the garden. We're limited by the pond and the buildings."

"How far can GPR penetrate?"

"From a few centimeters to a thousand meters, depending on the texture of the terrain," he said with confidence.

"Will snow or frozen ground be a problem?"

"No."

"We're doing it at night and can't chance being caught. How long do you think this will this take?"

"Fortunately, this is the very latest GPR, so the sweeps are wide, deep, and accurate. We should be able to finish in three to four hours, max."

"Too long. Although it'll be night, there still might be guards—or worse, listening devices or cameras in the garden," I said. "We'll have to pick the most likely area, scan it, and get out in an hour or two. Start at one in the morning and finish by three, at the latest."

"Okay. We'll eliminate crosshatch sweeps. They take too long. Just parallel runs, straight up and back."

"Fine," I said. "If we find something, we can come back another night to dig."

"Do you have a backup plan if we come up empty?"

"Yeah, Krasinski Gardens. It expanded after the war to include Swietojerska Street, which had been part of the ghetto. The Jewish Historical Institute director emailed me to say that they'd explored an old house on Swietojerska five years ago, at Marek Edelman's suggestion. They found two human corpses and some personal documents."

"We can map that the next day."

"This all may be a wild goose chase," I said. "The director was no longer certain there really was a third milk canister. Maybe just a rumor."

"Now you tell me. Too late. We're here, and we'll look. Sounds like there's plenty to cover during the next few days."

∽

We parked on Nowolipie Street around midnight, sat in the truck, and waited until we were sure all was quiet.

"Excited?" I asked Jurek.

He nodded. "Maybe more scared than excited. What happens if we get caught?"

"Helluva time to be asking."

"Yeah, I know. So what happens?"

I told him about the last known trespasser, captured as a spy.

Even in the moonlight I could see his face blanch. "I guess we don't want to be caught."

"You got that right."

We unloaded the GPR half an hour later but left the shovels and pickax in the truck. Jurek had fitted the GPR with an extra muffler, so the sound of the motor was just a low vibration. We passed by the twin lions, and my heart tangoed as we began the search.

Using moonlight, Jurek guided the GPR over the ground. His eyes stayed glued to the laptop-sized radar screen in front of him. I walked alongside, my eyes searching the surrounding area for any movement. I didn't know what I'd do if I did see someone approach us. Fortunately, the cold February night—probably in the low twenties—with snow flurries made it unlikely that anyone would be around. No guards were patrolling and certainly no lovers trying for a quickie on a park bench.

33

Walking the frozen garden and having to detour around the pagodas and the lake and trees and other obstacles made me realize the futility of what we were doing. The topography had changed dramatically since this ground was part of the ghetto. It would be easy for a milk canister to stay lost forever beneath the concrete foundations of the new road out front or the embassy's new buildings. The container could be sunk at the bottom of the pond, tangled in the roots beneath new trees, or any number of other places. The original tin boxes and milk canisters had been found within five years of war's end, when most of the original ghetto landscape was still untouched and could be excavated. It had all changed.

After an hour and a half, I called it quits.

"We're done. Too many hiding places we can't screen, and I don't want to push our luck about getting caught. Tomorrow, we'll try Krasinski Gardens, but I don't have my hopes up."

Jurek dropped me back at the hotel, where I ate breakfast and lay down for a brief rest; I'd been up most of the night. "Brief" turned into four hours. I woke, had lunch, and called Jurek; we headed to Krasinski Gardens in early afternoon.

The garden was the site of the Krasinski Palace, a large, ornate, white-brick two-story building with a green-tile roof, built by that wealthy family in the late 1600s. Rebuilt after bombing during the war, the palace now served as the Polish National Library. The garden extended between Dluga and Swietojerska Streets and surrounded a pond with a spouting fountain—easily accessible to our GPR.

My expectations were low, and my heartbeat stayed steady. It took only two hours to prove I was right; we came up empty. Obviously, we could not search the palace or other buildings on the property, as the museum director had done several years ago.

"What's next?" Jurek broke into my thoughts. "You done? Back home?"

"One last shot. There's this old man, a retired doctor who lived through the war, who I want to talk to—if I can get past his guard dog. Then I'm finished."

CHAPTER 10

"If nothing else, you're persistent," Marek Edelman's daughter, Elzbieta, said as she opened the front door, guarding it with her foot, as usual. "What do you want now?"

"I'd like to talk with your father, just briefly."

"About the war?"

"About where he told the institute director to search for hidden ghetto material."

"Who's at the door, Bieta?" Marek Edelman said, walking toward us. "Ah, yes, my fellow heart doctor. Goerner, wasn't it? Good to see you again. You've brought another friend. Come in, come in. Bieta, some coffee, please."

Edelman ushered us into the small living room. I introduced Jurek.

"How can I help this time?" Edelman asked.

I told him about our fruitless GPR searches in the two gardens.

"Yes, the topography has all changed. If there ever was a third milk canister, I'm afraid it's likely buried forever."

"Is any part of the ghetto unchanged that we might explore?"

He thought for a moment. "Yes, surprisingly, there is."

The room was silent as I waited for him to reveal this secret. He played it along, seeming to savor the suspense. Bieta arrived with coffee and cookies, placed them on a small table, and left. Edelman poured, and we sipped and snacked.

Finally, he spoke.

"Unbelievably, the Nozyk Synagogue, right smack in the middle of the ghetto, was built in the late 1800s, and the Nazis left it intact during the war. They burned down just about everything else. The synagogue needed some repairs after the war, and we added a new wing, but we still use it today, pretty much as it was seventy-five years ago. The Nazis converted it into a horse stable to humiliate us but also to use. They left it intact."

"Did you search for the milk canister?" I asked.

He smiled. "From top to bottom, five years ago. Practically tore the synagogue apart. Nothing."

This was my last chance, and I wasn't going home without a try. "Is it possible for me to visit, maybe talk with the rabbi?"

"Of course. Rabbi Abraham Kleinman is an old friend and a very nice person. I'll call him now if you wish; see if he's busy."

"Wonderful. Yes, please."

Edelman left the room but soon returned. "He'd be happy to see you; show you the synagogue. Go right over. It's on Twarda Street, next to Grzybowska Square."

I stood and held out my hand. "Dr. Edelman, it's been an honor to meet you and talk with you, sir. Your exploits during the war are legendary, as was your career as a cardiologist. God bless you, sir, and thank you so much for your hospitality."

"Good luck with your search. You are right. That spoon is important for your family."

The day was clear as we stood in front of the Nozyk Synagogue, a large, rectangular neo-Romanesque building of yellow-tan stone with a central domed entrance, flanked by two smaller wings. I rang the front bell, and Rabbi Kleinman answered—a short, slim man with a round, gentle face, long gray beard, and mustache. Bristly gray eyebrows draped sparkling blue eyes. A kippah covered his gray hair.

"Gentlemen," he said, smiling and extending his hand, "welcome to the Nozyk Synagogue. Please come in."

I introduced myself and Jurek. "Thank you for seeing us, Rabbi. It's a great pleasure to meet you and see this wonderful synagogue."

Before we walked into the main sanctuary, he handed us black kippahs to cover our heads.

The interior had off-white walls and was divided into three long aisles, leading to the dais, with balconies on both sides, probably for the women. Twenty or thirty rows of dark wood seats lined the floor from wall to wall. Intricate chandeliers hung from a domed ceiling.

We sat in the first row in front of the dais, and I looked around, thinking what these walls had witnessed seventy-five years ago.

I'd never been in a synagogue, but it all somehow felt familiar—no, not familiar like I'd been here before, but familiar comfortable, almost like I belonged. It was an unnerving feeling. Perhaps it was the warmth of Rabbi Kleinman that made me feel so at ease. Whatever it was made me feel connected to the silver spoon even more.

"So how can I help you?" he asked.

I related my story, from the spoon onward.

"I'm afraid I agree with Marek Edelman, Gabe." He shook his head. "The third milk canister is most likely lost, if it existed in the first place."

"Yes, I'm beginning to accept that, Rabbi. But I'd be interested in what happened here. Can you tell me a little of the history leading up to the Nazi takeover of the synagogue? Was there any warning?"

"I was not here at the time, of course," Kleinman said with a small smile, "but the tale handed down was that spies had warned the rabbi of what was coming, and he hid the Torah scrolls and prayer books to prevent desecration."

"Where?"

"You're not Jewish, are you?" he asked with crinkly eyes.

"No, Polish Catholic."

"In Judaism, sacred documents are kept in a place where they cannot be destroyed or sullied, called the *genizah*, which in Hebrew means reserved or hidden." Kleinman said this was usually a special room set aside in the synagogue exclusively for that purpose. Since the rabbi and congregation knew the Nazis would be taking over the building, they buried the Torah scrolls and prayer books in the Jewish cemetery, at the northwest end of the ghetto, just outside its walls.

"Are they still buried?" I asked. My heart started to pitter-patter again.

"Oh, yes. After the war, the rabbi replaced everything with new Torah scrolls and prayer books to rid the Nazi stench and left the old ones buried in the cemetery."

"Rabbi Kleinman, I know this will seem like an incredible request, and we've just met, but would it be possible to go to the—what did you call it—*genizah*—and exhume the scrolls?"

He looked startled; then he seemed to ponder. He ran two fingers through his beard in long, smooth strokes. "It's interesting that you ask," he said, looking toward the dais where I figured the present Torah scrolls were kept, "and not so outlandish. I've thought of doing that many times since I became rabbi here, ten years ago—just to be able to look at the old Torah scrolls and hold them, since they go back several hundred years. So, yes, we could. I would want to get the approval of the president of my congregation, but it is possible."

My pitter-patter heartbeat gave way to gallops.

"When might we do this?"

"Tomorrow? Let me check with the president and also with the people at the Jewish cemetery and get back to you."

CHAPTER 11

Jurek drove me back to my hotel. I used WhatsApp to call Cassie and brought her up-to-date.

"Wonderful, Gabe," she said, as excited as I. "Good luck."

I called Wik and met him for dinner at the hotel. We split a bottle of Milosz pinot noir recommended by our waiter, along with the national dish of Poland, bigos stew made from pork and spicy Polish sausage. The wine was not quite like a bottle from Willamette or the meat from Saint Elmo, but both were nice enough.

I tossed and turned through much of the night with dreams that alternated between digging up an empty casket and finding one filled with disintegrated papers that could not be interpreted. Finally, I drifted to sleep until the alarm sounded.

I showered, dressed, and met Wik for breakfast. "I hope you slept better than I."

"Probably. I'm not used to wine with dinner, and it put me in a trance. Any word yet?"

I shook my head. "Hopefully, before we finish breakfast." I started to hold up crossed fingers, but then changed my mind.

We each had downed two eggs over easy, bacon, fried potatoes, and toast when my cell phone vibrated. I listened, said yes, and pumped my fist. We hailed a cab to the Jewish cemetery on Okopowa Street and met Rabbi Kleinman at the entrance.

"Good morning, Rabbi."

"A very good morning to you both. The grave we want is in the section of mass graves for victims of the Warsaw ghetto uprising. It should be dug up and waiting for us. Follow me."

We walked through a thick forest of trees and underbrush that had grown around and between hundreds of headstones of various sizes, shapes, and conditions; it looked nothing like manicured cemeteries in the States. As I viewed nature's clutter amid the graves, I had the crazy thought that the cemetery looked busy and lived in.

Winter had stripped the trees bare of leaves to reveal their true selves. The same thing might be happening to me.

We came to a freshly dug grave, where an attendant had set up a table. On it stood a large, unlocked, rusty metal casket.

My gallop rhythm was too fast to count, my breathing uncontrolled, and I was sweating in thirty-degree weather.

"Ready, Gabe?"

"I am, Rabbi. Please proceed."

He flipped back the lid of the casket. Inside were neatly piled prayer books and three Torah scrolls. But no diaries, pictures, or any handwritten papers like I'd seen collected from the metal boxes and milk canisters of the Ringelblum Archive.

My heart thudded to a stop. My breathing quit, and I shivered in the cold. This was the end of the line, the end of my chase. All for nothing. Strike three. I was out.

Rabbi Kleinman removed the cloth covering of one of the Torah scrolls, held it to his lips for a dry kiss, and set it aside. He laid the Torah on the table and unrolled the parchment scroll.

As he did, showers of handwritten and typed papers, rolled flat between the parchment pages of the Torah, flew out, fluttered in the wind and covered the table and ground in layers, much like the leaves that littered the cemetery paths. We raced to catch each page.

The more the rabbi unfurled, the more pages flew. He unrolled from the beginning of Genesis to the end of Deuteronomy. With each twist of the scroll, additional pages tumbled from their hiding places.

He repeated the procedure with the second scroll and the third, and more pages cascaded.

We flipped through pages of the prayer books and uncovered additional concealed writings. After three hours, diaries, poems, pictures, and memories were finally freed from seventy-five years of hiding. There was no third milk canister. It was a casket.

I wanted to jump up and dance, cry out, sing, or do something insane, but I resisted. We were in a graveyard, after all, and although we'd found the treasure, I still didn't know if that pile of papers held any information about Ari's spoon.

We captured every page and returned to the synagogue. Rabbi Kleinman phoned ten congregants, as well as representatives from the Ringelblum Archive, to help us collate the bonanza we'd uncovered. I helped as much as I could, but I was limited because all the writings were in Yiddish and Polish.

I paced up and down the aisles of the synagogue, hoping to hear someone cry out that they'd found writing about a ghetto family named Holmberg. After three nervous hours, someone did.

"Here's an archive written by a Jakob Holmberg. Is that what you're looking for?"

"Yes! Yes!"

Thank you, God! Thank you, Jesus! Thank you, Rabbi Kleinman.

I was on a plane back to Indianapolis. It would take several weeks for them to create an official translation of Jakob Holmberg's memoir. They promised to email it to me as soon as it was available.

Three weeks later, on a Saturday morning, the memoir arrived, and the words written by Jakob Holmberg would transform my life forever.

PART II

CHAPTER 12

Warsaw, Poland

The date is May 16, 1943.

I'm at Father Boduen's Children's Home, recovering from a Gestapo bullet wound in my side. Three sons of bitches chased and fired at me as I fled from them in downtown Warsaw six days ago. I made it to the Home, where they've tended my wound and hidden me.

Today also happens to be the official end to the Warsaw Ghetto Uprising. The Nazis blew up our precious Great Synagogue of Warsaw and declared our rebellion finished, though some Jews are still fighting, and a handful of buildings are still standing, like the Nozyk Synagogue.

During my recovery, word reached me that members of the Oyneg Shabbos, led by Emanuel Ringelblum, were asking all of us who'd lived in the ghetto to create an archive of our journey for the world to know what had happened. They intend to hide the documents until the war ends and then publish them.

I'm not certain why I've survived this long or whether I'll survive the rest of the war. But I feel I've been spared so far to be able to tell a story, a true story, about what happened in the Warsaw ghetto. I'm writing what I remember, starting with the bombing on

September 1, 1939, when I was just sixteen. I plan to fill these pages with detailed recollections of the last four years. Our suffering has been an unimaginable, horribly effective teacher that has battered, bent, and reshaped the Jewish people into a new way of living—and dying. I will explain in these pages. It is my hope that the future will avenge what the present cannot.

When I'm finished writing, I'll give these archives to a courier to deliver to Emanuel Ringelblum, assuming he's still alive.

If you're reading this, I was successful.

CHAPTER 13

On Friday, September 1, 1939, at 5:00 a.m., the shrill blast of an air raid siren pierced the quiet Warsaw night and jarred me from sleep. Moments later, my father pounded on the door to my room.

"Jakob, get up! Out of bed! We must go to the bomb shelter. Now! Nazi planes are coming."

We had feared the German invasion for some time. Border skirmishes between our Polish army and the Germans over the last few months stirred rumors that both sides were preparing for war. Late the night before, Radio Warsaw had announced that a group of soldiers in Polish uniforms had attacked the German Gleiwitz radio station. Hitler claimed Poland had started the war and planned to retaliate. Our government had denied the accusation, insisting it was Nazis dressed as Poles, a ploy to provide Hitler an excuse to attack. In the final analysis, it didn't much matter what we said. Hitler would do whatever he wanted, and no one could stop him.

I bolted from bed and slipped on pants, a shirt, and shoes. I glanced behind the window shade before I ran to the stairs. The night was dark—a total blackout with all lights off and windows covered, as our government had mandated.

The small, windowless concrete storeroom in the basement was already crowded with families from the other ten flats in our building. There was barely room for my parents and me to squeeze in. People lined the cinderblock walls, many still in nightclothes covered by bathrobes hastily thrown across their shoulders. A few had remembered to bring government-issued gas masks, and some had bags of food. The ventilation fan was weak, and the room was stuffy, with thirty or forty bodies breathing the same air. Two bare light bulbs, hanging from the ceiling at each end of the room, created eerie contrasting shadows on the walls.

I scanned the faces of my neighbors. Most were wide-eyed with raised brows and pale, frightened looks. Families huddled together, arms thrown protectively around each other, whispering softly, shielding children in the middle. Several families had very young children who screamed in terror. Mothers tried to quiet them with bottles of milk or bared breasts.

I was also frightened but tried to act grown up and not show it. My parents, Solomon and Ada, and I stood in a tight circle holding hands, waiting for the first bombs to hit, praying they would spare our building.

I looked at my father, who seemed quite calm, and compared myself to him. He was a big man, over six feet tall and thickly muscled from working in a steel mill as a young man. I'd just reached six feet, but, at age sixteen, I was still developing and hoped to be taller than he. We both had what are considered "good looks"; that is, Aryan features and not Jewish: blond and blue-eyed with straight noses and square jaws. Mother was not so lucky and had "bad" looks: a prominent nose, brown hair, and dark Semitic features. I thought she was beautiful, but maybe all sons think that of their mothers.

Rachel Glowinski greeted me, leaving her family of six to come over and say hello. I smiled and waved and wedged myself between people to meet her halfway. We elbowed our way to a corner of the room for a little privacy. She was my age and lived with three sisters and her parents in a two-room flat, one floor above us. Over the past two years I'd watched her blossom into curvaceous womanhood, with flashing blue eyes and lustrous, thick hazel hair down to her shoulders—definitely "good" looks. Sometimes I imagined her taking a shower, and that drove me crazy.

Her beauty was matched by fearlessness. The year before, two nasty Polish girls were tormenting her girlfriend Sarah after school. "Dirty Jew, dirty Jew, just an ugly dirty Jew," they chanted over and over. When the bullying turned physical and they began to shove Sarah from one to the other, Rachel came flying over. She plowed into them, whacking one girl to the ground and belting the other in the teeth. Both ran off crying, and the harassment stopped.

I stood as close to Rachel as I could and asked if she was scared. I really wanted to hug her to me.

She gave me a tiny smile. "Yeah, maybe a little. But we're going to get through this, one way or another. It'll be rough for a while, but our guys'll kick their asses."

"Like you did the two girls beating up Sarah."

She grinned. "Worse."

"I hope you're right."

"I am. You'll see. They're brave men."

Rachel's mother called, and she returned to her family.

"Be safe," I shouted as she shouldered her way through the crowd.

After almost an hour without an explosion, the babies stopped crying, and people began to relax. They made room to sit on the floor, chatting sociably with each other. The adrenaline rush wore off, and eyelids drooped, heads nodded, and many dozed, catching up on the past night's truncated sleep. Maybe Rachel was right, and our planes had headed off an attack.

My parents and I found a bit of space and slid to the floor. We braced our backs against the wall, with Mama in the middle. She looked tiny between us. She came up to Papa's shoulder and probably was half his weight.

"Papa, maybe it was a false alarm." I didn't really believe that but hoped we might be spared. I wasn't sure what I wanted to do with my life—I thought about being a writer—but whatever I did,

I didn't want it to end at age sixteen in the concrete basement of our apartment building.

He shook his head. "No, Jakob. If it was, they'd sound the all-clear signal. I think the Luftwaffe may be waiting for daylight so they can see where to drop the bombs."

It turned out Papa was right, as usual. I know kids are supposed to see their parents in a different light as they grow up, maybe that they are not as smart, but Papa always had been my role model, my hero, and he was right more times than not. I loved Mama and she loved me, but I respected and admired Papa. He made the big decisions for the family.

We dozed, off and on, for about an hour, our bodies propped against each other, until the sirens blasted again. I heard a rumble to the west, like distant thunder. It gradually grew louder as the squadrons of planes got closer. People held each other and started to cry and moan. It was hard not to be scared with bombs blowing up all around us. People had to be thinking, *Does this one have my name on it or the person sitting next to me?*

I heard them plead with God.

"Please dear God."

"God, I don't want to die—not like this."

"God, spare my children—my children."

"Save us, oh Lord."

"Where is God?"

"What God?"

"There is no God."

Bombs dropped in clusters of deafening explosions, one falling right after the other, followed by a brief, eerie silence and then isolated blasts at longer intervals. The pattern repeated, probably as fresh waves of bombers flew over. Our building shook when bombs exploded close by and triggered white clouds of dust from the walls and ceiling. We held handkerchiefs over our mouths and noses to avoid inhaling the floating debris.

The babies started crying again, joined by panicking adults. Families clutched each other, most open-mouthed with fright.

Faces blanched with terror. Some crossed themselves, fell to their knees, and prayed. A few had brought a Bible with them and read from it, turning pages hurriedly. The rest seemed frozen in place.

"Papa, do you think our planes can chase the Germans away?" I heard the pleading in my own voice, hoping we could defend ourselves. I searched his face and stared into his eyes for reassurance.

Instead, I got a blink and a shrug. Papa tried to remain unruffled, but I could read anxiety in his eyes.

"Good question, Jakob. Maybe, but I don't really know. Germany's been building an army for at least five years. We only started a year ago. We'll soon find out, but I'm afraid it'll be the Germans."

The bombing continued in cycles for several hours. One bomb hit so close it might've nicked a corner of our building. We threw our arms over our heads as the building shook and the dust billowed.

Gradually, the explosions slowed and stopped. The roar of the planes grew distant and then faded to silence. An all-clear siren wailed, and we shuffled slowly out of the room and onto the stairs, back to our flats. Friends reached out to close neighbors for reassurance.

I looked for Rachel, but she was surrounded by her sisters, who were crying, and I didn't want to interfere.

"What happens now, Papa?" I asked as we returned to our flat. "What will the Germans do?"

"I don't know, Jakob. It all depends on that madman, Adolf Hitler, and what his plans are. I think this is just the beginning."

"More bombing?"

"Probably, followed by troops in our city. And then—who knows? Meanwhile, I'm going outside to see if any neighbors need help. Come with me."

The devastation around us was vast and hard to believe. Our building had been spared, but many others on Leszno Street had been reduced to piles of rubble—amorphous mounds of concrete, brick, and shattered glass. Broken furniture poked through the wreckage like arms reaching for help. Bodies and pieces of bodies lay among the ruins, with cries from some still trapped inside. Men were digging with anything at hand to try to save those still alive.

"Help me, please." It was a young boy, pinned under a concrete column with a pile of bricks sitting on his chest.

"C'mon, Jakob, help me dig him out."

We removed the bricks and, with two other men, lifted the concrete column off his body. He smiled a grateful thanks, took a deep breath, and died.

The streets were filled with people shouting and screaming, many staggering like drunks and bleeding from wounds. Hackney cabs and cars raced through the streets, narrowly avoiding people and each other, speeding the injured to hospitals and clinics.

Animals seemed to be screaming as well. Horses on hind legs whinnied and clawed the air, dogs barked and ran in crazy circles, and they died in the street.

Fires blazed in many areas, gutting the remains of some buildings and feeding on new ones. The fire department was overwhelmed. We joined one line of people filling buckets of water. We worked for about an hour, passing buckets to a group of five men who were trying to contain a fire and prevent it from spreading to an untouched building. The fire won, and we gave up.

Dust from collapsed buildings and smoke from fires choked the cool fall air, and a dense powdered fog blanketed everything like snow, reducing visibility and making breathing difficult. I held a handkerchief over my face, and Papa twisted a scarf over his.

Even though the planes had left, destruction continued as damaged buildings, wounded but precariously still upright, began to topple. Balconies fell away. Other buildings crashed completely as foundations crumpled. People walked in the center of the street or stood in open squares to avoid falling debris.

Papa and I remained outdoors until nightfall, helping wherever we could. Finally, exhausted and covered with dust and dirt, we returned home for a late supper. Mama made us undress in the pantry and change clothes. She had cooked a beet soup that we devoured, along with thick slices of rye bread—the last loaf from the store, she said.

CHAPTER 14

Over the next month, I learned very quickly which army would prevail. Our ground troops, some still fighting with sabers on horseback, fought bravely but were no match for more than two thousand German tanks and heavy artillery that crossed our borders from the east, north, and south in a giant pincer movement.

German guns were particularly frightening. Called the "fearsome 88s," their artillery shot 88mm shells, each weighing more than thirty pounds, at tanks and planes—and at us. At least with bombs, we had some warning. Not with the 88s. They burst on the scene and exploded like a lightning strike. Being frightened by one was a good sign because it meant you hadn't been killed—yet.

The Germans owned the skies as well as the ground. Our planes were old and slow, and more than a thousand German Stukas outgunned them. Those dive bombers and ground-attack aircraft commandeered the skies by early September and were mostly unchallenged as they bombarded us day and night.

When we weren't in the air-raid shelter, Papa and I ventured out to help where we could. We carried bodies from the street and buried them as fast as we could, sometimes in a nearby park or garden. The stench of rotting corpses was awful. We'd come home and scrub our skin raw; we'd stand in the pantry and hand our clothes to Mama to wash, but the smell lingered, and I knew it would be with me forever.

One afternoon, we were walking in the street when four or five men ran by.

"What do you think it is, Papa?"

"I don't know, Jakob. Let's find out."

We followed them around the corner, where a horse lay dead in the middle of the street. The men were butchering it, carving off chunks of meat and sharing it with a crowd that rapidly gathered around the fallen animal.

Horse meat—*ugh!* But we were all starving. We balked at eating dogs and cats, and buried them, sometimes in the same graves as the humans. But horse meat, when you're ravenous, wasn't so bad.

The worst day came in late September—Monday, September 25, beginning at 8:00 a.m., to be exact. The air was turning cold, presaging a rough winter.

The Luftwaffe threw everything they had at us. The bombing and artillery shelling became so relentless and frightening that one of our generals said over the radio that the Germans were trying to take Poland by terror rather than by force.

Papa said we were close to the end. Almost half the buildings in Warsaw had been destroyed—twice as many in the Jewish section of the city as in other parts—and forty thousand citizens had been killed. We later learned it was even worse at the front lines, where seventy thousand men died and more than six hundred thousand were taken prisoner.

We named September 25 Black Monday. Poland surrendered two days later, and shortly after that, the Nazis put boots on the ground in Warsaw. Persecution began in earnest when Mayor Starzynski surrendered Warsaw to a German Wehrmacht officer on that fateful day, September 27, 1939. We were now a captive population.

That population swelled as Germans herded Jewish refugees from other Polish cities into Warsaw. People overflowed the city, and housing, food, and water shortages became even more critical.

Electricity was mostly nonexistent; the newspaper shuttered; and Radio Warsaw was bombed silent. Except for propaganda transmissions to wireless radios from Radio Berlin and Radio Moscow, we were completely isolated.

While Poland had experienced anti-Semitism over many years—blaming Jews for Polish economic and governmental woes and trouble with other nations, like Germany, despite thousands of Jews having fought and died for Poland in World War I—when Hitler took over Germany, he fanned anti-Semitic flames to heights never before seen. He was intent on creating a pure Aryan race of Germans uncontaminated by *Untermenchen*—undesirables—like us Jews but also Slavs, Jehovah's Witnesses, Russians, gypsies, mentally or physically handicapped, Romani, and homosexuals.

"Papa, look," I said on our walk, pointing to a new poster hanging from a building wall near Muranowski Square. It decreed that as of September 29, all Jewish businesses must be transferred to German "trustees," who could not retain any Jewish employees and must revoke any Jewish pensions. Jews could no longer own or manage apartment buildings and could only sell products or produce on streets populated by other Jews.

Even the university was impacted. The University of Warsaw separated Jews in lecture halls and made them sit on a Jewish bench on the left side of the hall, apart from Aryans. They labeled the books in which students wrote examination answers as "Aryan" or "Jew."

As we walked, an armored car rolled slowly past, driven by a soldier wearing an olive-green Wehrmacht uniform. Another soldier in the passenger's seat held a megaphone out the window and, in German-accented Polish, announced that the German army was handing out bowls of vegetable soup and black bread at multiple sites throughout the city for all the citizens of Warsaw.

"Papa, maybe they're not so bad after all. They don't want us to starve." I looked at him for confirmation, but his face displayed skepticism.

"Maybe, but I doubt it. It's a smart move, Jakob. Showing us their good side at the beginning. Let's get on the line. We'll bring a surprise for Mama. But don't get your hopes up. Their goodwill won't last. Hope can be a dangerous emotion, son. You need it to keep your spirits up, but it can lead to false expectations that can be disastrous."

The day was cool but clear as we hurried several blocks to Leszno Street across from the courthouse, where a line had already formed. Starving Poles jostled for position, holding tin bowls distributed by two men wearing Wehrmacht uniforms, like the men in the car. Standing next to them was a German soldier, keeping a watchful eye on the people in line. He wore a gray-green uniform with an insignia bearing two lightning bolts and a human skull, which showed he was a member of the Einsatzgruppen, a Nazi paramilitary death squad composed of men selected from the SS and Gestapo.

The SS were the *Schutzstaffel*, originally Hitler's personal bodyguards, while the Gestapo were the *Geheime Staatspolizei* or Secret State Police. Except for having different leaders in charge, the three performed many overlapping duties, which tended to blur major distinctions among them. All three groups killed with little or no provocation.

One soldier ladled steaming soup from a huge black metal vat placed on the sidewalk, while the other handed out two thin slices of black bread to each person. The aroma of the food was overpowering and made me realize how starved I was. I wasn't fat to begin with, but I'd lost fifteen pounds in the last two weeks, and my clothes were starting to hang on me. I had to add holes to my belt to shorten it and keep my pants from falling around my knees.

The line was long and slow-moving. Ahead was a bearded man

dressed in a black jacket, pants, and round brimmed hat, and a woman wearing a long black dress and a dark shawl covering her hair. They were part of more than three million Jews living in Poland since the end of World War I, making us the largest minority—about 10 percent of the Polish population. We'd felt pretty safe, integrated into the Polish community, until now. Mostly, we left them alone, and they returned the favor.

Two young men up ahead walked alongside the long line and tried several times to cut in, but ranks closed and wouldn't let them. They stood talking together, and I saw them point to the Jewish man and woman.

Their behavior alarmed me. "Papa, those men up ahead—"

"I see them, son. Just stay in line. Keep quiet." Papa's face showed awareness but no anxiety.

"But they're—"

I watched, speechless, as the men approached the Jewish couple. They said something in Polish, shoved the couple out of the line, and took their place. The men laughed as the bearded man tripped and fell, tearing a hole in the pants over his knee. When he regained his feet, he ran at the men and pushed back. A scuffle began.

One of the Poles yelled in German, *"Hier sind Juden! Hier sind Juden!"* Here are Jews!

The Einsatzgruppen soldier ran over and pulled the men apart. Without hesitation, he drew his pistol and, from two feet away, shot the Jewish man in the head and then killed his wife. He holstered his weapon and sauntered to the soup kettle without a backward look.

The two Poles took the Jews' place in the line again, laughing and congratulating each other with handshakes and pats on the back.

"Papa, do something!" I was shaking with a mixture of rage and fear.

"Jakob, hush! Do not call attention to us. Just stay in line." Papa looked around. His face was pale, his mouth open, and his eyes dilated.

My papa was frightened.

I stared at him as I would a stranger. I couldn't believe what he'd said, what'd just happened. I was frightened too, but how could we stand by and do nothing?

"Papa, how can you—" I continued to look at him, my hand over my mouth.

He gazed straight ahead and wouldn't even glance at me. "We want to get our soup, Jakob," he said through clenched teeth. "We *need* to get our soup. We've had little to eat for days. I'm not about to quarrel with armed Germans and get shot for my efforts. They're not going to be here forever. And when they leave, life will return to what it was. I want us to be alive when that happens. You either adapt or you perish, son. Remember that. Adapt or perish."

I tugged at his sleeve, my eyes still fixed on him. "But Papa—"

"Enough! Silence!" He pulled his arm from my grasp. His mouth was set in a grim line, eyes squinted, and forehead creased. He was angry at me!

I dropped my hand and stopped talking. It was no use. He wasn't going to budge. This was a different father than the one I'd known five minutes ago.

The line continued forward; all eyes averted from the dead husband and wife bleeding on the sidewalk.

Suddenly, two young boys—maybe eight or nine—burst through the line and ran to the bodies. I figured they were children of the slain couple and would fall on them, crying.

Fall they did, but they quickly rummaged through the couple's pockets, seized whatever they found, and sped off within a minute. No one tried to stop them. The two Poles just laughed.

When our turn came, we filled our bowls, took the bread, and walked toward our building in total silence. I was stunned by the tragedy, the German's indifference, and Papa's response.

The more I thought about what'd happened, the angrier I got— at the two Polish men who started it, the German who finished it, and all the Germans who had invaded us. I pictured a family, probably with young children, waiting for the return of the husband

and wife and panicking as the hours passed. I wondered if anyone would retrieve the bodies, identify the man and woman, provide a decent burial, and care for the family they'd left.

And mostly, I feared for all of us, if this was foretelling what was to come. We weren't a particularly religious family, but I did believe in God and wondered, if He existed, how He could let this carnage happen.

We didn't talk much as we finished the soup and bread at our kitchen table. Mama asked what it was like, being on a food line, but Papa didn't tell her about the killings, and neither did I. I excused myself as soon as we finished and went outside. I needed air—and to get away from my father.

I spotted Rachel as she was leaving her apartment, and we walked together. The Germans had imposed an eight o'clock curfew, so we couldn't stay out long. They threatened that violators would be shot.

I told her what we'd witnessed.

She stopped and stared at me. Her eyes teared, and she shook her head. "Good God, that's horrible, Jakob. Just horrible. That poor family. We got soup and bread also. Our line was at Tlomackie Square, near the synagogue, but we had no problems."

"I'm so mad at everyone, including my father." I clenched and unclenched my fists. But I was sad also at having lost the father I thought I had.

"Be fair, Jakob. What could he do? Really." Her face was composed, calm, reasonable. "They would've killed him like they did the man and woman. And probably shot you too."

"I suppose. But it seemed like he didn't even get angry." I slapped the side of my leg in frustration.

"I'm sure he did and just didn't show it, which was smart." She gave me a tight smile. "We've got to be very careful when Germans are around. There's no telling what they might do, especially if they can kill like that without remorse and not get into trouble. You're better off keeping your feelings to yourself."

We walked in silence for a while, our arms at our sides. When our hands brushed, I thought about taking hers. I wanted to but didn't. I'd never held a girl's hand before. When our hands brushed again, I glanced at her.

"Yeah." She grinned. "So what are you going to do about it?"

I took her hand. She squeezed mine.

CHAPTER 15

Anti-Semitism escalated over the next several months in a series of additional German decrees. It seemed every day brought new and greater restrictions, starting with a ban on Jewish emigration. Then the Germans froze Jewish bank accounts and limited the amount of money Jews could earn or possess, eliminated social welfare programs, and began forced labor. They wanted us impoverished and totally at their mercy.

We tried to maintain life as near to normal as we could, wearing our usual street clothes and restarting public schools, jobs, welfare groups, and hospitals, but the Germans made it impossible for us to regain or retain any sense of normality. Just staying alive consumed most of our resources and the hours each day.

We had to surrender our radios. Failure to do so was punishable by death. Nazis mandated a Jewish census and issued identification papers called *Kennkarten*, stamped *Jude*. Jews were ordered to wear a white armband with a blue Star of David on their upper right arms, and every Jewish shop had to display a Star of David in the window. Months later, the Germans changed the star to yellow on a black background, inscribed with the word *Jude* and worn on clothes over the chest.

We joked to lessen the impact. "Did you hear the story about Hitler? Somehow, he gets through the pearly gates and sees Jesus walking in paradise without an armband. Furious, he orders, 'Arrest that Jew walking without an armband.' Saint Peter replies, 'Leave him alone; he's the boss's son.'"

Oppression tightened as winter approached. Jewish schools and synagogues were closed, and public worship forbidden. Jewish lawyers were banned from work, and Jewish doctors could only care for other Jews. We were forbidden to ride public trams, except in cars marked "For Jews." We had to remove our hats and step aside for any German in uniform walking on the sidewalk.

Interracial relations were outlawed so the Nazis could keep their bloodline "pure," uncontaminated by Jewish "vermin." A Jew caught dating a non-Jew would be imprisoned, and intermarriage was forbidden. Food ration cards were issued that allowed Poles 2,613 calories per day, and Jews 184. We could only use them in Jewish grocery stores. Jews couldn't own fur coats or jewels. All gold and silver had to be forfeited to the Reich, under penalty of being shot.

A black market materialized to avoid starvation, and Poles didn't mind selling Jews a loaf of bread or bottle of milk if we paid ten times the Aryan cost. Most of us couldn't afford those prices. Soon, we could be recognized by shirts, pants, and dresses many sizes too big that hung in loose folds from emaciated bodies.

With each new decree, I became more and more angry. I'd storm out of the apartment and pace up and down Leszno Street, keeping an eye out for Germans. We had to worry about the Gestapo and SS, as well as the Wehrmacht and Einsatzgruppen. The Nazis had fostered communities of hate.

Rachel often joined me. She'd take my hand and talk softly to calm me down. We'd remove our Jewish stars—they'd become a stigma that invited ugly responses from passersby. Polish hoodlums, as well as the Nazis, randomly beat up anyone who was wearing one. They especially liked older people and women, who were easy targets.

We were better off financially than many because Papa had earned a good salary before the war and had had the foresight to withdraw cash from the bank before the invasion. Also, because Rachel and I both had the "good" looks that could pass for Aryan, we'd shop for food in an Aryan grocery store blocks from our building, where we were not known. Such shopping was risky. If the Gestapo caught us not wearing an armband and carrying food bought at an Aryan grocery store, we'd be imprisoned or shot on the spot.

There was another risk that I learned the first day we shopped together. The grocery store was one large room with shelves on all four walls and a short counter where the clerk tallied up and bagged what I'd bought—milk, cheese, a chicken, a small piece of beef, vegetables, and bread.

I was carrying the bag as we left the store, with the fresh loaf protruding from the top. We'd walked maybe ten steps when Rachel screamed—but too late. A young boy ran up behind me, snatched the bread, and took off. I handed the bag to Rachel and chased him. When I finally caught the little thief, he'd already gobbled down almost half the loaf, and there wasn't much I could do.

"I was hungry," he cried and crumpled to the sidewalk. "I haven't eaten in three days."

"Where're your parents?" I studied him. He was maybe ten years old, filthy, skinny as a rail, with big, round, protruding eyes that seemed even bigger because of his sunken cheeks and matted hair. He smelled of sewage, and I suspected that was where he'd been living.

"The Gestapo," he sobbed. "They came in the middle of the night and took my papa. They said he was a traitor, but he wasn't. He was a professor at the university. They dragged him outside and shot him, along with two university friends from the next building. Mama tried to save him, but they killed her too. I hid in the closet." He broke down again, head in his hands, weeping.

I gave him the rest of the bread, some cheese, and the beef, and all the zlotys I had with me. He was just one of hundreds—maybe thousands—of youngsters living on the street who'd been orphaned when their parents were shot, imprisoned, or conscripted for forced labor by the Germans.

We ate a light dinner of vegetables and cheese that night, saving the chicken for the next night. My parents said I'd done the right thing.

After we finished and Mama was cleaning up, Papa asked me to walk with him. January and February had been particularly harsh. Now it was March but still freezing outside. We bundled up with scarfs and sweaters under our jackets. Still, I shivered as we stepped outside.

Papa was silent for a while, hands in his pockets, deep in thought. I waited for him to break the stillness. Finally, we stopped walking, and he turned to me. His face was drawn, serious.

"Son, I know I've disappointed you ever since the soup line back in September." His eyes were sad.

I nodded. We'd not talked much since then. Certainly not as much as we had before the invasion. We used to play chess but had stopped.

"I've thought a lot about what happened in these months since the Nazi occupation. You're old enough to make up your own mind, but I want to share my thoughts." He looked at me for confirmation. "We have to select our battles carefully. The Nazis are monsters and kill without remorse. We don't have their powerful weapons, and even if we did, I doubt we could kill as easily as they do."

I didn't know what to say so I remained silent. He'd aged, it seemed to me. The lines in his face had grown deeper and more numerous and his hair more gray. Dark bags under his eyes made him look tired.

"What I want to tell you"—Papa stopped talking and looked around to be sure no one was close enough to overhear—"is that I am doing something. I became a member of the Judenrat in October."

"I don't know what that is."

Papa stretched his arm across my shoulders and drew me close.

"The Germans ordered us to form a council of twenty-four elders to help them govern the Jews."

"Why would they do that?"

"They think it looks like we're governing ourselves, and that will help maintain peace and prevent panic. Of course, it's just an illusion. We must follow their orders."

"Then why do it?"

"It gives me a reason to meet with other Jewish leaders and make plans."

"Like what?"

"That, my son, I cannot discuss. I've already told you more than I should. Mama doesn't know any of this, but it was important to me that you didn't think I was a coward."

I wanted to tell him I loved him, that what he did was okay. "Papa, I—"

He held up his hand to silence me. "Jakob, like most young people, you're impatient and want action now. What you don't know is that things are about to get worse. Warsaw has become a dumping ground for Jews rounded up by the Germans from all over. We've had outbreaks of typhus and tuberculosis, especially where Jews are living in close quarters and with poor sanitation. The German authority is threatening to force all of us to move into one area as an excuse to contain the infections."

"Are you sick?"

He didn't look well, but he shook his head. "The Gestapo is going into each neighborhood, Jews as well as non-Jews, and systematically killing leaders, newspaper reporters, artists, musicians, intellectuals—anyone they think poses a threat to them. Thirty, forty, maybe even fifty have been dragged into the street and murdered in cold blood. That's probably why they killed the father of the young boy who stole your bread. The Nazis have also formed a Jewish Police force, made up of Jewish thugs willing to do their bidding to save their own necks. So now we've got to watch out for the Nazis, the Polish Police, and the Jewish Police."

"What are you going to do?" I asked.

His lips creased—a determined look. "That I cannot say. But we are doing something."

"Can I help?"

"Maybe. But not yet."

I searched his face. "Are you at risk like the boy's father?"

"I don't know, but that's why I don't want you to do anything just yet. I was a chief mechanical engineer, and that may qualify me as an intellectual or leader in their eyes. I don't think the Germans would've put me on the Judenrat if they were planning to arrest me—or do worse. But I'm involved with some other things that pose a danger. I cannot tell you because you can't confess to something you don't know. Also, if I'm exposed and caught, you need to be around for Mama."

I threw my arms around his waist, and we hugged.

He wasn't afraid after all. He was adapting.

CHAPTER 16

Spring of 1940 melted the snow, and the weather slowly warmed. The streets were crowded as more people poured into Warsaw. Three and four families crammed together in living space barely big enough for one. The number of homeless on the street increased. Hygiene became a larger issue, and more cases of typhus and tuberculosis emerged, especially in the rundown and more congested buildings, where we lived on top of each other.

Rachel and I had gotten into the habit of walking each morning and sometimes after dinner, holding hands and talking about lots of things—even a future together, when all this was over. The night before, as we entered our building just before the curfew, the lobby was dark, and she had stood close, looking up into my face. I pulled her to me and kissed her. It was our first, a gentle kiss, but our passions had been building, and when I felt her breasts press against my chest, even through my clothes, I got an erection. I couldn't help it. I didn't know if she could feel me, but she didn't pull away, and we stayed like that, close together, until we heard footsteps.

On a clear morning in mid-April, I was late for our usual walk. When I came out, Rachel was gone. I checked her apartment, but her mother said she'd left at her regular time to meet me in front of our building.

What could have happened? This was not at all like her. She would've waited for me or knocked on my door. Something was wrong, and I started to panic. I walked Leszno Street, first in one direction and then the other. The trees had started leafing and the sky was blue—far too nice a day for anything bad.

In the afternoon, I spotted her turning the corner at Solna onto Leszno and hurrying toward our building. I walked fast to meet her. I wanted to run and grab her into my arms, but that would've attracted too much attention.

"What happened?" I asked. "And what is that awful smell?" I held my nose.

Her face was chalk white, which made the dark mascara lines running down her cheeks look even darker. She held her green jacket tightly across her chest, but her pink blouse was rolled into a ball in her hand. While the day was sunny, it was still cool, and I didn't understand why she wasn't wearing her blouse.

She remained silent until we entered the lobby of our building. Then she collapsed into my arms, moaning, a dark sound from deep within.

"What, Rachel? What is it? What happened?" I hugged her to me, stroked her hair, and tried to calm her down.

Her whole body shook. Her groans slowed after several minutes, and she caught her breath. "Let's go to your apartment. My sisters will be in mine."

Papa was at a Judenrat meeting, and Mama was at a friend's apartment. We sat down in the tiny kitchen, and I got her a glass of water. She threw the blouse to the floor. It smelled like the sewer. She pulled the green jacket closer.

"I was standing in front of our building this morning, like I always do, waiting for you, when two Nazis drove by in a car. I was wearing my armband. They stopped in front of the building. I almost ran inside, but I was determined to show them I wasn't afraid. Stupid! One Nazi—he was Gestapo—got out of the car and came up to me. 'We need help to clean,' he said in Polish. 'Get in the car.'

"I tried to break away, but he grabbed my arm and dragged me to his car. Another girl about my age was in the back seat with her face in her hands, crying. She wore the Star of David armband also. He pushed me next to her, slammed the door, and got into the front seat. We drove off. 'You won't be hurt,' he said, turning to look at us. 'We just want you to clean some clothes and bathrooms.' The girl—I think her name was Helena—stopped crying but couldn't stop shaking. She tried to whisper something to me, but the Gestapo told her to be quiet. She groped for my hand, and I held hers. It was icy cold and clammy.

"We drove about ten minutes, and then the car slowed on Pawia Street, in front of the Pawiak Prison. I was so scared they were going to lock us up for no reason. A Gestapo guard waved the car through a metal gate that blocked the entrance, and we parked in front of a tall iron door."

She paused and shivered. Her eyes went vacant.

I reached across the table and took her hand. It was ice cold and shaking, just as she'd described Helena's. Tears trickled down her cheeks, darkening the mascara lines already smudged. I ached for whatever'd happened to her and feared the worst. I squeezed her hand and waited in silence. Several minutes passed.

She took a deep breath. "Somebody inside opened the iron door, and the Gestapo pig took the two of us inside the prison. He gripped my arm with one fist and Helena with his other. We walked down a long, dark, cold hallway enclosed by gray stone walls. I think there were cells on both sides—I could hear yelling or screaming—but I couldn't see clearly.

"We stopped in a small, windowless room with three unmade beds. He said they were the living quarters of the Gestapo guards who ran the prison. He pointed to a pile of dirty clothes on the floor. There was a pail of water on the floor alongside the clothes and a bar of yellow soap. He pushed Helena to the floor next to the pile. 'Wash the clothes,' he said. 'I will come back in one hour. Be sure everything is clean.'

"Then he led me through the room to three bathrooms in the back. They stank. There were no windows and barely enough light to see. 'Clean them,' he ordered, pointing to the toilets. I looked around for cleaning stuff but didn't see any. I asked, 'Do you have rags or a brush I can use? Soap?' 'Use your shirt,' he snapped. I stared at him like he was crazy. He slapped my face and yelled, 'Don't you dare look at me like that, Jew bitch. Clean them! Now!'

"I turned away from him and took off my jacket and blouse—I had my bra on underneath. I wrapped my jacket back over me. When I turned around, he smirked and stared but didn't say anything. I flushed the toilets, wet my blouse in the sink, found some soap, and began scrubbing. He stayed a few minutes, watching, and then left."

Rachel buried her face in her hands, and her sobbing began. I got up, knelt beside her chair, and pulled her close to stop her shaking. I could feel her heart racing. She took a deep breath and gently pushed me away. I sat back down at the table; she wiped her eyes and continued. I was seething as I opened and closed my fists. I feared what might come next. I wanted to kill the bastard.

"He came back in about an hour, checked the toilets, and grunted, 'Okay.' I tried to wash my blouse in the sink, but I couldn't get rid of the stench. He took me to the room where we'd left Helena. She was sitting on the floor, holding a pair of white underpants stained with … stained with … shit. She seemed stunned. There was a hole in the seat of the pants. She'd rubbed too hard to get them clean. The Gestapo pig cursed and yelled. 'Stupid bitch, you ruined the pants.'"

Rachel stopped and wrapped her arms around her body. She could barely talk. I waited. She took a deep gulp of air. "He drew his gun and shot her in the head!"

"Oh God!" I jumped up, furious, helpless. Son of a bitch! I couldn't believe it. I remembered the Jewish couple on the soup line.

Rachel started crying again. I went to her, and she collapsed into my arms, her body convulsed in sobs.

I heard the door to the apartment open and close, and Mama walked into the kitchen. She stopped when she saw us. "What is this, Jakob? What's going on?" Her tone was suspicious. "And what is that awful smell?"

I explained.

"My poor child," Mama said, softening. She put down her purse and rushed to Rachel. She pushed me aside and took Rachel in her arms. "How horrible." She turned to me. "Go outside, Jakob. I'll help Rachel." She bent down, picked up the blouse and held her nose. "We can start by washing this."

CHAPTER 17

Our lives were about to get worse.

The Nazi command issued orders on Yom Kippur—Saturday, October 12, 1940—by decrees posted around Warsaw and over loudspeakers from trucks driven throughout the city. All Jews were forced to move into one of the poorest and most rundown sections of Warsaw, just east of the Jewish cemetery, extending from near the Umschlagplatz train-loading station at the north end, to Sienna Street south, and from Zelanza Street on the west to an irregular eastern border, wider in the north—called the Large Ghetto—than in the south—called the Small Ghetto. Poles living in the ghetto area had to vacate, and Jews living outside that area had to move in. The order displaced more than 250,000 people.

An eighteen-kilometer brick wall, built by forced Jewish labor, three meters high and topped with imbedded glass shards, enclosed the entire compound, officially called the Warsaw Jewish District but known to all as the Warsaw Ghetto. Twenty-two gates, heavily guarded at all hours, led in and out of the ghetto. The Judenrat was ordered to implement the move and determine where four hundred thousand inhabitants—30 percent of Warsaw's entire population—would live in a total of seventy-three streets, or just over 4 percent of all the streets in Warsaw. The whole area was a little more than three square kilometers.

We had two weeks to move—until November 1; later extended another two weeks to November 15. Jews could only take belongings that could be carried by hand or in a pushcart. Everything else had to be left behind.

"Papa, but why? We've done nothing wrong. Why do we have to leave our home?" I asked as we packed our belongings. Our three-room apartment had a small kitchen, a tiny bedroom for me, and a bigger one for my parents but would be huge compared to what we were moving into.

"Right or wrong has nothing to do with it, Jakob. Only who's most powerful and in control. The Nazis say it's because of infections they want to control and wall off, but it's really an excuse to control us, to contain all Jews in one walled-in space."

"What if we don't move and stay where we are? Maybe they'll forget about us," I said, stuffing clothes into a pillowcase.

Papa stopped filling boxes and considered what I'd said, a rueful look on his face. "Not likely. The Nazis will search every building after the move to be sure all the Jews have been rounded up. Any Jew caught on the Aryan side will probably be shot, a lesson to anyone else who's hiding."

I tossed the pillowcase into my old baby carriage, which mama had resurrected to push into the ghetto. "Why should we just submit, meek as lambs? What would happen if we all banded together and fought them? They have guns, but we outnumber them. We could ambush them with knives or clubs or maybe steal their weapons."

Papa grimaced and shook his head. "You're not alone in that thinking, Jakob, but it won't happen. We outnumber them, but that's including people too old or too young to fight. Our actual fighting force would be much smaller, and that's assuming everyone of fighting age would join the battle—not likely. Most Poles wouldn't raise a finger to help the Jews. Although the Germans consider themselves superior to the Poles, they don't treat them as badly as they treat us."

I was intrigued by the first thing Papa had said. "Who else agrees with me?"

"It's a secular labor party called the Bund, made up of socialist Jews who want to fight. They tried to join with a Polish underground, but that failed. They did successfully fight many of the Polish hoodlums who were beating up Jews a while back."

"Maybe we'll be better off, living with just Jewish neighbors," Mama said with a smile.

I didn't really believe her. Papa's face showed he didn't either.

The day of our move was not particularly cold, but we still wore all the clothes we could put on, including multiple pairs of socks, three shirts, several pairs of pants, and a sweater beneath our coats. Mama wore the three dresses she owned. Though we were all skinny, the extra layers of clothes made us look fat and well nourished. The giveaway was our gaunt faces. Clothes couldn't hide sunken cheeks, bony foreheads, and teeth protruding through paper-thin lips.

Papa pulled a two-wheeled wooden cart loaded with food, blankets, sheets, kitchenware, some books, and other valuables. I pushed the baby carriage filled with the rest of our clothes, stuffed pillowcases, family pictures, and some valuables hidden in a false bottom. Mama carried two more pillowcases overstuffed with the rest of what we needed. We had to leave all our furniture, wall hangings, and a big potbellied stove that'd kept us warm through many cold winter nights. Whatever Polish family took over our flat would inherit a bonanza.

Our non-Jewish neighbors could barely wait until we left. Some lined up in the hall outside apartments being vacated to be the first to claim empty rooms and grab belongings. Though we'd made friends with many, not one came to say goodbye. Rather, it was good riddance.

Rachel and her family had left the day before. I'd asked Papa, as a member of the Judenrat, to make sure their apartment was in the same building as ours. They had two rooms for the six of them on the floor below us.

Privacy became a distant memory as refugees poured into the ghetto, and people had to share space. Some of the wealthier Jews paid for better living quarters, but among poorer Jews, six or eight people often shared a one-room apartment. Living while packed like sardines was brutal, and nerves became frayed. Fights were frequent as occupants had to take turns cooking, sleeping, and using the toilet.

On November 16, 1940, the Nazis sealed the ghetto tight, and we were locked in. Just as Papa had predicted, Jews trapped on the Aryan side after that date without permission papers were sent to Pawiak Prison or shot in the street.

Food became even more scarce, and we depended on a new enterprise of black-market smuggling, dominated by a legion of pint-sized soldiers. Youngsters, both boys and girls, found ingenious and daring ways to slip in and out of the ghetto—through cracks in the walls or buildings, holes dug under the wall, or past guards distracted or bribed at the gates. This bantam army of tiny giants stole or begged food and merchandise on the Aryan side and smuggled it back for their own families or to sell on street corners.

Like the boy who grabbed my bread many months earlier, little snatchers lurked outside grocery stores and bakeries and preyed on unsuspecting shoppers. Returning, they'd find a deserted stretch of wall and toss a stone over the top. If the stone was promptly relaunched, they knew a Jewish receiver was waiting. The diminutive soldiers then extracted their collected bounty from large pockets or secret clothes linings and threw it over the wall to the waiting collaborator. Getting caught on either side meant a bullet in the head, but without food, it was death anyway.

We also depended on certain ghetto guards who closed their eyes for zlotys or precious family possessions. They allowed ghetto garbage collectors to leave with a load of smelly refuse and return with a cargo of food, or they permitted a hearse to exit with the dead and reenter with produce for the living. We funneled milk and water into the ghetto through pipes hidden on the Aryan side.

The ghetto was rundown, with half of the buildings damaged

by the bombings and in need of repair. Motorized vehicles were banned, except for trams marked for Jews, and most of the streets were crowded with people walking.

When we heard a car motor, we hid because we knew it had to be Gestapo or SS, and that meant trouble. Getting caught resulted in a beating, at the minimum, or conscription for a work detail, or—at the worst—a bullet.

One afternoon several weeks after our move, Rachel and I heard a car approaching as we walked down Leszno Street. Along with people near us, we ducked into a nearby hallway. An old man with a long white beard and traditional long sideburn curls apparently didn't hear the car coming. He continued walking with a limp, leaning on a cane.

"Old man," I shouted, "come hide with us."

He must have been deaf or didn't understand Polish because he just kept walking.

I repeated it in Yiddish—"*Alt mentsh, kum do mit aundz*"—but he still didn't respond.

I started to go after him to drag him to safety, but before I could, the car pulled alongside and stopped. A driver and three Gestapo jumped out of the car and formed a tight circle around the old man. Initially startled, he faced them defiantly.

"*Vas vilstu?*" he shouted in Yiddish. What do you want? His voice was strong.

"*Wir verstehen nicht Jiddisch,*" the Nazi answered in German. We don't understand Yiddish. He was broad-shouldered and stood tall, arrogant, with hands on his hips and a fake smile on his face.

"*Gey avek. Lozn mir aleyn,*" the old man said. Go away. Leave me alone. He gave a backhanded wave to the German.

"*Wir verstehen nicht Jiddisch,*" the Nazi repeated. "*Tanz für uns Juden.*" Dance for us, Jew. The Gestapos clapped and laughed, enjoying themselves.

"*Geyn tsu genem!*" the old man shouted. Go to hell.

The Nazi performed a few dance steps, pointed to the Jew, and said, "*Jetzt machst du es.*" Now you do it.

"*Geyn tsu genem!*" the old man shouted again. He poked the big Gestapo's chest with his cane.

The Gestapo seized the cane and cracked it across his knee. He nodded to his two buddies. They pinned the old man's arms. The Gestapo reached into his pocket and withdrew a folding knife. He flipped open the blade and pointed to the knife and then to the Jew's curls. He repeated his dance step; then pointed to the Jew.

The pantomimed conversation was clear: Dance, or get your hair cut.

The Jew shouted again, "*Geyn tsu genem!*"

The Gestapo transferred the knife to his left hand, made a fist with his right, and smashed the Jew in the face. The old man's legs buckled. He would've fallen to the pavement, had not the Nazi on each side held him up. With the old man stunned, the Gestapo cut off his side curls.

When the Jew regained consciousness, he looked down to see the curls at his feet. He sucked in a mouthful of air and moaned, "*Oy vey iz mir.*" Tears formed in his eyes.

"I've got to help him," I whispered to Rachel. "I recognize two of those bastards."

"Who are they?"

"The tall one with the knife is Josef Blösche, but they call him Frankenstein. He's a sadistic killer. I think he stores up the need to kill like in a savings account and then makes a withdrawal. He and the fat one to his left, Heinrich Klaustermeyer, drive along the ghetto streets randomly shooting anybody walking nearby. If they don't find strollers, they shoot at people looking out of their windows."

I moved to help the old Jew. Anger had replaced my fear.

Rachel grabbed my arm. "They'll kill you. Stay here."

I looked around to see if anyone in our small group hiding in the doorway would help. Heads shook no. My mind flashed back to the soup line and what I'd expected my father to do. Now that it was my turn, I realized the helplessness of the situation.

I suppose you could call me a coward—that's how I'd thought of my papa, initially—but when faced with the reality, it was different, overwhelming, as it must have been for him. Even though I was not afraid, there was nothing I could do. The Gestapo were four; I was one. They had guns; I had none. I remembered what Papa had said: "Adapt or perish."

"*Ir baren basterdz. Ikh sheltn aykh aun ayere kinder,*" the old man shouted. You fucking bastards. I curse you and your children.

The Nazi obviously didn't understand him. He did his dance again and pointed the tip of his knife at the old man's beard.

"*Geyn tsu genem!*" the old man cried again.

Frankenstein grabbed hold of the end of the beard and began to slice it off. The Jew kicked and struggled, turning his head side to side, but it was no use. The Nazi, laughing, held up the gray trophy.

The Jew reared his head back and spat—*ptui!*—in the German's face. "*Hobn a gute gelekhter itst, ir mamzer!*" he screamed. Have a good laugh now, you bastard!

Frankenstein drew his gun and pointed it at the old man's face for a long moment. Then he wiped the Jew's spittle off his face, smiled, and pulled the trigger.

The old man fell backward, dead before his skull cracked and bled on the sidewalk. Frankenstein unzipped his pants and urinated on the body. He threw an arm across Klaustermeyer's shoulder. Laughing, they sauntered to the car and sped off.

Rachel and I were numb, with a combination of fear, anger, and hatred. How they could kill so callously, without remorse, transcended any understanding. Their capacity for evil was unlimited. I could almost hear the rage building in my gut.

I wanted revenge, but how could I get it? How would I adapt? I did not intend to perish.

CHAPTER 18

My walks with Rachel became the highlight of my day. It was the only time we could be alone, surrounded by scores of other walkers. Every room in every building still standing was crowded. More than half the buildings had collapsed, and we walked around or wove our way through huge piles of rubble that obstructed sidewalks and streets.

We shared our deepest hopes and darkest secrets and had to be satisfied with emotional intimacy. Privacy was impossible for more than a quick kiss and fleeting hug. That was probably just as well but made for some very cold showers and lonely nights.

While some fortunate Jews found employment in German-owned factories or shops, both in and out of the ghetto, most were unemployed. Scrawny beggars of all ages, near starvation, lined the streets. Children had the most success and at times were "loaned" to childless couples for that purpose.

"Haks Rakhmunes! A shtikel broit?" Have mercy! A little bread? It was a common plea, heard on almost every street corner.

One cold December afternoon, I walked with Rachel along Leszno Street near the courthouse in the ghetto. We were bundled with two sweaters beneath our jackets. Mine was my father's old leather jacket, and Rachel wore her usual green jacket.

We came upon a woman bent on one knee and talking earnestly

with a little boy, maybe six or seven. His arms and legs poked like broomsticks from raggedy clothes. His pale face was drawn and teary as he held an empty tin cup, sobbing. When we approached, the woman stood and draped a protective arm across the little boy's shoulders.

She wore a nurse's uniform beneath a heavy black overcoat. She looked fairly young, maybe thirty. She had dark hair and a round face with twinkly, kindly brown eyes and full, red lips. Most striking was her tiny size. She was less than five feet tall and probably forty kilograms.

"Do you have any food with you?" she asked without preamble. "Jerzy says he hasn't eaten in two days."

I put a hand in my pocket, rummaged around, and found a sweet biscuit I'd been saving for Rachel. I held it out to the boy, who snatched it, greedily popped it into his mouth, and started chewing.

Sad eyes suddenly brightened as the sugary taste hit his palate. Silently, he held out his hand for more, but I had nothing else and shook my head. The sad look and tears returned.

The woman faced us. "I'm Irena Sendler," she said, "and this little boy just told me his name, Jerzy Rudnicki. He says the Nazis took his parents to Pawiak Prison last week, and he's been living on the street ever since. I'm going to try to find a home for him."

"Hi," I said, extending my hand. "I'm Jakob Holmberg, and this is my good friend Rachel Glowinski."

"Holmberg," Irena said, studying my face. "Is your father Solomon Holmberg, a member of the Judenrat?"

My eyebrows rose. "Yes, do you know him?"

She nodded. "A very good man. Smart and helpful with the settlement. He did a fine job—or as fine as he could, under the circumstances. I work at CENTOS, just a couple of blocks from here, down Leszno Street, near the courthouse." She pointed.

"What's CENTOS?" Rachel asked.

"The National Society for the Care of Orphans, part of the Jewish social self-help organization we've formed here in the ghetto. We're stretched to the limit, with more orphans than we can handle and more people coming in every day. That's why so many little tykes like this boy are out on the street, begging. We've run out of space, food, heat, blankets—you name it. Orphans are literally freezing to death on the street."

"How awful. Can we do anything? Can my papa help?"

"Talk to him; see what he can do. I have some homes on the Aryan side where I could place youngsters, but I obviously can't move them out of the ghetto past the Nazi guards."

"I will. Meantime, Jerzy can stay with us. It's a bit crowded, but we'll find room for one more."

"Bless you." Irena bent on one knee again to talk to the boy. "It'll be okay, Jerzy. I promise. I'll come visit, and you won't need to stay there long."

His eyes got big. He seemed more afraid than grateful.

I reached my hand toward him, but he backed up, pressed against the wall, and started to cry.

"He's been pretty traumatized, seeing men take his parents," Irena said.

"Damn Gestapo." I turned to Rachel and nodded toward Jerzy.

Rachel knelt alongside Irena and held out her hand. Jerzy hesitantly took it.

Rachel drew him toward her, inch by inch, like a fisherman reeling in a catch, and then slowly and tenderly lifted him into her arms. She hushed his crying and stroked his hair, and the tyke lay his head on her shoulder. She stood and kissed his cheek, and he closed his eyes. He must've been exhausted.

My heart swelled at the tenderness of the scene, just the pure sweetness of emotion, seeing a little lost soul find an oasis of hope in this desert of madness. At that moment, I decided I wanted Rachel to be my wife, to be the mother of my children.

We said goodbye to Irena and made plans to meet the following day. We walked to our building, with Jerzy asleep on Rachel's shoulder the whole way. When we went inside the building, he woke, looked around with frantic eyes, and started sobbing again.

"I want my mommy," he cried.

"Shush, little one," Rachel said. "Shush. It's going to be okay. We'll find your mommy, but first, how would you like some bread and butter? And maybe a glass of milk? Yes? Or a cup of soup?"

He nodded and gave a tiny smile.

"Okay, then, stop crying and come with me. We'll go find the food." She took him into her flat.

I went to mine. Mama was preparing dinner. I told her what had happened.

"That poor thing," she said, shaking her head, her eyes welling. "To be orphaned at such an age and left without anyone. I hope Papa can help." She glanced at the clock. "He'll be home shortly."

"Irena Sendler is an extraordinary woman," Papa said after dinner, when I'd told him what'd happened. "She's Christian; lives in a nice safe flat on the Aryan side but has made it her life's work to help Jews in the ghetto. She once told me that her father raised her with the philosophy, 'If you see someone drowning, you must jump into the water to save him, even if you cannot swim.' And that's what she lives by."

He pushed back from the table and crossed his legs. "She runs CENTOS, as she told you, and goes in and out of the ghetto several times a day, using some sort of an epidemic health control pass, smuggling in food, medicines, whatever's needed. She knows the Germans are deathly afraid of catching typhus, and she uses that scare tactic to her advantage." He gave a short laugh. "She's even commandeered the hospital's ambulance to smuggle grain, meat, vegetables, and other necessities hidden under stretchers in the back. She's fearless. So far, she's not been caught, and the Nazis don't know who she really is or how big is the operation she runs."

"She said she has placement homes for orphans on the Aryan side but can't get the children out," I said, watching his face.

82

"That's a problem. The Nazis only let out Jews with a work pass who are employed on the Aryan side. No one else can leave."

"Can you do something?" My voice was hopeful.

"I'll try but not likely." He shook his head. "Times are getting even harder. There's some talk about the Nazis beginning a transport system, resettling Jews east to God knows where. I think Irena and her friends are basically on their own."

CHAPTER 19

When I stopped for Rachel the next day, I saw Jerzy in her apartment. Her sisters were doting on him. "At last, we have a little brother," they shouted, laughing and playing together. He giggled and ran about the room with them.

I told Rachel what Papa had said about Irena as we neared the courthouse. When we got close, we saw she had another child with her, a little girl with golden curls, several years younger than Jerzy. The youngster was sound asleep in Irena's arms.

"How brave are you?" were Irena's first words, searching my face and then Rachel's.

I sucked in a deep breath, let it out slowly, and looked at Rachel. She was grinning!

"I think one of us may be braver than the other," Rachel said with a nod, punching me lightly on the shoulder. "But neither of us scares easily."

I thought about the couple killed on the soup line and the old Jewish man murdered on the street, and maybe Rachel remembered her friend shot while cleaning underwear. We didn't know the risks Irena was talking about, but our hatred of the Germans gave us strength and perhaps a false sense of bravado.

"You both can be trusted. Right?"

"Yes," we answered simultaneously.

"Follow me. We're smuggling this little three-year-old out of the ghetto to a home on the Aryan side. Girls are easier to place with non-Jewish families than boys because Gentiles can raise them without fear that a circumcision would betray the child. Anyone caught harboring a Jew is executed immediately, along with the entire family and sometimes neighbors too."

Rachel peered at the child. "She's a beautiful little girl."

Irena smiled and said in a soft voice, "Actually, *she* is a *he*. We've made him look like a girl in a dress, so if we're stopped, the Gestapo won't pull his pants down."

Rachel and I looked at each other and smiled at the clever deception.

We trailed Irena as she walked toward the courthouse. I was scared, but finally, this was a chance to *do* something.

"I don't know if you're aware," Irena said, dropping her voice, "that the courthouse sits half in the ghetto and half on the Aryan side of the wall. The Nazis were stupid to divide it like that, but it's to our advantage. The ghetto entrance is in front of us here on Leszno Street, while the entrance on Ogrodowa Street opens to the Aryan side. That's where we're going to exit."

She put a finger to her lips and walked up the steps from Leszno into the courthouse. The entrance was a vaulted two-story room with a dark marble floor, white walls, and thick, round columns supporting the ceiling. Irena made a quick right turn and unlocked a door with a key she removed from her purse. We walked down a flight of stairs into the basement.

Irena took a flashlight from her purse. She whispered, "We're beneath the courthouse in a basement tunnel that leads to the Aryan side. I gave the janitor, Stanislaw, five hundred zloty to leave the connecting door unlocked." She walked ahead, shining the flashlight, and we followed. The little boy stirred in her arms but remained asleep. She came to a door and tugged, but it didn't open.

"Damn!" she let out in a loud breath. "This was supposed to be unlocked."

A man materialized from the shadows. He flipped on a flashlight in his hand. "Where you going?" he asked.

I heard Irena gasp. "Who're you? Where's Stanislaw?"

The man was short and fat with the red, watery eyes of an alcoholic. His clothes were ragged, and he held an unlit cigar stub in his mouth. "Maybe this was his day off, or maybe he's sick, or maybe the Gestapo took him to Pawiak Prison. Point is, he ain't here, is he?"

"How much?" Irena asked, resignation in her voice.

"Maybe nothing, and I just call the Gestapo that you're smuggling a baby, probably a Jew, to the Aryan side. How'd you like that?"

"Look, don't fool with me," Irena said, authority replacing resignation. "I've got friends who will mess you up badly."

"Do you, now. And who might they be?" Fat Man stood tall and tried to look intimidating.

Irena glanced at me. I stepped forward, took the long flashlight from her, and held it in my hand like a club. Then I stood in front of the man. I was at least a head taller and much younger. I'd never been in a fight before, but I clenched the flashlight like I knew what I was doing.

Fat Man looked me over, backed away, and said, "Thousand zlotys."

"I already paid Stanislaw five hundred."

Fat Man stared at me and then at the flashlight in my hand. "Okay, five hundred."

Irena handed the baby to Rachel, opened her purse, and removed the money. "Open the door first," she said.

Fat Man pulled out a key and opened the door. Irena handed him the zlotys. We walked through the open door and heard it close, the lock clicking behind us.

"Well, that was interesting," Irena said. She took back the flashlight and let out a long sigh.

"More than interesting," I said, holding up my shaking hands. "I've never been in a fight in my life."

Irena smiled. "Could've fooled me."

"And me," Rachel added. "I guess now we know who really is brave." She held up her fists in a mock fight.

"Will he call the Gestapo?" I asked.

"Maybe, but I doubt it." Her look was convincing, even in the dark. This lady didn't scare easily. "That was just a typical shakedown for money. I always carry extra zlotys. There are informers, blackmailers, and all sorts of crooks who pull stuff like that. Sometimes a *szmalcowniki*, or Jew betrayer, will stop you on the street on the Aryan side if you look Jewish and threaten to call the Gestapo if you don't give them money. They'll come up behind you and meow like a cat. That's the signal to let you know they're going to call the Gestapo unless you pay the blackmail. Sheltering a Jew has been called 'keeping cats.'"

She continued to walk, and we followed.

"That's crazy," Rachel said. "So what do you do?"

"You've got to stand up to them, just like this guy," she said over her shoulder. "They don't want a fight, just the money. They'll take the bribe and disappear."

"Will this route remain safe for you?" Rachel asked.

Irena stopped and ran fingers through her hair. "I suppose he might make good on his threat. I have other ways to get these kids out."

We walked a few feet until we came to a flight of stairs.

Irena paused again. "Let's have a minute to let the adrenaline settle. Take off your armbands," she said. "When we walk up these stairs"—she pointed—"you will become Polish Aryans."

After a little rest, she started up the stairs, and we followed. "Act with confidence. Don't be afraid to look people in the eye as you walk. Just act natural."

My armpits were wet, and I was breathing fast. Fat Man had made me realize how unprepared I was for what we were doing. And now, we were going to pose as Aryans. I looked at Rachel.

She smiled calmly and took my hand. "No big deal," she whispered. "We don't look Jewish."

"Yeah," I whispered back, "but if we're stopped, we have no papers."

Irena overheard and turned around. "Yes, you do." She handed me the young boy to hold. "Inside his blanket are two envelopes. Reach in, and slip them out. Those are new Polish identity papers, a Kennkarte for you and one for Rachel. They're perfect forgeries, and neither is stamped Jude. On this side of the wall, you're both Polish Aryans, not Jews."

I looked at her in amazement. "How did you know we'd agree to help? How did you get these made so quickly?"

"One question at a time." She laughed as we walked out the courthouse onto Ogrodowa Street. "I sensed you would when you offered to take little Jerzy. We employ an expert forger who fakes many kinds of official documents for us. Your new identity papers were routine. He had them ready in an hour."

We followed Irena toward Mirowski Square on the Aryan side of the wall.

The difference from the ghetto was dramatic. Buildings were mostly intact, and the streets wide and clean, with many kinds of motorized traffic whizzing up and down. People bustled along, dressed in winter finery, faces full and red-cheeked. They didn't need layers of clothes to look fat. Stores displayed merchandise in large front windows, and brimming baskets of food outside grocery stores made me drool.

I saw very few beggars and suspected those who begged were likely from the ghetto and in grave danger of being arrested by the SS, who guarded the ghetto gates.

We walked past a checkpoint where several SS loitered, smoking cigarettes and drinking beer. One of them whistled at Rachel and then shouted in Polish, "Hey, pretty lady, want a drink of my beer?" He held his bottle in Rachel's direction.

"Just keep walking," Irena said, breathless. "Ignore them." She picked up the pace. "This is different. They're trouble."

The SS called again, but Rachel didn't respond. He flipped his cigarette to the street, ground it out with his boot, and sauntered toward us, holding the beer forward as an offering. "I don't like to be ignored," he said with a forced smile. He stopped in front of Rachel and blocked her path. "Especially by such a pretty lady." He was thin-faced, pockmarked, and leering. He reached to lift up her chin, but she gently pushed his hand away.

"Thanks for the compliment," Rachel said, smiling back at him, drawing her green jacket close across her chest, "but I'm a married lady. This is my baby girl"—she pointed to the little one Irena was carrying—"and this is my husband."

He studied Rachel and then looked at me. "I don't see a wedding ring."

"Sold it for food for the baby," Rachel answered without a pause. "Rations don't go very far when you have a third mouth to feed. Maybe you could get us more. How about some fresh milk?"

The SS looked at the little child. "You're pretty young to have such an old baby."

"My goodness, another compliment! My baby girl's only two, and I'm seventeen. My husband"—she nodded at me—"was very eager to have children."

His face darkened with disbelief, eyebrows bunched and lips pursed thin. Two of his fellow guards strolled over. One had more stripes.

"I am Oberführer Schmidt. Is there a problem here?" His body language said, *I am in charge.*

"No, none that—" Rachel started to say.

"Yes, sir, Oberführer, there is a problem. This pretty lady is just ignoring me. She won't even take a drink of my beer."

Schmidt shook his finger at Rachel. "That's not a polite way to treat the SS, young lady. Germans, especially the SS, deserve more respect from you Poles. After all, we are now your masters. Show me your papers—all three of you," he said, holding out his hand.

"Why, certainly, Oberführer," Irena responded in a pleasant tone, pulling her Kennkarte out.

I reached for mine with a trembling hand. Rachel's and my identity papers had different last names. He'd know Rachel was lying, that our papers were forgeries, and that maybe we were Jews. He'd make me pull down my pants, and then we'd be shot—or at least I would.

All this flashed in a microsecond as he read Irena's Kennkarte.

A commotion at the checkpoint diverted his attention. The remaining guard had caught one of the little smugglers, who was putting up a good battle against a man twice his size. The guard ripped open the boy's coat, and food spilled out onto the street— far more than he could've gotten begging. The boy broke loose and bolted, and the guard tripped over the food, trying to catch him.

The Oberführer dropped Irena's Kennkarte, and he and his men ran to head off the escaping little fugitive.

"Come quickly," Irena said. "Follow me." She picked up her Kennkarte and walked off at a rapid pace, fast enough to get away but not so fast that we'd attract attention. She led us east toward Zelaznej Bramy Square and from there to the Saski Gardens. We followed along a winding path to the back of the gardens and sat on a bench to catch our breath, concealed from the street by a thick grove of trees.

"That was too close," Irena said, looking at Rachel. She shuddered. "Bribing the fat man was routine, but those were the SS, as bad as the Gestapo. You had quick thinking about being married, but your identity papers would've given you away."

"I'm sorry," Rachel said, finally looking scared. Tiny beads of sweat glistened on her forehead. "It just popped into my head. I didn't like where the conversation was heading."

Irena smiled at the two of us. "Maybe I'd better prepare another set of papers with the same surnames?"

"Fine with me," I said, pulling Rachel to me. I kissed her cheek. "She can have my surname anytime. The sooner the better."

"Are you proposing?" Rachel asked. Her composure had returned, and her eyes twinkled. "If you are, you have to do it properly."

I got down on one knee in front of her, took her hands in mine, and looked up at her. "Will you marry me?" I asked. As I said the words, one part of my brain yelled, *You're crazy.* Another part said, *Do it now. She's going to be your lifelong partner.*

Rachel made the decision. "Yes, if we live through this nightmare." She blinked back tears and smiled.

"Why wait?" I said, standing and taking her in my arms.

Rachel became quiet, thinking. "First, I need my parents' permission. Next, we have no means of support or a place to live. Third, either of us could be captured or killed at any moment. Fourth, now's no time to have a child. Fifth, we're pretty young—"

"Okay, okay," I said with a chuckle. "I get the picture. But we can at least get engaged."

The baby in Irena's arms stirred. "Enough, you two lovebirds. We need to take this little one to a home before the Luminal sedative wears off. So move this along. I'm not a minister or a rabbi, but I now pronounce you two engaged."

We laughed.

Irena slipped a silver ring off her finger and handed it to me. "The engaged man may put this ring on the finger of the engaged woman."

"Thank you, Irena. I'm touched, but I can't take this." I pushed her hand away.

She shook her head. "Please. I have great hopes for the two of you, not just for your own future but in helping me meet the needs of people in the ghetto. This will seal your and my relationship, just as it seals the two of you."

I hugged her and took the ring. Rachel and I faced each other, much like we might at a wedding ceremony. We gazed into each other's eyes as she held out her hand, and I slipped the ring on her finger. Then we kissed, long and passionately. I silently prayed that we'd both live through this insanity, and she'd become my wife when it was all over.

"Okay, break it up," Irena said, already walking off. "Delivery time."

CHAPTER 20

The Germans were right to fear a typhus epidemic. Our close quarters, lack of personal hygiene or sanitation, and starvation diets all increased the risk of infection. Added to this, corpses of people who died outdoors from starvation or typhus or were shot by the Gestapo were piled at the sides of the streets, stripped of their clothes, and left to decompose. Passersby covered the bodies with old newspapers topped by stones to keep the papers from blowing away. Every morning, stiff bodies were loaded like slabs of firewood onto a horse-drawn wagon, destined for a mass grave.

Lice infested everything—our clothes, hair, and homes. Whenever possible, we smuggled in vials of typhus vaccine, hidden in the false bottoms of handbags, coat linings, or brassieres padded with multiple small pockets. So many women wore them that it was a joke that living in the ghetto made women's breasts enlarge.

The Germans began reducing the size of the ghetto in October 1941, claiming it was to stop the smuggling and to control the typhus epidemic that was averaging a thousand new cases each week. The SS sometimes allowed an ambulance to carry those who were very sick to hospitals on the Aryan side.

Irena viewed this as a smuggler's dream. Counting on the Germans' fear of infection, she hid sedated little ones under dirty, foul-smelling bloody blankets in the same bed as the sick or even bundled in coffins shared with a corpse and carried out in the ambulance. The ambulance driver had a dog he'd trained to bark and whine on command so when they went through the checkpoint, noise from the dog would obscure any sounds from youngsters waking if the sedatives wore off. Annoyed guards quickly waved the ambulance through. Some children were concealed in burlap sacks or garbage bags slung over the shoulders of workmen trekking to Aryan factories and delivered at the back doors of homes, like a bag of groceries or laundry.

Irena was very creative. One morning, when Rachel and I met her for our usual day to help smuggle babies out and food and medical supplies in, she asked, "What do you know about the sewers?"

"That carry human waste?" I asked.

"None other. I've bribed a city worker for a map of these underground passages. They're perfect secret tunnels under the wall. Three main lines with multiple tributaries. We'll enter by lifting a metal manhole cover on the ghetto side, descend on iron rungs fixed to the wall, and drop the last few feet into the most god-awful–smelling knee-high waterway of excrement you've ever seen, and then rise like a filthy phoenix on the Aryan side. Sound like fun?"

It didn't, but that's what we did. The first time we went, we trailed Irena, with one baby strapped to Rachel's back and another to mine. After that, Rachel and I traveled alone, following the map to navigate twists and turns. I never did master the routes; I often got lost and had to backtrack to find our bearings. Being trapped in the sewer was not a pleasant prospect.

When we emerged, we tried to find someplace to clean our shoes and pants but were not always successful. Most times, the people we met understood where we'd come from and just wrinkled their noses.

If placement had not yet been arranged for the orphans, we used Father Boduen's Children's Home on the Aryan side as a stopover until a foster home could be found. This was especially necessary for children who had "bad" facial appearances; that is, who looked Jewish and, if caught, would be killed.

The entrance to the Boduen's Children's Home was like a church sitting behind a brick wall. Often called "a gateway to life," the home took babies of all denominations from families whose members had been killed, resettled, arrested, or just disappeared, as well as sometimes from Poles who had agreed to provide a foster home for a Jewish child but became frightened of discovery and gave up the child to the Boduen's Children's Home.

The Gestapo inspected the Home frequently to check the children's documents that proved their Christian identity. Birth certificates of Christian children who had died were especially valuable. Their deaths were never reported to the authorities and their documents were "revised" to provide a name and registry number for an incoming Jewish arrival.

Nuns at the home taught older Jewish children the Lord's Prayer and the Catechism of the Catholic Church to prepare them for drills the Gestapo used to uncover Jewish children posing as Catholics. Any stumble, such as mixing up matins, morning prayers, with vespers, evening prayers, led to "advanced" interrogation techniques.

Irena kept a list of the names and addresses of relocated orphans, as well as their new identities, to make certain the children would be returned to their birth parents after the war—if the parents survived and could be found—so the children could reclaim their Jewish identity. Irena and a friend named Jaga hid the lists in a glass milk jar they buried at night beneath an apple tree in Jaga's backyard. Every so often, they'd dig up the jar to add new names and then rebury it. Irena swore Jaga and us to secrecy.

When we couldn't smuggle an orphan out of the ghetto, Irena appealed to Dr. Janusz Korczak, a Jewish pediatrician who ran a ghetto orphanage of two hundred children at 16 Sienna Street near the southern border of the ghetto. He was famous in Poland, with a radio program before the war called *Old Doctor* and as an author of over twenty books for children and adults. In fact, his real name was Henryk Goldszmit, but he wrote under the pen name of Janusz Korczak and that was how he was known. As a child, I'd read his most famous book, *King Matt the First*, about a boy who became king and tried to reform his kingdom. I treasured it. One of his popular adult books was called *How to Love a Child*.

I was nervous when I met him. Irena had told me so much about him; he'd become a living legend. Because he was so famous, the Nazis had offered him asylum out of the ghetto on several occasions, but he refused to abandon his orphans.

His assistant, Stefa, an older woman with a sweet face, escorted us to his office, a tiny cubicle in the orphanage, barely large enough for a desk, a few chairs, and a tiny sofa. A small window opened onto a dirt playground where I could see a group of five- or six-year-olds playing. "He's the most wonderful man I've ever known," Stefa whispered, flashing the doctor an adoring glance as she left.

He looked to be in his sixties. Bald, with a mostly gray mustache and tousled goatee, he wore wire-rimmed round glasses that accentuated his blue eyes and gave him a professorial look. He had a slight build and appeared frail; he walked with a cane after imprisonment and injuries from a Gestapo beating for refusing to wear the Jewish armband, rather than his Polish uniform.

"So you two are Irena's latest recruits," Dr. Korczak said, smiling. He offered us his hand. "She must have an army by now. It's a pleasure to meet you both."

"Thank you, sir," I said, smiling in return and standing stiff, like a soldier at attention. I felt I was in the presence of an important person and didn't know quite how to act. "It's a great honor to meet you, sir. Irena has told us so much about you."

"Relax and stop with the 'sir.' I'm Janusz." He spread his hands out, palms up, as he sat down on the sofa and motioned us to the chairs.

"I can't say that, sir," I said, sitting down. "How about Dr. Korczak?" He nodded. "That'll do fine."

"Thank you for accepting little Yitzhak," Rachel said, watching the children through the window. Stefa had taken him by the hand

and was introducing him to a group on the playground who'd been jumping rope.

"I'm sure he'll fit right in. Just one more mouth to feed." Korczak sighed. He seemed tired, worn out. He looked it also, his face haggard, eyes bloodshot.

"That's difficult?" I asked.

"Oh, yes. My staff and I often go door-to-door to beg for food when we run out of black-market groceries. There's never enough in the ghetto, as I'm sure you're aware. Irena helps whenever she can. The children seem to thrive, despite the shortages. I weigh them each Sabbath to be sure they're gaining."

"How can you afford black-market prices?" I asked. The reality of providing support for two hundred orphans, plus a staff of a dozen, struck home.

"Irena has contacts—I think in England—who receive donations from Jewish organizations all over the world, especially America. She smuggles in the money and shares what she can with us. It's enough to keep us going."

"Do you miss practicing as a pediatrician?" Rachel asked, studying a graduation certificate from the University of Warsaw that hung over his desk.

He smiled, glanced at the certificate, and then looked out the window. "No. These children are my life," he said, pointing. "I'm able to raise them the way I think they should be raised, as I've written in many of my books and in this diary I keep." He took a black leather-bound book from his desk and held it up for us to see.

"And that is?" Rachel asked.

"With respect, independence, and equality, rather than by authoritarian control at the hands of an adult who does not understand or care about their world. That's what the Germans are doing to us—treating us like children without regard for our feelings and our world, locking us up in this god-awful ghetto prison. I refuse to inflict that behavior on the children, so I've created their own world. They live in a protected bubble—at least, so far—within the Nazi domain. I treat them as equals; I respect them, and they, in return, respect me. The older children help run the orphanage, hold an internal court of honor, and publish a weekly newspaper under my guidance."

Rachel's eyes grew moist. "That's beautiful," she said, "to be insulated from the daily horrors we're living with."

He smiled, and his eyes filled also. They lit up as he said, "It's my greatest gift, one that sustains me every waking hour of every day. When you save children, you save the future of the world with all its myriad possibilities. It's my dream they'll grow up to become healthy, normal adults with no scars from this madness."

"Will we ever see that kind of world again?" I asked, depressed at the thought.

Dr. Korczak shook his head, a sad look on his face. "Not as long as Nazis control it."

"How long do you think that will be?"

"I wish I knew, Jakob. I wish I knew." He shook his head again. "One more day is too long."

CHAPTER 21

Rumors were a way of life in the ghetto. They spread faster than typhus. Since we had no access to phones or radio, it was hard to check their validity.

Several underground newspapers were secretly circulated. Workers risked their lives to print information about the war that they'd learned from spies outside our walls. The newspaper moved from one hiding place to another in the dead of night to avoid detection. The Nazis had issued a decree that "as long as the secret press continues to appear, there will be executions" and called such activities treasonous.

The latest idea floating in the spring air of 1942 was a new settlement in a place called Treblinka, ninety kilometers northeast of Warsaw. People who'd seen that camp said it'd been built without barracks, so it was not likely we'd be sent there to work.

Other rumors from a handful of people who had escaped the Lublin ghetto, located about 170 kilometers southeast of Warsaw, were more ominous. They talked about Jews packed into cattle cars and transported to Belzec, a town 130 kilometers southeast from Lublin. A young boy who'd escaped from Belzec said it was a killing camp, where Jews were systematically gassed to death. No one believed such an outlandish story. Reports emerged about liquidation of ghettos in Lwow and Krakow, with inhabitants also transported to Belzec and gassed. Still, no one believed.

At dinner, I asked Papa what he knew about what was going on and whether these reports held any truth. As a member of the Judenrat, he was always current on ghetto happenings. He also seemed to have an inside track to the newspaper and regularly brought home a copy as soon as it was printed.

He stopped eating and laid down his fork to consider my question. He pushed back from the table, unsmiling, with sad eyes. "Only rumors so far, Jakob, but I'm worried—very worried. Gassing Jews seems far-fetched, even considering the cruelty of the Gestapo and SS. I would think we're too valuable a workforce to kill. There's talk about moving us east to work camps to help supply the German army, which would fit with keeping us alive."

I took my last bite of potato and slurped the soup. "What kind of work camps? Supply them with what?"

"Don't talk with your mouth full," Mama interrupted. "You know better."

"Yes, Mama." My eyebrows rose in exasperation. "I'm not eight years old."

"All the more reason to know better." She stood with hands on hips, shaking a wooden spoon at me.

She was serious, but I had to fight not to laugh. I was nineteen, two inches taller than Papa, and a hundred pounds heavier than Mama. We were living hand-to-mouth, barely surviving on black-market food. The Gestapo and SS were killing people every day in broad daylight for no reason; we'd just heard rumors of camps gassing Jews to death; and Mama was scolding me about talking with my mouth full.

"Jakob, you know you can't win an argument with your mother. I haven't won a fight in twenty-two years. Just do as you're told."

"We don't fight, Solomon. We discuss," she said, clearing the table and giving him a fake scowl.

He chuckled. "I haven't won one of those either. So what were we talking about, Jakob? I've lost track." He threw his hands in the air, looking at Mama.

"Work camps to supply Germans."

He nodded, returning his gaze to me. "Ah, yes. I don't know what kind of work. Could be on farms to grow food or tend animals or maybe work in factories that manufacture whatever Germans need, like arms, planes, or tanks. I've no information yet."

"It can't be that new place, Treblinka, can it? I heard it was built without barracks so there'd be no place for us to live."

⁓

The rumors worsened. A week later, Papa brought home a newspaper with stories about more death camps—one in Sobibor, almost three hundred kilometers southeast of Warsaw, and another in Chelmno, just east of Lublin.

Miraculously, three people sentenced to death in Chelmno escaped through the woods at night and told how almost one hundred thousand Jews had been gassed in just two months the year before. They related chilling details of how new arrivals were told they were going to take a shower. They were given a bar of soap and a towel, made to strip, and then led to gas chambers. The newspaper story also reaffirmed the killings in Belzec, saying that no one ever returned from that killing factory.

"This is terribly frightening, if true," Papa said, his face grim. "We discussed it at a Judenrat meeting. We also heard that the Nazis had some sort of a meeting in a small town outside Berlin called Wannsee in January. We don't have specifics, just that a Nazi named Eichmann has been put in charge of the Reich Central Security Office to deal with the Jews."

I glanced at Mama, but she showed no surprise, so apparently, Papa had told her about joining the Judenrat.

"But there is still doubt among many that stories about mass killings are actually true," he continued. "Some members of the

Judenrat received letters from relatives in Chelmno and Sobibor, saying how well they were being treated after resettling."

"Papa, how do you know the Nazis didn't send those letters just to fool us?" One of my friends had told me his cousin had received a letter from his brother, who'd died two years ago.

"Could be. Equally disconcerting is more talk of emptying our ghetto, moving us to Treblinka."

"Maybe they've built barracks there by now," Mama said, hope in her voice, "so we can go there to work and have a place to live."

Papa's face darkened, in no way agreeing with Mama. He ran a hand over a two days' growth of beard. "I hope you're right," he said. "I only hope you're right."

I wondered what it would take to get Jews to stand and fight. They seemed to think sacrifice, blood, and tears were part of our heritage, required to keep our traditions alive.

That was indeed a part of our history.

But enough is enough of being treated like vermin, I thought. *Armed resistance is the only way to end this insanity, the only thing Nazis will respect. They'll kill ten or even a hundred of us for every one of them we kill, but it's now time to stop adapting and start acting, or we will surely all perish!*

CHAPTER 22

The pounding on the door seemed part of my dream. In the dream, I was in my bedroom with Rachel. We'd just kissed, and I was unbuttoning her blouse. She had her hands on my belt, undoing the buckle. Her mother was pounding on the bedroom door to save her daughter from ruin.

The door splintered with a loud *crack* and shocked me from my dream. It took me a second or two to get my bearings.

I heard Nazis shouting and realized the *crack* was real.

"Alle raus! Jetzt! Hände hoch! Alle raus!" Everybody out! Now! Hands up! Everybody out!

This was no dream. This was a nightmare.

I jumped out of bed. My erection shriveled to nothing in seconds as I slipped on my bathrobe, knotted the belt, and ran into the kitchen. Our front door was shattered and rocked loosely on its hinges. It was three o'clock in the morning.

Mama and Papa stood next to the kitchen table, wearing bathrobes, staring at five men in gray-green Gestapo uniforms. A red armband with a white circle and a black swastika in the middle encircled each man's right biceps. None drew a weapon, but they didn't need to.

One man walked forward to stand directly in front of Papa, his face inches from Papa's, and stared unblinkingly into his eyes.

Mama took two steps back, wringing her hands. The man looked more Jewish than German, with thick bushy eyebrows, a swarthy complexion, and a prominent nose.

"I am First Lieutenant Ludwig Brandt, chief of the Gestapo's Jewish department in Warsaw," he said in Polish. He removed a paper from his shirt pocket, unfolded it, and read aloud. "Solomon Holmberg, you are hereby placed under arrest for being a member of a group of Jews that has been publishing an illegal secret newspaper. If you are found guilty of this violation, the penalty will be imprisonment and death. Do you have anything to say in your defense?"

Mama swayed on her feet, and Papa gasped and sucked in a mouthful of air. Their faces drained white; I'm sure mine did also. Mama now hid behind Papa, hands over her face, crying silently. Papa brushed the palm of his hand across his forehead to wipe away glistening sweat. My knees were shaking, my breathing fast, and my pulse too fast to count. I tried to lick my lips, but I had no saliva.

"I don't know what you're talking about. I'm a mechanical engineer and know nothing about publishing newspapers," Papa said haltingly, massaging the muscles over his chest with his fingers. His voice quivered; he dropped his eyes and stared at the floor.

"How about mimeograph machines and a printing press? Do you know anything about them? How to build them? How to operate them? How they copy papers at a fast rate? As a mechanical engineer, surely you must know." Brandt sneered at Papa.

Papa shook his head unconvincingly. "I do not."

"It will go easier for you if you confess. If not, we will bring you to 25 Szucha Avenue. Do you know what that is?"

Papa shook his head again.

"Gestapo headquarters, a nice place for interrogation by my friends." He nodded at the other four. Two of them opened and closed fists and displayed fake smiles. "We have many effective methods to get confessions, and you will sing like a pretty bird; I promise. If you survive their questioning, you will be transported—you'll need a stretcher by then—to Pawiak Prison, where you'll be executed. We like to use hanging since it's more economical than wasting a bullet on a Jew, and it makes a good scene for public education."

Mama's knees buckled. She collapsed to the floor. I ran to her and helped her sit on a kitchen chair. I wet a towel and put it across the back of her neck. She cradled her arms on the table and buried her head in them.

"Or maybe we will ask your son to describe your activities." Brandt turned to me. "What's your name, boy?"

"J-Ja-Jakob."

"And what do you know about what your father's doing, Jakob?"

"Nothing." Papa had been smart not to tell me.

"Oh, I doubt that. Perhaps we'll have to question you at 25 Szucha, along with your father."

My knees started to give way, and I had to grab the back of a kitchen chair to keep from collapsing, like Mama.

"Let me be perfectly clear about this, Solomon Holmberg. During the night, we found your underground printing press in the basement of a building on Mila Street and arrested your editor and three associates. At Gestapo headquarters, later in the evening, they happily gave us all the information we needed, including your name and how you helped build and set up the printing press. Sadly, they died during their interrogation. I wanted to give you a chance to tell us yourself and spare you the questioning, but you chose not to. That's too bad. It's time for you to come along with us."

The Gestapo chief nodded to the other four men, who quickly surrounded my father and cuffed his hands behind his back.

My mother sprang to life, ran to Brandt, and grabbed hold of his shirt. Tears ran down her cheeks as she pleaded with him. "Wait! No! Stop! Please! Leave him alone. Give him a chance to promise not to do it anymore."

Brandt seized her wrists, yanked her hands off him, and shoved her aside. I caught her to keep her from falling. She was weeping uncontrollably.

My father didn't say anything. I think he was numb or in shock.

His mouth hung open, and his eyes were wide but stared, unseeing, straight ahead. His bunched eyebrows formed deep, dark furrows.

The men pushed him toward the door, and he staggered like a drunk in a trance. He stumbled when he tripped over the threshold and looked back at Mama with the most sorrowful expression, one I will remember my entire life.

They led him out of the apartment and down the stairs to the street.

I ran to Mama and put my arms around her. She quivered like a wounded animal, mute, arms at her sides, with an expression as sorrowful as Papa's.

"It'll be okay, Mama," I said stupidly. "We'll get the Judenrat to help get him out of jail. Maybe Irena can raise some money for a bribe. I'll—"

A single gunshot rang out.

I ran to the window. My father lay face down on the sidewalk, blood oozing from the back of his head. The Gestapo got into a car and drove off, leaving him there.

I raced down the stairs, screaming, "Papa! Papa!" I ran to him, fell to my knees, and cradled his head in my lap. Mama followed and collapsed onto his body, her arms around his shoulders and her face burrowed into his neck, crying hysterically. His warm blood oozed onto my hands, my shirt, and my pants, but I barely noticed. We just wept and held him close.

Rachel must have heard the gunshot because she came running outside. She gasped. There were no words. The three of us just held onto each other, sobbing and rocking back and forth, stroking Papa's body as it grew cold.

After a while, we regained some composure. Together, we lifted Papa and carried him upstairs to our flat and laid him on the bed.

We buried Papa the next day in the Jewish cemetery. Neighbors in our building came so we had a minyan to say Kaddish.

The night the Gestapo killed Papa was Friday, April 17, 1942. I learned the next day that a major German *Aktion* had taken place. During the night, groups of five or six Gestapos had stormed ghetto homes, searching for prominent Jews from a list of sixty, all associated with underground newspapers. The Gestapo had found fifty-two of the sixty, dragged them to the street, and executed them, as they had my father. An eyewitness survivor reported that the Jewish Police had provided the list to the Gestapo. We'd been betrayed by one of our own.

Because the streets ran red, the night was called "Night of Blood."

For weeks after that, Nazis randomly killed ten to fifteen Jews every night. They shot on a whim, without rhyme or reason. The merest chance determined whether you lived or died. Someone would happen to be walking by, say, from the grocery store or a visit to a neighbor, and *bam*, they would get a bullet in the head.

Ghetto residents lived in terror of hearing a knock on their doors, of having to walk outside. In early May, 110 Jews imprisoned in Pawiak Prison for illegally crossing to the Aryan side were publicly executed.

Prior to the Night of Blood, we lived each day, knowing the ghetto "rules" and how to bend them and still stay alive within the confines of the Nazi boundaries. April 17 and the murders afterward eroded any sense of stability, of foundation, of knowing what to do to stay safe.

The ghetto had become a jungle, with predators lurking behind every building, and survival became an even greater challenge.

CHAPTER 23

After Papa's funeral, Rachel spent a great deal of time in our apartment, helping me support Mama. We sat shiva for seven days and then tried to resume near-normal activities. But Mama was too depressed. She rarely left her room and seemed to live on a slice or two of toast for days on end. I didn't think it possible, but she lost more weight and looked like a skeleton. She said she didn't want to live without Papa.

Rachel and I talked a lot, especially after Mama went to bed, keeping our voices low to not disturb her. We'd stay up late sitting at the kitchen table, drinking weak tea, and eating whatever we'd been able to salvage. The underground printing presses started again, and sometimes we'd have a newspaper to read. That was dangerous, and we'd tear it into tiny pieces to flush down the toilet after we finished.

"The Germans are liquidating the ghetto with these random killings," Rachel said one evening in early May, after reading seventeen names of people killed the night before.

"Do you know why?" I asked. I spread my hands, palms up.

"Because they're murderers."

"True, but that's not the reason." I shook my head. "They want to instill so much fear that we'll do exactly as we're told and be afraid that the slightest disobedience will trigger a bullet in the head."

"It will." She trembled.

"Only if we continue to do nothing and let them get away with it." I stood and paced the small room in stockinged feet, keeping quiet because of Mama. For me, the Night of Blood ended the old, passive ways. "I want a new beginning, Rachel. I can't take any more. I *won't* take any more." I sat back down.

"You and I can't defeat the Nazis, Jakob," Rachel said in a quiet voice. She reached across the table and put her hand on mine.

"Of course not, but I want revenge—or die trying." I raised my hand to slam the table, but a look from Rachel stopped me. "I want the Nazis to pay for what they've done. I want them to fear a Jewish reprisal after each act against us." I pointed a finger at my chest and jabbed several times. "They may end up killing me, but it'll be on my terms, while I'm killing them, not when they decide to shoot me for amusement while I'm walking down the street."

"How will you start?"

I made a fist and punched an imaginary target. "By searching for the Jewish Police traitor who gave the Gestapo the list that got Papa killed. There must be resistance groups I could join."

"No, not you. *Us.* We could join," Rachel said, her look serious.

"Are you sure? There's a good chance of getting killed."

"I know, but I want to help—under one condition." She smiled.

"What?" I asked and leaned toward her.

"That you marry me."

I jumped up, grabbing the back of the chair just before it crashed to the floor. Rachel giggled and put a finger to her lips for silence. "Are you serious?"

"Absolutely." She stood and came into my arms, her lips an inch from mine, body pressed tightly against me. "We love each other. I'm not going to risk losing you before we've had a chance to have a child. If I die, I want to die as a wife and a mother, not an old maid."

"Wait." I held her at arm's length. "Didn't you tell me when we got engaged in the park that now was no time to have a child?"

She nodded. "I did, and I was probably right, but that was two years ago, and I've changed my mind. A woman can do that, you know."

We both laughed.

"Holding little ones for Irena made me want a baby of my own—to love, to nurture, to protect as best we can in these terrible times." Her face softened with that tender look I'd seen when she first held little Jerzy two years earlier, and I'd fallen in love.

"We're nineteen. My mother had two babies by that age. That's part of being alive, of being a woman, and I want that experience."

"But think—how will you be able to move about the ghetto with a big belly?"

"I'm young; I'll manage. Besides, that won't stop me until I'm in my ninth month. I'll keep up with you until then."

I recognized her look and knew not to argue. "Do I have to get down on my knee again to propose?"

She laughed. "No, once is enough."

I held her in my arms. "Kiss me, my wife-to-be. I love you."

When we told Mama and Rachel's parents the next day, they agreed. Mama smiled for the first time since Papa died and kissed us both.

"You're supposed to wait a year after the death of a parent," Mama said, "but I understand and give you my blessings."

Since the Nazis had forbidden public worship, we got married in our apartment, with only Rachel's family, Mama, and Irena Sendler attending. Rachel held a small bouquet of flowers that Irena had snipped from the Saski Gardens, where we'd become engaged.

We stood under an improvised chuppah—a sheet held up by bedposts—while the neighborhood rabbi pronounced us man and wife, a month to the day after Papa had been slain.

Mama provided an old, chipped glass wrapped in a towel, and I smashed it under my foot as everyone shouted, *"Mazel tov!"* We celebrated with a chocolate cake that Irena had managed to sneak in. Mama provided a pair of precious brooches from Papa for me to give to Rachel as a wedding present.

Our wedding night started out like the dream I'd had a month earlier, with a passionate kiss, me unbuttoning Rachel's blouse, and her unbuckling my belt. The only pounding this time was my heart against my rib cage as I carried to bed the woman I loved.

CHAPTER 24

It didn't take long to make contact with Mordechai Anielewicz, the commander in chief of the *Zydowska Organizacja Bojowa*. The ZOB was the Jewish fighting organization in the ghetto. We arranged to meet in a rundown apartment at 32 Zamenhofa Street. He cautioned me to be sure I wasn't followed.

On our walk over, I told Rachel a story I'd heard about Anielewicz. A year before, the Nazis had ordered the Jewish Police to kidnap young males for work details in German labor camps. When two policemen burst into his apartment, Anielewicz beat them up, leaving them alive but unconscious. He fled to another hideout and sent a message to everyone in the ZOB to do the same—to resist recruitment. He'd told them to not become complacent, to fight being a slave in mind and body, and to not accept the present situation. *Revolt against the reality* were his words. That might have been the real start of Jewish resistance.

A guard at the door demanded we show our Kennkarten. She took her time analyzing them with a magnifying glass, front and back, checking for forgery. She explained that the ZOB was very concerned about Nazis posing as Jews and infiltrating the organization.

Angel, as he was nicknamed, was a lot younger than I'd imagined—early twenties, most likely. He had a medium build, square jaw, greenish eyes, and dark hair, cut short. His voice was quiet and gentle, but there was steel in it, a resolve that was the unmistakable mark of a leader. His softness was his strength. During difficult times, people turned to leaders. Angel was one.

His clothes were ordinary. No uniforms for the ZOB, especially no hats. With heads bare, they would not have to doff their hats to the Germans they passed on the sidewalk.

Angel was sitting at a wooden table, studying a book on military tactics, when the guard led us into the small room, bare except for the table and chairs. Next to Angel was an attractive woman of about the same age. She had curly red hair and bright eyes, high cheekbones, and smooth skin. She was reading a copy of an underground newspaper.

Angel rose to greet us. "Welcome to the ZOB headquarters. Please join us." He turned to the woman. "This is my dearest and most trusted companion, Mira Fuchrer. Mira, meet the newlyweds, Rachel and Jakob Holmberg."

"Newlyweds, eh?" Mira said, rising and coming over. She shook my hand and hugged Rachel, kissing both cheeks. *"Mazel tov.* When?"

"A month ago, May 17," Rachel said, beaming. "We didn't want to wait any longer, war or no war."

"I don't blame you," Mira said, looking from Rachel to Angel. "We've discussed it also. Maybe we'll follow your example. Come." She took Rachel by the arm. "Sit down with us."

"Sorry if I've caused you trouble," I said in an undertone to Angel.

"Not a problem, Jakob." He smiled at Mira. "We'll get married soon." He motioned me to sit. "Can I offer you both something? Water? Tea?"

"Thank you, no."

"Tell me why you want to join us. It's dangerous work." He searched our faces intently, as if he was trying to penetrate our brains for what had made us decide to fight.

I told him about my father, about the old Jew and Frankenstein, and Irena's work and that we'd had enough of the Nazi killings. Rachel related her cleaning nightmare.

"I know Irena Sendler. She's already saved hundreds of children, smuggled out of the ghetto, and hundreds more, if not thousands, by smuggling food and medicine in. She has a large network of people helping and money from Jews all over the world. An amazing woman. What we're going to do will be more dangerous and not so benevolent. Do you know anything about resistance fighting?"

"Nothing."

"Guns?"

We shook our heads.

His eyebrows arched, and he looked away, his face thoughtful. After several moments, he said, "I can imagine some of what you're feeling—about your father and the other experiences. But this cannot be a personal crusade, Jakob and Rachel. While I hope we find and deal with the Jewish traitor—we want him ourselves— what we're doing is about all of us and for all of us." He swept his hand around, taking in the entire ghetto. "About what Nazis are doing to Jews throughout Warsaw and elsewhere. In a month—" He stopped. "What do you know about the ZOB?"

"That you're a resistance force fighting the Nazis here in the ghetto."

He nodded. "Let me give you a bit of history. I was raised in a one-room flat in the Powisle District of Warsaw, a mean, crime-ridden slum, where I fought anti-Semitic Poles almost every day. I helped my parents run a grocery store. We were dirt poor. One of my jobs as a kid was to paint leftover fish with red dye so they could be sold as fresh."

We all laughed.

"When I got older, my younger brother and I formed a gang that fought back and made the Poles leave us alone. Later, I met Mira, and we fell in love. When the Germans invaded Warsaw, we left for Vilna, but I knew we had to come back to help. We did and tried to start a resistance group."

"That's why we're here," Rachel said.

Angel nodded. "It's been an uphill battle, a real struggle to motivate Jews to fight. They don't believe stories about the gassings and fear more killings if we fight back. The Bund wouldn't join us and only some of the Zionist youth organizations have. Most Jews do nothing except pray that God will create a miracle—maybe part the ghetto wall, like He parted the Red Sea. It's not going to happen."

"That's what my papa said."

"We had the start of a fighting force—until April."

"What happened?"

"Pinkus Karlyn was a leader of the Communist Polish Workers Party. He, several other Zionist leaders, and I met in January to create what we called the Anti-Fascist Bloc resistance. During the April 17 purge that caught your father, Pinkus and the others were nabbed while using the underground press to print recruitment material. The whole resistance framework crumbled, so we have to start over."

He paused and sipped his tea. "We're short of everything—recruits, money, guns—everything we need to convince the Nazis there will be consequences to what they do, even if it costs us our lives. I started to tell you earlier what's going to change all of this, change all of our lives."

"And that is …?"

He dropped his voice, and we leaned on the table toward him. "Deportations."

"I've heard rumors."

"This will be more than rumors, Jakob." He steepled his fingers in front of him. "We've inside information that they'll begin in a month. The Nazis want to eradicate the entire Jewish population. They decided that at a conference in Wannsee in January. Anyone without a job working for the Germans or not a Judenrat member or member of the Jewish Police will be deported."

I shook my head, incredulous. "That's four hundred thousand people. To where?"

"Treblinka, probably. By train."

"I've heard Treblinka doesn't have barracks."

Angel was silent a long time. He stared into space, scratched the side of his nose, and sipped his tea. He remained silent. We waited.

Finally, he spoke. "If you decide to join us, that will be your first assignment. Once the deportations start, we need to find out whether Jews are being moved to new *living* accommodations or new *dying* accommodations. There are no prisoner barracks in the main Treblinka camp. No factories. No collection of people. We've had reports from contacts that thousands enter, but no one leaves. Someone has to go to Treblinka to confirm what's going on."

I looked at Rachel. She was nodding her head yes. "We'll do that, Rachel and I."

"You're sure? It'll be dangerous."

"We're sure."

CHAPTER 25

On July 20, about a week after I met with Angel, there was a knock on our door. Even though it was early afternoon, it frightened us. I stood to open it, but Mama pushed Rachel and me into the small bedroom.

She opened the front door a crack and peeked out. It was the Judenrat chairman, Adam Czerniakow.

"I'm sorry if I scared you, but I need to speak with Jakob," he said.

We came out of the bedroom, greeted him, and all sat down at the kitchen table. Mama boiled water for tea.

"Jakob," Czerniakow said, his face serious, "I heard a rumor you're going to join Mordechai Anielewicz's resistance group and that he told you deportations are about to begin. True?"

Mama gasped. I hadn't told her about the meeting.

I sucked in a deep breath. "Where'd you hear that?"

He waved the air in front of him, swatting away my query. "The ghetto has no secrets. People see and people talk. Because your father and I were good friends, I'm warning you not to believe the deportation lies. The SS has issued a decree that anyone spreading such lies will be shot for treason. Several have been shot already. And stay away from Anielewicz. He'll get you killed."

❦

Angel was right. Two days later, on July 22, 1942, the Nazis issued a new decree that *all Jews living in Warsaw, regardless of sex and age, will be evacuated*. The order, effective immediately, mandated that by four o'clock that afternoon and every day thereafter, the Jewish Police, backed by the SS, must deliver six thousand Jews to the Umschlagplatz for transportation to Treblinka.

Jews employed by Germans, members of the Judenrat and Jewish Police, staffs of Jewish hospitals and sanitation squads, and Jews already hospitalized in Jewish hospitals, too sick to be moved, were exempted.

We were sitting at the kitchen table, debating how the order would be enforced if people hid in the ghetto, when I saw flashes of white flicker past the kitchen window.

"Look, Mama—snow in July?" I grabbed Rachel's hand, and we went outside. In contrast to the usual crowds, Leszno Street was deserted, except for occasional persons walking quickly to and from buildings. Clouds of white feathers drifted down and blew like snow in the wind, coating the sidewalk and street. I looked up to see men and women hanging out of apartment windows, ripping the downy contents from stuffed pillows and comforters and discharging them into the air.

"What are you doing?" I shouted to a woman in our building who was dumping eiderdown from a third-floor window.

"Making room to travel. The SS said only fifteen kilograms per person in a small valise. We'll restuff the comforters and pillows when we're resettled in Treblinka."

Resettled in Treblinka. How would the Nazis resettle four hundred thousand people, all funneled through the Umschlagplatz? We had to see what it was like.

As Rachel and I neared the train station, we saw columns of Jews, four abreast, being marched at double pace toward the loading dock. SS and Jewish Police with clubs, whips, and snarling German shepherds held the ragtag group of adults and children in line, whipping stragglers to keep up.

This was no simple resettlement. SS and Jewish Police grabbed any stray person walking in the street and forced them to join the march. We found out later that each Jewish policeman was responsible for recruiting at least five people daily to the Umschlagplatz, or the SS would kidnap them and their family as substitutes.

We followed at a distance, concealed in doorways and hugging the sides of buildings to remain unnoticed.

The train-loading station was located in the northernmost part of the ghetto, an open area alongside railroad tracks, on which stood a row of wooden cattle cars. Swarms of people, herded together into a confined area, milled about, clutching small suitcases or parcels tied with twine.

Faces displayed fear and anguish; some cried, others yelled, several were vomiting. Mothers cradled hungry infants in their arms or grasped the hands of small children as well as each other. Young ones separated from parents wailed in fear. Many older folks collapsed to the ground and prayed, reciting the *Shema*. There were no sanitary facilities, so people urinated in their pants and defecated in the grass.

It was a scene of chaos and terror. The SS barked orders and instructed everyone to leave their luggage on the station platform. The bags would travel on a different train, they said, and be returned after settlement in Treblinka. Rachel and I exchanged doubtful looks. Their belongings would more likely go to the SS.

We watched with increasing horror as the SS crammed Jews so tightly into the cattle cars that they could only stand, bodies crushed against each other. Intermittent gun shots were a fatal reminder not to resist the loading process. Those who dared were left bleeding, to die where they fell.

When no more bodies could be wedged into the train, the SS slammed the doors shut and locked them in place. A single, tiny, barred window, head-high, was the only opening. Screams and moans came from the incarcerated people, begging to be let out; they cried for water, to urinate, to breathe, to eat.

We hid for several hours on nearby Stawki Street, barely talking as we tried to block out the heartbreaking cries. We stayed until all of the cars were crammed with a hundred or more souls and the

Deutsche Reichbahn chugged away with its first load of innocents to be "resettled" in Treblinka.

At least another thousand waited for the next train in the adjacent field. We could see in the distance additional groups being herded toward the Umschlagplatz in long lines of four across to fulfill the daily quota of six thousand. We learned that those not loaded into the last train were held over as reserves until morning, when the process started again. Without food or water, they'd spend the night in the field or imprisoned in one of the nearby deserted buildings.

On our return to our apartment, we bumped into Irena, hurrying along Leszno Street.

"Have you heard—" she began.

"Yes. We've just come from the Umschlagplatz," Rachel said. "It's horrible, worse than we could've imagined." Her lips quivered, and tears filled her eyes. She couldn't continue.

"I know. I'm trying to smuggle out as many youngsters as possible before their parents get deported. We may be able to save ten to fifteen children a day."

"While the Nazis take six thousand," I said.

"The hardest part is to convince parents we might be able to save their child if they give him or her up. I've got a legion of assistants knocking on ghetto doors, trying to do this. But how do you convince parents to hand over their child to a complete stranger, with no guarantee the child will survive or that they'll be reunited after the war. Many say no."

"Who can blame them?" I said.

"I agree. Some believe the Nazis' resettlement promises and refuse. For others, the idea that their Jewish child might be raised in a Christian home or by nuns in a monastery is unthinkable. It was different with the orphans because we were their only hope. Now ..." She left it unfinished.

"What about the Korczak orphanage?" Rachel asked.

Irena shook her head. "I think it's full. Besides, it's subject to deportation orders also. But that's an idea. Why don't we check with the good Dr. Korczak first thing tomorrow morning?"

CHAPTER 26

Rachel and I met Irena early the next morning, and we walked together to 16 Sienna Street. Irena was unusually quiet.

"Something wrong?" I asked. "Second thoughts about the Korczak orphanage?"

"No. Just more bad news," she said. "You remember Adam Czerniakow, the Judenrat chairman?"

I nodded. "He was a good friend of my father and paid us a recent visit. What about him?"

"He committed suicide. Swallowed cyanide. He said the Nazis lied to him that they wouldn't deport children, and as head of the Judenrat, he couldn't face giving orders to do that."

"That's so sad," Rachel said. "Who'll replace him?"

"I don't know, but I'm sure the Nazis will find somebody."

We walked silently for a while, immersed in our own thoughts. Taking cyanide required courage, but it was the easy way out compared to standing up to the Nazis and resisting their orders. Importantly, we'd lost a respected leader in the ghetto, someone to whom all listened, whose leadership might have made a difference.

"We're close to the Korczak orphanage," Irena said as we crossed onto Sienna Street. "It's still early, so I expect they'll all be asleep."

∽

The courtyard was full—not with children but with SS troops. They were swarming all over like ants. Czerniakow had been right this time.

"Oh my God, those poor children. They must be frightened to death. We've got to help Dr. Korczak," Irena said.

"What can we do, Irena?" I asked. "We're outnumbered ten to one."

"We're going to find him. My health pass will get us in. You have your Polish Kennkarten?"

We nodded.

"Good. You'll be my assistants. Let's go." She was off to the front door of the orphanage before we had a chance to respond, and we trailed in her wake.

Irena flashed her pass for the SS officer at the door and told him we were conducting a health checkup on the orphans before deportation. He let us in.

We found Janusz Korczak in the dining room of the orphanage, calmly helping servers dish out breakfast to the children. When he saw us, he put a finger to his lips and nodded for us to follow. He led us to his office.

Once inside he closed the door and showed his true feelings.

"Those bastards," he snarled, pointing at shadows as they flitted by the window. "They came banging on the door before we even woke. Scared the little ones to death. It took us forever to quiet them and get them cleaned up and into the dining room for breakfast."

"What's going to happen?"

"The SS are emptying the entire orphanage, Irena. Deporting all of us to Treblinka—staff, children, all of us. Resettlement, they say. Ha! It's a gas chamber. And there's nothing you or I can do—not unless you've got an army to fight these murderous bastards."

"We don't now, but we're working on it," I said.

He pointed to his medical certificate, still hanging framed on the wall. "My one goal was to save these children so they could grow up to lead normal lives. That's not going to happen. If they survive deportation—and that's a big if—the trauma will scar them forever. I've got to protect them from that."

"How?" I asked.

"By making this seem like a normal outing, a walk in the park, pleasant and dignified."

"How can we help?" Rachel asked.

"With the youngsters. Get them dressed in their best uniforms, faces washed, hair combed, and ready for a pleasant journey to the Umschlagplatz."

An hour later, the children lined up outside the building in neat rows of four, encircled by the SS. In contrast to the bedlam we'd watched at the Umschlagplatz the day before, total order prevailed. They were dressed in clean blue-denim uniforms, faces scrubbed, and hair combed. They stood quietly as they listened to Dr. Korczak's words.

"We will be going on a long walk," he said. "We will give each of you a small jar of water, and you can take one personal item. Your teachers and I will stay with you. I want you to think about the story of *King Matt the First* and how he behaved when he was captured near the end of the story. Who remembers?"

Several hands rose. Korczak nodded at them in turn.

"He was brave."

"That's true. What else?"

"He was calm."

"Yes, he was."

"He was dignified."

"Correct. Now, I want you all to act like King Matt as we walk and whatever happens after that. Remember: brave, calm, and dignified. Can you do that?"

There followed a chorus of yeses. One boy asked, "Where are we going?"

"We will first walk to the Umschlagplatz to go on a train ride. After that, I'm not sure, but I hope it will be like summer camp, with fresh air, trees, and little animals, like rabbits and squirrels. We can play games."

Korczak walked up and down the rows of two hundred children, followed by his assistant, Stefa, and a dozen helpers. He paused to hug and reassure each anxious child, to provide a bright smile for scared faces, and to pat the heads of the older ones.

Suddenly, we heard, "Rachel! Rachel!" A young boy broke rank and came running toward us. It was Jerzy Rudnicki!

He'd grown in the last two years and gained weight. He looked like a healthy youngster as he jumped into Rachel's arms and squealed in delight.

She hugged him and swung him around in circles. "Jerzy, Jerzy, I've missed you. So have my sisters. How are you?" Tears rolled down her cheeks.

She set him down, and he ran to Irena; then to me.

"I'm fine. Dr. Korczak takes good care of us. We have good food to eat, and he reads us books. But I like being with you best. You're here to get me, right?" His face was shining with hope.

Rachel's expression turned panicky as she looked at Korczak. He shook his head.

"Not this time, Jerzy. Maybe a little later, after—"

His cries interrupted her. "I want to go with you. Dr. Korczak, I want to go with Rachel. I want to live with her and her sisters."

"Jerzy, we have to go for a walk first, and then on a train ride," Korczak said.

Jerzy's crying intensified.

Stefa approached Korczak, whispered in his ear, and handed him a green flag. He held it out to the boy.

"Jerzy, remember how King Matt waved this green flag? What did it mean?"

"That he was free," Jerzy answered in between sobs.

"Correct. You take this flag. You can be King Matt and lead us on our march. We'll follow you. Okay?"

A grin replaced the tears as Jerzy grabbed the flag and walked to the head of the group, shoulders braced. He turned briefly, smiled, and waved at us. "I'll see you when we come back," he shouted. "I want to live with you and your family."

I watched Rachel bite her lip to keep from crying out loud. She nodded, waved, and brushed away tears.

Dr. Korczak carried a little girl in one arm and held Jerzy's hand with the other as he led the group out of the orphanage and onto Sliska Street, singing a marching song. They turned north on Zelazna and crossed the bridge over Chlodna to leave the smaller ghetto and enter the larger one. We followed behind.

The sun rose, and the little ones began to tire.

We were astonished to see the SS and Jewish Police, instead of prodding and beating, slow the pace to accommodate the stragglers. None laid a hand on the children; they formed a protective flank, shielding them from heckling onlookers and stone-throwers.

The five-kilometer trek took about three hours, and we arrived at the Umschlagplatz, hot and tired. The children looked spent, as did Dr. Korczak; his face was pale and sweaty. Like the marching SS, the guards at the Umschlagplatz withheld their whips, guns, and cudgels and kept their snarling dogs at bay. They watched silently, respectfully, as the children collapsed on the dirt in the field next to the railway siding to rest and drink what was left of their water. We tried to approach Jerzy, but the guards stopped us.

Around noon, with the hot sun beating down, loading began. The SS sprang into action, shoving, whipping, and clubbing people into the cattle cars but leaving Dr. Korczak's group untouched. Then the Jewish Police commander, a man named Schmerling, ordered Dr. Korczak to prepare the children for loading. They rose as a group, the strong helping the weak to stand.

Before they marched to the trains, an SS officer entered the field, strode to Dr. Korczak, and presented him with a document. All movement ceased. The SS stopped, arms at their sides, and quieted the yelping dogs as all eyes focused on Dr. Korczak.

He took out a pair of glasses from a jacket pocket, opened the envelope, and scanned the document. He looked at the SS officer, then at the children, and read the document again, this time more slowly. Very deliberately he held up the paper for all to see, shook his head, and ripped it to shreds, letting the pieces fly free in the breeze.

In a loud voice, he said, "You do not leave a sick child in the middle of the night, and you do not leave children at a time like this." He flicked a backhanded dismissal at the SS officer, spun around, opened his arms, and smiled at the children.

A stillness descended over the entire Umschlagplatz as the children again formed orderly columns of four. Dr. Korczak led them out of the field to the cattle cars in a stately procession, heads held high and shoulders back, again singing the fighting song. The Jewish Police spontaneously lined up on each side of them, stood at attention, and saluted as the children, true to their beloved Dr. Korczak and King Matt the First, boarded the train, brave, calm, and dignified.

Jerzy was the last to enter. He turned, waved the green flag at us, and shouted, "I love you, Rachel. I'll see you as soon as we get back."

Rachel blew him a kiss as the SS rolled the heavy train door shut and bolted it. Not a child cried; not a whimper was heard. The silent, noble protest of Dr. Korczak and his courageous children spoke louder than words.

CHAPTER 27

Deportations continued to meet the daily quota. Every day, six thousand people were listed to assemble at the Umschlagplatz. Those souls brave enough to ignore the order hid in attics or basements when they heard a knock at the door. Merciless, Nazis blocked off streets and searched the ghetto, house to house, room by room. They ripped up floorboards and punctured walls. After dark, people snuck around the streets, toting knapsacks filled with their belongings as they tried to outguess where the next SS blockade and building search would take place.

"Alle Juden Raus!" the SS shouted as they stormed a building. All Jews out! They came out slowly, dejectedly, and were corralled into a group on the street in front of the building. Some still wore bedclothes; others came packed with belongings. Frightened eyes searched for familiar faces of relatives or friends. The SS seized anyone walking by and marched all under guard to the train station. Those who resisted were executed instantly.

Work papers provided some protection against deportation, at least initially, and immediately snowballed the price of that document to thousands of zlotys. Owning a sewing machine—proof of gainful employment by the Germans—was like possessing gold, and the price of that common object also escalated out of sight.

As the population shrank, the Nazis hit on a new approach. They offered three kilograms of bread and one kilogram of marmalade to anyone who volunteered to be deported. The thought of three freshly baked, brown-crusted loaves, swimming in sweet jam, drove the starving population crazy. So many ravenous people flocked to the Umschlagplatz that the trains couldn't handle the increased load, even though they now left twice daily with twelve thousand people aboard.

Many had to spend three or four days in the field, waiting in line to get the promised foods and board the train. By this time, the field was covered in human waste, and each step sank into puddles of urine or excrement. Despite a belly full of bread and jam, total despair lined every face, as hope faded and people realized they might have reached the last moments of their lives.

Irena told us she'd increased her efforts to save ghetto children and took even more risks to sneak them out.

"I was almost executed yesterday," she said casually one morning, almost as an afterthought, as we sipped breakfast tea in our flat.

"Good God! What happened?" I asked.

"I went to smuggle Anna Grynstein out of the ghetto and place her in a nice home. She was a starving seven-year-old, just skin and bones, maybe weighing thirteen or fourteen kilos. She clung to her mother, sobbing, when I went to get her. The family was on the next day's deportation list, and it was only a matter of time before they'd be caught and brought to the Umschlagplatz.

"Anna only spoke Yiddish. I was afraid to give her a sedative because she was so frail, so I asked her mother to explain that she must remain quiet during the trip—no talking at all once we were on the Aryan side. Anna nodded that she understood. I took her by the hand, and we used the courthouse to cross the wall."

"Was the janitor there this time?" I remembered, all too well, facing off Fat Man with a flashlight.

"Stanislaw, yes; no problem. He was happy with five hundred zlotys and unlocked the door. We exited on Ogrodowa Street on the Aryan side, like before, walked to the tram station, and boarded the next tram. It was full, so I held Anna, light as a feather, on my lap. Eventually, the rocking of the tram put her to sleep with her head snuggled on my shoulder.

"All was fine until we hit a bump in the road that jarred her awake. She sat up with a frightened look on her face—not knowing *where* she was or remembering who *I* was—and screamed in Yiddish, '*Ikh vein meyn mami!*' I want my mommy, over and over, and then started sobbing. I couldn't quiet her. The lady sitting next to me jumped up, stood in the aisle, pointed at Anna, and yelled, 'She's a Jew! She's a Jew!'"

"Good God! What did you do?" Rachel asked, eyes wide with fear.

"Before I could do anything, two Gestapo hurried over. They must have been sitting in the back of the tram because I didn't see them when we boarded. If I had, I would've never gotten on. They were big. The younger one looked mean, with a Hitler mustache; the older one was maybe a little nicer. They ordered the driver to stop the tram. Mustache grabbed me by an arm, and the other took Anna. They dragged us off the tram and pulled us along the street until we came to a park. I didn't know where I was, but it seemed like a quiet residential area. Anna was so frightened that she'd stopped crying and was just stone mute, staring in fear at these two huge men."

"Wasn't there anyone around?" Rachel asked.

"Yes, but no one stopped. In fact, they shielded their faces and looked away as they walked by to avoid witnessing an execution. The Gestapo made us get down on our knees in the grass with our hands behind our heads. I kept waiting for the bullet. We were both shaking so hard that we could barely stay upright.

"The Gestapo walked a short distance away and spoke in

whispers. I couldn't make out what they were saying. When they returned, the older one told Mustache to leave, and he'd finish this mess. Mustache said no, he wanted to do it—to kill us. It'd be his first kill, and he wanted to see how it felt. He said it with a smile on his face. The older one must've outranked him because he ordered Mustache away, saying they were late for a meeting, and he should report in. Mustache finally caught the next tram.

"The Gestapo pushed us deeper into the park to an area surrounded by a cluster of trees that hid us from the street. He ordered us down on our knees again and drew his Luger, and I thought it was all over. '*Ich habe eine Tochter in Ihrem Alter in Berlin,*' the Nazi said. I have a daughter her age in Berlin.

"Then he fired two bullets into the ground next to me, turned, and walked away. Anna and I collapsed into the grass." Stoic Irena fought back tears and took deep breaths as she struggled to contain her emotions.

We waited for her to continue. Finally, I asked, "What happened then?"

"We hid in the park until it got dark. Poor Anna. She'll be traumatized for life, doubly so if her parents are killed. She didn't speak until we boarded the last tram. We finally made it to Father Boduen's Children's Home. Anna will stay there a few days until she's placed."

Irena sat silently a few moments and stared into space, apparently lost in her own world. Then she wiped her eyes and blew her nose.

She managed a tight smile and said, "Might I have some more tea, please? With a cookie, if you have one."

CHAPTER 28

Rachel and I were impatient for Mordechai Anielewicz to contact us. I wondered how much worse living conditions had to get before the resistance took action. Finally, he sent a message that he wanted to meet at 32 Zamenhofa Street, same as before.

When we arrived, he motioned us to chairs at the table. This time, his frustrations boiled over.

"It's still hard to find recruits to build a resistance force, despite the horrific deportations. Even after the Gestapo began hanging bright-red posters around Warsaw, listing the names of fifteen or twenty people executed daily at Pawiak Prison, our friends still call me a provocateur, an instigator. They raise the same objections: 'Our life is to suffer—we've done so for over two thousand years. Treblinka is only a labor camp. Why would they give us bread if they planned to kill us? If the Nazis kill some of us, the rest of us will still survive. If we kill one of them, they'll kill a hundred of us.'"

"So what can we do?" I asked.

"We need eyewitness proof of what's happening at Treblinka. I must convince people it's a death camp, not a work camp. I need you"—he looked at me and then Rachel—"both to discover the truth."

I took Rachel's hand and held it up with mine. "We're ready."

"A friend, Max Frydrych, works at the Warsaw Danzig Terminal.

He'll board the Warsaw-Malkinia train line with you to Sokolow, about 120 kilometers from Warsaw. A railroad spur there branches off to Treblinka, thirty-five kilometers away. You get off the train five kilometers from the camp and walk the rest of the way through the woods. Max knows the area well. Scout out the camp, and return the same way. We'll publish your report in the next issue of *On Guard*, our latest newspaper. What do you think?"

"How long will the trip take?" I asked.

"Three or four days, at most."

"Dangerous?" Rachel asked, her face serious.

"No riskier than what you've been doing for Irena. I'll loan you a 9mm Luger pistol that one of our cleaning ladies stole from a Nazi bedroom. I have only seven bullets, but that should be enough. If it's not, having more probably wouldn't help."

Rachel sucked in a sharp breath.

Angel reached into a drawer and pulled out the gun. "I'll load it, but you can't target practice. Just point and shoot. Could you kill, if you had to?"

I thought for a moment before answering. "Good question. I can sit here and say yes, but if and when the time comes, I don't know."

"Hopefully, you won't need to."

⚬⚬

Once it was dark, we sneaked out through the sewer, met Max, and cleaned up at the Warsaw Danzig Terminal.

Max was a short, sinewy guy, bald, with a face battered like an ex-boxer and cat-like slanted eyes. He didn't talk as we boarded the Warsaw-Malkinia train line. He guided us to an empty train compartment for a few hours' sleep and said he'd wake us when it was time to get off.

Two hours later, he knocked as the train slowed before reaching Treblinka. We jumped off the rear car and headed for the woods, carrying backpacks with food and water. The moon was full as we followed Max to the outskirts of the Treblinka camp. We hid among the dense trees on a small hill overlooking the camp until daylight.

When the sun rose, Max pointed and described the layout in detail. "Treblinka's basically two camps a kilometer or two apart." He handed me the binoculars. "You're looking at Treblinka I, the forced-labor camp. Before the war, it was a gravel pit." His hand moved to the right. "Over there, you can see prisoners digging in the quarry for construction material. They dig all day, get a cup of watery soup and a piece of bread for dinner, and collapse for the night until the digging resumes the next morning. Prisoners work every day until they die or are killed."

I scanned the camp with the binoculars. A three-meter double-layered barbed-wire fence enclosed two sets of barracks; I assumed one for men and one for women. The rumors about there being no barracks were wrong.

In the quarry at the side of the camp, prisoners hacked up stone with pickaxes and carried away the pieces in large buckets. They looked emaciated, and I marveled that they could still wield axes and carry buckets. Multiple guards stood at the perimeter with whips and guns, prodding the slackers.

I grimaced and handed the binoculars to Rachel.

"How many people would you estimate?" I asked.

Max pulled an earlobe. "Folks in town tell me about a thousand working prisoners. That doesn't include another five hundred who chop wood in the forest to fuel the crematory fire pits. And another five hundred women who just clean uniforms."

"What about Treblinka II?" Rachel asked, gesturing with the binoculars toward the other camp.

Max shrugged and rubbed his lobe again, this time more gently. "Good question but much more a mystery. Townspeople are forbidden within two kilometers of Treblinka II. They only know that trainloads of people come in and no one leaves. No supplies arrive to feed the thousands who enter daily, yet the camp chops and burns lots of firewood every day. I think that tells a story. But we know very little about what actually goes on in the camp."

He checked his watch. "Should be a trainload arriving from Warsaw in about fifteen minutes. Let's move a little closer so we're at a better vantage point when they unload."

He led the way deeper through the woods. When Treblinka II was in sight, we sat back against some pine trees and watched the train tracks. We heard the train rumbling before we saw it round the bend and stop at a flat receiving area alongside the train tracks. In moments, organized bedlam erupted.

SS guards in military uniforms, armed with whips, guns, clubs, and German shepherds, materialized to corral the thousands who descended from the train cars. Passengers looked exhausted and desperate. They stumbled along, a swarm of heartbroken humanity, many held upright by others. Their gestures told us they were pleading for water or food. The SS guards separated men from women, healthy from weak, and ignored cries from anguished families torn apart. They herded them into rows of four and marched them from the landing area around a huge dirt mound, where they disappeared from view. Horrified, we watched guards shoot those too weak to walk unaided and leave the bodies where they fell.

After the train emptied, a group of male prisoners in striped pajamas gathered on the platform. They entered each train car, dragged out the dead, and piled the bodies alongside the others. A crew of women prisoners followed, carrying buckets of water and rags. The whole process was very organized and was finished in less than an hour.

"What happens behind that dirt mound, Max?" I took the binoculars from Rachel and tried to focus beyond the mound. "I can't see anything. Can we get closer?"

"Too dangerous in broad daylight. Wait until dark. You two take a rest until then. I'll keep watch."

Rachel and I ate a bit of food and drank water from our canteens. We lay down in the grass and closed our eyes. I tried to block out the horrific images we'd just seen. The August day was sunny but not especially hot, and we were comfortable in the shade on a bed of leaves.

Physically and emotionally exhausted, we fell asleep until an overpowering acrid smell hit us. Plumes of black smoke rose from the other side of the dirt mound. It wasn't hard to imagine what was burning. I tried breathing through a handkerchief, but I couldn't filter out the smell of lives literally going up in smoke. I shuddered and gave thanks that Mama and Rachel's family were still alive.

We waited until two hours after sunset to sneak close to Treblinka II. This would be the most dangerous part of our mission. If we couldn't see what was happening, we might have to cut through the barbed-wire fence—and it could be electrified—to enter the camp. The risk of being captured was great. Also, the cut fence would leave a telltale sign that we wanted to avoid. But we had to find out what was concealed behind that dirt mound. My heart pounded at the thought.

We'd just set out toward the camp when Rachel whispered, "I hear something over there." She pointed to the perimeter of the camp. Her hand was shaking.

CHAPTER 29

"Give me the binoculars, Max," I whispered. I focused on the path leading from the camp.

"See anything?" Max asked.

"A man. Not in uniform."

"Careful," Max said, backing away. "Could be SS. Maybe we've been spotted."

I held the binoculars in place with one hand and reached for the Luger in my belt. "He's alone, walking in our direction. Hide back there." I nodded at a clump of bushes several yards away. "Come out if we need help."

Rachel and I ducked behind a large tree. I gripped the loaded Luger, my finger alongside the trigger guard. In that moment, I knew I could kill, but the sound would alert the SS in the camp.

The man hurried along a path, glancing over his shoulder every few steps. He didn't see us until he practically fell into my arms.

"Jesus Christ!" he exclaimed. He was shrunken, his eyes red and runny, and gray hair tangled in dirty clumps, matching a scraggly beard. His clothes hung loose on a tall, skeletal frame and reeked of sweat and urine.

"Who are you?" I pointed the Luger at him and waved to Max, who emerged from the bushes.

The man raised both hands over his head. "Don't shoot. I'm

Yitzhak Brachstein. I've been a prisoner for four months. From the Krakow ghetto. Do you have any food?"

"How did you escape?" Max asked, handing him a piece of cheese and the rest of the sausage.

He reached for the food and talked while he chewed. I laughed to myself. Mama would not have approved.

"My job was to remove the dead from the train after the living were unloaded," he said, cheeks bulging. "With the last transport, I swapped my prisoner uniform for this dead man's clothes." He ran a hand over his shirt and pants. "One of the cleaning ladies helped me hide the body. I stayed on board until the train pulled out again. When it slowed to pass through the security gate, I jumped off." He sucked on his teeth and ran his tongue around them, searching for more crumbs.

"Why didn't you stay on the train to get out of here?" Rachel asked.

Brachstein shook his head. "The SS search the train after it leaves Treblinka and would've found me." He took a deep breath and asked, "Who're you?"

I explained and tucked the Luger back under my belt. "Tell us about Treblinka II."

His eyes clouded, and he gagged several times, barely keeping down the food. "If hell exists, it's here. God doesn't."

"Doesn't exist or doesn't live here?" I asked.

"Either. Both." Brachstein stopped and stared at the camp, shaking his head and breathing fast. He seemed to have a mixture of emotions. "This is a death camp run by murderers without consciences." He pointed with a quivering finger. "Everything is fake, except the slaughtering. The train station is fake. See that big clock? Fake. The ticket window lists fake train schedules to and from fake cities. A cashier gives out fake receipts for valuables to be returned when passengers leave on the next fake train."

"Why?" Rachel asked.

He flashed a grim smile. "Makes it seem like a real railroad station and reduces panic when the trains arrive every morning and afternoon to unload six or eight thousand more Jews. The SS even play Mozart or Wagner on loudspeakers to keep everyone calm when they step off the train."

"On their way to the gas chambers?" I asked.

"Yes, hidden from the offloading area by that huge dirt mound." He pointed again. "See it? Looks like a wall."

I nodded. "Go on."

"Right behind there, new arrivals get sent to an undressing area, have their heads shaved, and are told they're going to take a shower and get deloused. Healthy ones go to Treblinka I. The rest are given a bar of soap and a towel—more fake stuff—and then led to the gas chambers that look like showers. They get locked in. Killing takes twenty minutes. Bodies are removed and gold teeth extracted, and then bodies are burned in open-air pits or buried. The SS kill twelve to fifteen thousand Jews every day." He sounded like a jaded tour guide escorting us through a museum.

"How many gas chambers?" I asked.

"Three but more in construction—maybe six, maybe ten. Who knows? They gas people with carbon monoxide piped in from tank engines, not like in Auschwitz where I heard they use cyanide. Zyklon B kills in half the time. It takes us longer—about three hours to strip, shave, gas, and burn or bury three thousand people, so about a thousand an hour. Trains come in twice a day, and we work twelve to fifteen hours every day to keep up with the load." His face clouded, but he still recited in a monotone.

I stared at Brachstein and struggled for words. "I can't believe what I just heard you say."

"What'd I say?" His brow wrinkled in concentration.

I kept staring at him and shook my head in disbelief.

A thousand an hour—we work twelve to fifteen hours every day to keep up with the load.

"You said it so matter-of-factly, like maintaining a schedule for hauling a load of lumber or manufacturing a quota of pots and pans, not killing thousands of human beings according to a timetable."

He stood robot-like, showing no feeling, while my insides

churned. The viciousness, the depravity—it tore me apart. How could a person with an ounce of humanity do this to a fellow human being?

He looked back at me and blinked a few times, as if he didn't understand.

"You started out all teary-eyed and shook up, telling us about Treblinka being hell and that God's not here. Now you talk like killing was just a job you had to do; orders you had to follow," Rachel said. "Was your remorse an act?"

Brachstein shifted his gaze from me to Rachel and stood open-mouthed, as still as a statue. Gradually, in slow motion, as if something had just dawned on him or had just broken through his consciousness and scaled the protective wall he'd built, the apparent indifference disintegrated. His face crumbled, and his eyes filled. His lips quivered, and he started to tremble, just a little at first and then violently. He fell to the ground on his knees, face buried in his hands, sobbing uncontrollably. He stayed like that for several minutes. When the sobs slowed, he stood and wiped his eyes.

"Th-th-they made us," he managed to say. "They made us do it. We had no choice."

"Everyone has a choice," I said. I knew I sounded arrogant, but what he'd said just pissed me off. "The consequences may be ugly, but you had a choice. You could've said no."

"That's a pile of crap. Easy for you to say, sitting safe in the woods. In the camp, you refuse an order, you get shot. Immediately. It's that simple. You obey everything, do anything to stay alive. You can't know what it's like unless you were there, living minute to minute, starving every day, not knowing if your next breath would be your last. You do all you can to live one day longer, even if it means stealing your best friend's bread or volunteering him for the gas chamber instead of you. You become numb to the cruelty you see every day."

"How could you do that?" Rachel asked, incredulous. "Betray your friends?"

He tossed a backhand at her. "You're both so incredibly naïve!

Look down at that … that … that horrid place!" He pointed with a quivering finger and shuddered. "Look at me, at what I've become! Get it through your heads—this is a killing factory. Treblinka strips away every last vestige of compassion, of humanity, of who you are, right down to your core. And then, what are you left with?"

When we didn't answer, he said, "Survival instincts, that's what. Your own survival is all you think about, care about, every minute of every day. Living here degrades you to that one fundamental goal. Do whatever it takes to survive another minute, another hour, another day. We all carry hope until the end."

Irena's selfless work flashed through my mind, contradicting everything he'd said. She and others like her were Christians who risked their lives every day to save Jews. Still, they didn't live in Treblinka II. Even if they had, I couldn't believe they'd steal bread from a friend.

But would I? Would I choose to obey orders, knowing the consequence of refusing? Frankly, I didn't know and hoped I'd never be tested to find out.

"War dehumanizes the victor, but living in a killing camp dehumanizes victims as well," Brachstein said in a quiet voice. "Cruelty feeds on itself and breeds more cruelty. People become nameless numbers, no longer fathers and mothers, brothers and sisters, aunts and uncles. We are stripped of any individualization, of any identify, of any history. We no longer have hearts and brains or feelings. We become objects, not personalities. Killing is easier if the person is a faceless animal, a piece of trash you can grind under your foot."

He seemed to regain some self-control; he brushed himself off and squared his shoulders. "Maybe I would've been better off if I'd let them kill me or if I'd killed myself. I survived and have to live with the memory of all this"—he swept a hand toward the camp—"and all that I did to stay alive."

"What did you do before"—Rachel seemed to grope for words—"coming here?"

"I was a general surgeon in Cracow, where I saved lives every day, operating in a hospital. I had a wife, a daughter, five years old, and a son, seven. They were murdered the day we arrived—torn from my arms and gassed in the first hour; up in smoke in three. Maybe they were lucky, but I lost my humanity when I lost them. That's when I built a wall against what I was seeing and doing, especially what I was *feeling*. If I hadn't, I'd have gone crazy and committed suicide in a week."

He started sobbing again, face in his hands.

Rachel went to him and rested her hand on his shoulder. She embraced him.

We were silent. What was there to say about such inhumanity, such cruelty?

After several minutes, he quieted. "Am I proud of what I did here? No, of course not. Would I do it again?" He stared hard at Treblinka II, thinking. "Sadly, I probably would. Like my very sick patients who fought with all they had in the hospital to live another day, so would I."

He locked eyes with me. "And to your original question about keeping up with the load, if I hadn't, the SS would've made me a part of it."

I nodded. "Will you come back with us to tell your story?"

"Maybe, if you have anything more to eat."

CHAPTER 30

"So that's the story, Angel," I said, a day after we'd returned from Treblinka. "The place is horrible beyond belief. I felt like we were looking at hell—I mean, real, actual, physical hell."

I laid the Luger on the table.

He counted seven bullets and smiled. "Glad you didn't need this."

"Now you have an eyewitness account from a survivor. Better than just publishing a report in *On Guard*, Brachstein can talk in the ghetto and relate firsthand what he saw and lived through. Spread the word that deportation to Treblinka is a death sentence."

"Yeah, and he'd be shot before he made it past the first building. No, we've got to keep him hidden. Nourish him back to health, and maybe he'll join us later, fighting the bastards. Meanwhile, I'll write up your account, add his experience, and publish it without names in *On Guard*. We'll distribute the story throughout the ghetto and hope it mobilizes some doubters."

"Even better if we could sneak Brachstein out of Poland, maybe to England or America, to tell his story. Maybe that'd help mobilize worldwide support against the Nazis," I said.

Concern drew deep lines across Angel's forehead, and he ran his tongue over his lips. "Good thinking. Something to consider in the future."

The deportations continued, and by mid-August 1942, some two hundred thousand Jews had been transported to Treblinka and murdered. The Nazis blocked off parts of the ghetto as it emptied, boarded up buildings, and closed streets. Food trickled in at astronomical prices, and we'd often go days without eating.

Mama bartered her wedding ring, an heirloom diamond kept hidden from greedy German hands, for two loaves of bread and three apples. We heard of others who bargained away a solid gold necklace for a kilo of butter and a pure silver ingot for two moldy sausages.

Irena and her workforce tried to keep up with the demand as the number of orphans swelled. Parents, forced to the Umschlagplatz, often left their children in hiding, hoping they stood a better chance alone than facing certain death at Treblinka. Sometimes, a family waiting to board the cattle car sent their children running to flee the guards. Some kids were shot immediately. Others made it to safety and became part of Irena's burden.

We smuggled children out through every route imaginable—the sewers, the courthouse, cracks in the wall, or holes dug under it—and hid them in almost any truck, wagon, or cart that left the ghetto. About the only route we didn't use was flying over the wall.

But even that happened.

One evening, during a late-night walk despite the curfew, Rachel and I saw a young woman ahead of us on Leszno Street. She was hiding in the shadows, close to one of the buildings that bordered the wall. She was slight, maybe one and one-half meters tall, and dressed in a dark sweater and a black skirt, with a kerchief covering her hair. She cradled a bundle carefully in her arms. As we got closer, we could see she was nursing an infant, swathed head to toe in pink blankets. The woman finished nursing and laid the baby gently on the pavement. She bent, picked up a stone, and tossed it to the Aryan side. In a moment, a stone flew back.

The woman stooped again, picked up the baby, kissed and

hugged it tenderly, whispered something in its ear, and then tucked its head securely inside the blanket. She gripped the bundle tightly in both hands and swung it back and forth several times in an increasing arc to gain momentum. Bending at the waist and with a mighty heave, she hurled the bundle up and over the wall. Despite her supreme effort, it barely cleared the top layer of splintered glass. Within seconds, a stone sailed back, hopefully acknowledging successful receipt of the precious cargo.

The woman collapsed, groaning, her cheek against the wall and her hands splayed out on the bricks. Her fingers twitched, as if trying to recapture her love, expressing her sacrifice for the infant she'd bequeathed to someone on the Aryan side.

The young woman saw us as we approached and ran off. We heard her sobs fade in the distance.

Rachel gazed at me, her eyes moist. "That has to be one of the most heartbreaking decisions a mother could ever make."

I kissed away the tears running down her cheeks and held her close. "I'm sorry we didn't know. We might've been able to help."

"And how many more like her, I wonder, trying to protect their children?" Rachel said, trembling and burrowing into me. "I'm so glad I have you to protect us."

Something in her tone—maybe because she sounded so serious—made me pull away slightly so I could look into her eyes. "You know I will, but what brought that on? *Us*? What's happened? Something I don't know about?"

A smile played in the corner of her eyes. She unzipped her jacket and unbuttoned her blouse. She took my hand and placed it over her bare breast. "Notice anything different?" Her smile grew.

My initial thought was to pull my hand away. It was risky, standing on an open street after curfew, even though it was dark and late at night. But it was an offer I couldn't refuse, and I left my hand where she'd placed it, savoring the intimacy.

"What are you doing?" I hugged her close, hiding my hand in the crush between us, loving the contact.

"Want to take your hand away?" she teased.

I laughed. "Never, not even for a moment. I'll stay here forever."

"So what do you feel?" she asked, looking into my eyes.

I stared back at her. "All my love."

She shook her head. "No. Really. What do you feel?"

I smiled. "Your heart beating furiously."

"Anything else?"

I thought for a moment, felt her breast, and tried to ignore my erection. "You're bigger? Firmer?"

Her eyes danced in excitement. "And?"

"You're pregnant!"

"Finally! Men." She shook her head in amusement. "Yes, I'm pregnant."

I kissed her. "When did you know?"

"About a week ago. I wanted to be sure before I told you. Happy?"

My smile matched hers. "Delirious. Wonderful. I want to shout; tell the whole world! When are you due?"

"Early March—you can take your hand out now," she said with a laugh.

"Do I have to?"

"Now, yes; later, no."

I took my hand out, and she zipped up her jacket. I pressed her to me and kissed her long and lingering. We just stood there, with her head on my shoulder and my arms wrapped around her. It was surreal to think about where we were, where this was all happening, where I was living one of the most joyful moments of my nineteen years.

"I'm so happy for us, my dearest Rachel. Thank you for this blessing."

"Thank you too, dearest husband," she said with a short laugh. "The last time I checked, you played a role—small, but you did contribute." She smiled at me—that same tender, beautiful smile as when I fell in love with her.

I took her hand. "Come, let's go home. I don't want to lose this moment."

CHAPTER 31

T he Nazis stepped up deportations through the last half of August and into September 1942 with bulging trainloads of pathetic souls.

Irena increased her efforts as well, and we worked day and night to smuggle children out. We used the Boduen's Children's Home extensively, and from there, we placed many children in Catholic orphanages and convents, such as the Order of the Immaculate Conception on Grójecka Street and with the Sisters of Service Convent in Turkowice, a town about three hundred kilometers southeast of Warsaw. The children were given Polish names and issued new identity papers. They were baptized, taught their catechism, raised as Catholics, and told to never, ever reveal their Jewish past.

Many parents in the ghetto refused to give up their children under such circumstances. "We will not allow them to sacrifice their Jewish heritage. It's better they die as Jews than live as Catholics." These children made the cattle-car trip to Treblinka with their parents.

Other parents wanted to save their children at any cost. If Catholicism and baptism were the price, they were willing to pay. We told them the children could return to being Jewish after the war. I'm not certain anyone really believed that would happen, but at least it offered some comfort to grieving parents.

Deportations from Warsaw to Treblinka suddenly ended on September 21, 1942, the first day of Yom Kippur. We heard that the last trains deported sixty thousand people in two days, including many of the Jewish Police and their families who'd outlived their usefulness.

One of Irena's helpers, a nurse at the Jewish hospital in the ghetto, told us that on the last day of deportations, SS stormed the hospital and calmly shot in the head anyone who could not get out of bed to be deported. Doctors and nurses raced ahead of the SS to the upper floors to administer as many doses of cyanide as possible to the remaining patients to spare them the agony of the shootings and to allow them to die with dignity.

One young mother delivered an infant girl minutes before she heard the stomp of SS boots outside the delivery room. The mother lifted her newborn from her breast and, sobbing, handed her to the nurse. As the SS entered the room, the nurse held a pillow over the infant's face.

Before the SS reached the children's ward, the hospital staff spirited thirty children down the back stairs to the kitchen, where they were hidden among wooden potato boxes, carted out to a waiting truck, and driven off.

From almost a half million ghetto inhabitants, about thirty thousand legally remained in the ghetto, along with their families, as employees in German factories and workshops. These fortunate ones had received a work authorization paper in the final days that allowed them to live a while longer. In return, they labored twelve-hour days at manual-labor jobs. Some lucky garbage collectors and gravediggers ended up transporting whatever valuables families still possessed, hidden in their garbage or coffins, to trade on the Aryan side.

Another thirty thousand illegals were called the "wild ones" and hid in subterranean bunkers, attics, and basements of abandoned ghetto buildings. They were always on the move to avoid being discovered and instantly shot.

That was us.

Rachel, Mama, and I, along with Rachel's family, moved into an underground bunker on Muranowski Street in the northeast corner of the ghetto. It was a block from the now-deserted Umschlagplatz. I figured that would be an unlikely place for the Gestapo and SS to search since the deportations had ended. We dug into the basement of a bombed-out building, concealed the entrance with rubble, and moved in. The basement was just a small square room with stone walls that we divided in half with a rug hung from the ceiling. We had no electricity or running water, but it was safe—at least for now.

Irena continued her activities but with greater stealth and caution. She still lived on the Aryan side and used her official health pass to enter the ghetto daily. Rachel helped her smuggle children out, but I stopped. I was full time with Mordechai Anielewicz.

In October, Angel held a series of talks with several other groups of young men to form a battle organization. Our goal was to prepare for armed resistance, should the Nazis attempt to restart deportations. We knew about sixty thousand Jews were in hiding on the Aryan side of the wall, and they, along with us in the ghetto, were tempting targets for the Nazis.

Lack of weapons and money made it difficult to recruit resistance fighters, but Angel had made a start. As before, he was named commander in chief of the Zydowska Organizacja Bojowa, the Jewish Combat Organization, and Marek Edelman became second in command.

Angel introduced us to Marek. He was in his early twenties, slim, and dark-featured, with widely spaced eyes and a triangular face set off by a thick black mustache. He had a firm jawline.

"I've fought anti-Semitism my whole life, Jakob, but never like today. I'm not about to submit without a fight. I'd rather die with dignity, shooting at Nazis, than walk into a gas chamber. A Jew who dies silently leaves no trace, no memory, while a Jew who dies shooting becomes a story, a legend. I'm willing to die for something more important than my life."

This was my kind of guy. Marek managed to obtain several pistols from sympathetic members of the Polish Home Army fighting the Nazis outside the ghetto.

I was thrilled to be an early recruit in the ZOB. Our ghetto army would become—finally—a force of retribution. The Nazis had issued many proclamations against us, so we started by issuing one against them. We proclaimed that the ZOB would begin retaliatory measures against some members of the Judenrat and the Jewish Police who'd been Nazi collaborators. We sentenced them to death.

To put teeth in that decree, on October 29, we shot and killed Jakob Lejkin, commander of the Jewish Police. He'd been a vicious, brutal cop, implementing the ruthless bidding of the SS.

This one's for you, Papa, I said silently when Lejkin breathed his last.

Over the next several months, we followed this assassination with additional attacks on collaborators, blackmailers, and Jewish Police—names picked from *our* list. Though the beginning seemed trivial, for the first time, we were killing the enemy. We were victors, not victims. The vermin were biting those trying to eradicate them. Even the Polish Home Army was impressed and donated ten pistols and ammunition to the ZOB at the end of December.

CHAPTER 32

And then, perhaps, God returned to Warsaw.
Irena told us about a knock on her door just before curfew in late November 1942. Unexpected visits were suspicious and risky, often bringing bad news—or worse, the SS. She opened the door a crack and saw a short teenage girl with dark matted hair, a crooked smile, and gaunt cheekbones. She was trembling—from fear or the cold, Irena couldn't tell which. She wore a light-blue jacket and dark pants, torn at the knees and muddied at the cuffs. Irena said the girl's first whispered words were that she had money for her.

"I checked the hallway to be sure no one was listening, that the girl wasn't followed, and rushed her inside," Irena said. "She told me her name was Greta and took an envelope from a coat pocket. She said, 'You're Irena, the lady helping save Jews, right?' I flinched at that. So many Nazi informers infiltrate the ghetto, and this innocent-looking young lady might be a Gestapo spy."

Irena said Greta flipped the envelope onto the kitchen table, but Irena didn't pick it up. "I said, 'No, not at all. I don't know what you're talking about. Who sent you?'

"'Trojan. I'm your new contact from Zegota. The Germans killed my parents. I hate them.'

"I relaxed when I heard the password *Trojan* and reached for the envelope. Inside were five thousand zlotys and two blank Kennkarten identification papers."

"Wow," I said. "That'll help bribe some gatekeepers."

Irena nodded. "I sat Greta at the kitchen table. She looked half-starved. I got what was left from a loaf of bread and a jar of jam, and she gulped down big mouthfuls."

"Interesting that she didn't use any of the money to buy food," Rachel said.

"True. An honest girl. I asked her about Zegota. Greta told me that Zofia Kossak, a writer, and another woman activist named Wanda Krahelska founded an organization initially called the Jewish Relief Council. They invented a fake person, Konrad Zegota, as a substitute code name for the organization. Greta laughed when she said that Konrad Zegota soon made it to the top of the Gestapo's most-wanted list."

"Who are these women?" Rachel asked.

"Greta said they're both Catholics, like me, intent on saving Jews."

"This is wonderful but why?" I asked, suspicious that the Gestapo had planted a trap, despite the girl knowing the password.

"I asked Greta the same question. She said the women told her they were driven by their Christian consciousness. But that's just the beginning. Apparently, within a month, Jewish charities around the world joined, and Zegota now has international Jewry support. Zegota's also working with the Polish Home Army resistance fighters. Zegota has a lot of money and contacts in the Polish government in exile who are willing to help."

Maybe there was a God after all, but if there was, I thought His presence would likely only be temporary.

CHAPTER 33

I was right.

In early January 1943, I spotted increasing SS activity around the Umschlagplatz and moved our "wild" family to an isolated attic in a building on Gensia Street, six blocks away. I reported this renewed activity to Angel and wondered whether the Nazis were planning to resume deportations.

Angel told me that Reichsführer Heinrich Himmler had visited the ghetto on January 9 and was furious that his order to deport all Jews had not been carried out. It was likely that deportations would begin again.

His words proved prophetic. Early on January 18, 1943, a cold, windy Monday morning, with snowflakes drifting in the air and dense clouds hiding the sun, the Nazis launched another *Aktion*. Spies tipped off the SS where "wild ones" like us were hiding, and they surrounded multiple ghetto buildings, including our attic apartment. They forced several hundred Jews to come out, hands held high, or they'd be shot.

Rachel and I had gone on an overnight mission for Angel, but Mama was home. She, along with Rachel's family, had been caught, herded into the street, and marched along, four abreast, with the others on the way to the Umschlagplatz.

Angel sent a messenger to find us. Fortunately, we were only two blocks away and raced back to his headquarters.

"What happened? Is Mama all right? What about Rachel's family? What are we going to do?"

"We shouldn't have left them overnight," Rachel cried. "My parents are too old, and my sisters are too young."

Angel, in his quiet, unflustered fashion, had a plan all worked out.

The SS, true to form, kidnapped stragglers along the way to the Umschlagplatz. Fighters in the ZOB walked alongside the captive group and were soon conscripted to join their ranks. No one expected us to be armed, and the SS did not search us as they punched and pushed us to join the line.

I walked beside Mama but didn't say anything. Her head was down, watching her feet and dripping silent tears. Her arms were bent at the elbows, fists balled tight against her cheeks. Finally, seeing movement beside her, she turned, took one look at me, and gasped.

Before she could say anything, I said out of the corner of my mouth, "Mama, stay quiet; just keep walking, and keep your eyes on the person in front of you. When we cross Mila, duck your head and run toward Lubeckiega Street."

I watched Rachel infiltrate alongside her parents and sisters, two rows in front of me, and I assumed she told them the same thing.

As we approached the intersection of Mila and Zamenhofa, Angel tossed a grenade at a group of SS guards walking in a cluster and blew three of them to hell. That was our signal. Confusion erupted when ten of us drew weapons—courtesy of Zegota—and started shooting at the SS. The "wild ones" broke rank and ran for cover. The SS also ran but shot blindly into the captured group, killing at random.

Mama, fists now pumping, raced toward Lubeckiega, followed by Rachel's mom, dad, and sisters. After just a few strides, her mother tripped and fell, striking her head on the pavement. She sat, stunned, on the ground, a terrified look on her face.

An SS officer pointed his rifle at her, but before he could shoot, Rachel, despite her big belly, threw herself at him. They fell together in a tangle and scrambled for the rifle she'd knocked from his hands. He recovered first, grabbed the gun, and turned to shoot her.

I was only a few feet away and shot him in the head, splattering his blood and brains over Rachel and her mother. Brachstein was right: *survival is the basic instinct.* I grabbed each woman by an arm, and we ran toward Lubeckiega. We hid in a doorway, where her father was waiting, so they could catch their breath.

Rachel's mother was crying and trembling so violently that she had to lean against the building to keep from collapsing. Rachel stared at where we'd just been and shook her head in apparent disbelief. I gave them a few moments to calm down; then guided them to Mama.

I went back to help Angel and Marek. We chased the SS into the streets and killed another four before they disappeared out the ghetto gates. They'd killed five of our fighters, along with eight of the captured Jews, but we freed the rest of the group. No one went to the Umschlagplatz that day.

The retreating SS dropped weapons and ammunition that we quickly retrieved, along with uniforms from their dead. Some of our fighters, led by Angel and Marek, continued guerilla fighting over the next three days, ambushing SS and Gestapo and killing another seven. The Nazis soon feared entering our buildings, where we'd built fortified bunkers and hid fighters to ambush and kill.

We'd disrupted the Nazis' plans for the very first time and made them realize their *Aktions* would pay a price. The Germans were no longer invincible, no longer to be obeyed unquestionably, and we were no longer sheep led to slaughter. We'd made them bleed and felt immense pride at our success.

The January Uprising, as it became known in the underground newspapers, established our reputation as a fighting force and drew unsolicited volunteers to our ranks. Even the Polish Home Army congratulated us and began to share weapons, mostly smuggled into the ghetto through the sewers.

The Poles were convinced the Nazis would try to wipe them out, once they got rid of the Jews. By the end of January, they'd given us over fifty pistols and hand grenades, and we'd begun making our own Molotov cocktails. We reorganized and established guards and guard posts throughout the ghetto to keep watch on Nazi activities.

The remaining ghetto inhabitants, though buoyed by our success, feared retaliation. Hundreds of parents pleaded with Irena and her group to smuggle their children to safety. I started helping again when Rachel's big belly forced her to stop. She was due in several weeks. She'd started spotting the day after she tackled the SS officer, and the ghetto midwives wanted her on bed rest.

Irena had exhausted all her usual contacts to place children and had to find new ones. Mother Superior Matylda Getta of the Franciscan Sisters of the Family of Mary in Pludy was especially helpful. She administered more than twenty orphanages in the Warsaw area, but getting children out of the ghetto was challenging. Only four ghetto gates remained open, and they were closely guarded by SS who refused bribes. They no longer accepted Irena's health pass, so she could not enter through any of the four gates. The sewers were the only way in or out.

It didn't take long before the SS started deportations again. The thirty thousand workers with apparent work-immunity papers were now being carted to the Umschlagplatz and forced into trains to Treblinka. In addition to combing the ghetto for us wild ones, the Nazis were also patrolling the Aryan side, hunting for Jews hiding among the non-Jews. The cycle was unending.

CHAPTER 34

"Jake, we're going to have a baby," Rachel said in a loud whisper, her lips against my ear.

I woke with a start, sat up, and checked the room in the gray morning light. It took me a moment to get my bearings. This had been our third move since the January Uprising, most recently to a fortified bunker on Wolynska Street, several blocks from ZOB's headquarters at 29 Mila Street.

Rachel's family, my mama, Rachel, and I shared a single room carved out of the rubble beneath the building. We'd hung blankets and sheets to create privacy cubicles. It had no heat, electricity, or running water. The privy was outside—unpleasant to bare your bottom in the harsh winter of late February.

"I'm having contractions," Rachel said, a nervous quiver in her voice, "and my water just broke. You need to get the midwife."

Excited, I leaned over and kissed her and then hopped from the bed and slipped on a pair of pants over my undershorts.

"Contractions I understand," I said, tying my shoelaces, "but how could water break?"

She gave a short laugh. "Silly. It means my membranes ruptured and leaked fluid from the birth canal. Don't you know anything about women and childbirth?"

I'd been worried about her ever since she'd tackled the SS three weeks earlier and began spotting. She'd rested as much as she could, but the multiple moves to avoid the random searches by the SS took a toll.

I sat down on her side of the mattress and kissed her again. I put my hand on her belly and felt movement—little jolts from the baby. "I'm excited, but I thought you weren't due for another week."

"I'm a little early. The baby's been kicking a lot since the uprising and wants out."

"If it were smart, it would stay where it is—safer, and the food's more reliable."

We laughed together.

"Can I help?" The corner of the hanging sheet turned back, and Mama poked her head in.

"Come in, Mama," I said. "I'm going to find the midwife. She said she'd leave word at headquarters where she was staying."

In a moment, the sheet corner turned back again. "I overheard. What can I do?" said Rachel's mama.

"Hi, Mama. Might as well come in and join the party," Rachel said.

"How close are the contractions?" her mother asked.

"Maybe ten minutes. But they're starting to get closer."

"There's still a bit of time. Go, Jake, fetch the midwife. But be careful," my mama said.

I kissed Rachel again, gave her a gentle hug, and whispered, "See you soon." I slipped a 9mm Weiss pistol, courtesy of the Polish Home Army, into the waistband of my pants and grabbed the Karabiner 43 rifle that was propped near the entrance. I pulled on my coat and sneaked out, trying not to wake the others.

God bless Zegota. We'd been able to buy more arms and ammunition. I'd practiced and had become a pretty good shot. Not as good as Angel or Marek, but not too bad either.

I pulled back a canvas tarp we'd draped over the entrance to keep out the cold, and then lifted aside the debris that covered the tarp to make it blend with the rubble of the building.

I stopped and checked Wolynska Street carefully, looking for

Nazis. The sun was just rising. It was probably around seven in the morning. The snow from last night was pristine, and I saw no footprints near the entrance, so we hadn't been discovered.

The air was cold. I tightened the scarf around my neck and pulled the black knit cap down over my ears. Keeping to the shadows of the buildings, I turned up Zamenhofa and darted to the headquarters without seeing anyone.

The officer on duty told me where Nadia Grynberg, the midwife, was staying, and I went to get her. She was an elderly gray-haired woman with a thick waist and a comfortable chest; she was wearing a worn yellow dress covered with faded flowers. When I told her Rachel had started labor, she flashed a reassuring smile with cheery gray eyes and donned a coat, and we walked quickly back to our bunker.

I lifted the canvas over the bunker entrance, and we went straight to Rachel. The two mamas had rearranged the hanging sheets so Rachel had privacy on all sides. She was in bed, with them fussing over her.

She looked peaked, with a sweaty, pale face, and was groaning in the midst of a hard contraction. Her eyes were shut tight. One fist was clenched at her side, and the other was in her mouth as she bit down on a knuckle to stifle a scream.

Nadia went to her, bent her knees, and peered beneath the sheet.

"Push, Rachel, push," Nadia urged. "I can see the baby's head. It won't be long now. This will be a quick labor for a firstborn. Good job. Push! Hard!"

I felt woozy, and my forehead broke out in sweat. Splattering the blood and brains of the Nazi during the march to the Umschlagplatz several weeks ago didn't bother me, but just thinking about what was happening to my lovely wife beneath that sheet was more than I could handle.

"Do you need me, Nadia?" I asked, my voice tremulous. I was getting nauseated.

"I don't, but Rachel does. Stay with her, hold her hand, stroke her face, and whisper in her ear that you love her. I'll manage this end, and you manage that one," she said, her head hidden by the sheet. "It won't be long now."

I did all Nadia told me, but I don't think Rachel noticed. She was too busy groaning and pushing. But it helped me get my mind off what was happening.

The contractions grew more painful, lasted about a minute, and occurred more often. I wiped her sweaty face, held her hand, gave her sips of water, and added my voice to the chorus for her to push. The two mamas mostly watched but occasionally handed Rachel or Nadia something they requested.

And then the magic happened. Rachel gave a mighty grunt, a push, and …

I heard a slap; the baby cried, and Nadia shouted, "*Mazel tov*. You have a beautiful, healthy baby boy!"

Everyone in the room shouted, "*Mazel tov!*"

I wiped Rachel's face and kissed my beautiful wife. "Thank you, my darling, thank you." I poured a bit of water from the pitcher on the night table near the bed, and we toasted our new baby.

She smiled at me and looked up as Nadia laid the baby across her chest. Next to our wedding day, this was the happiest day of my life. I was bursting with joy, pride, and hope, and I cherished this day, February 27, 1943. Our son was the future. I'd willingly give my life to make sure he survived this hell.

"*Raus! Alle Juden Raus! Jetzt! Schnell!*" the SS shouted. Out! All Jews out! Now! Quickly!

CHAPTER 35

How could the SS have found us? The snow! I'd left footprints in the snow, leading in and out of our hideout!

Stupid! Stupid! Stupid!

The thump of the boots approached our curtained-off corner. The curtain ripped open. The Nazi stood there, feet wide apart, sneering, his rifle pointed at us.

"*Raus, Juden! Raus!*" He laughed and reached for the leg of my newborn son. I'd heard stories of the SS and Gestapo twirling infants by the leg and smashing their heads into a wall.

"No!" Rachel screamed and pulled the baby away, turning her back on the Nazi to shelter the boy with her body.

I grabbed the handle of the water pitcher and flung it at him. He managed to get off a shot just before the pitcher hit him in the chest and doused his face with water. He blinked multiple times to clear his eyes, enough for me to reach him and smash my fist into his face. He staggered backward and became entangled in the sheet hanging from the ceiling. I yanked the Weiss from my waistband and shot him in the chest. He twitched once and didn't move again.

"Jake, watch out!" Rachel shrieked.

I turned to see a second Nazi bolt across the room, firing wild shots. I wanted to return fire, but Rachel's sisters were in the way.

Just before he reached me, I had a clear view, and I shot him in the gut. He crashed, writhing on the floor, clutching his stomach. I finished him with a bullet in his head.

"Jake!" Rachel cried again.

I whirled, ready to shoot another Nazi but, instead, saw my mother lying on the floor, blood spurting from her chest. I ran to her. "Mama! Mama! No!"

I cradled her head in my arms, tears obscuring my vision. She was panting rapidly, barely able to breathe as blood bubbled from her nose and mouth. Rachel threw a towel from the bed, and I pressed it against Mama's chest. But it was no use. Her eyes glazed over as she whispered, "I love you," and Mama died in my arms.

My most cherished day had turned into my worst nightmare. I hadn't pulled the trigger, but I'd caused Mama's death as surely as if I had. She paid with her life for my carelessness.

The room was in turmoil. Rachel's sisters were screaming. They ran to their parents for protection. Everyone was looking for a place to hide. Nadia was sitting on the floor, swaying back and forth, incoherent, repeating over and over, "Oh, no. Oh, no."

Our new son was wailing at the top of his lungs. Rachel held him against her chest and rocked him, trying to soothe him in low, comforting tones. "It's okay, baby; it's okay," she whispered, as tears dripped down her cheeks.

And I sat with Mama's head in my lap, sobbing, "I'm sorry, Mama. I'm so sorry."

Just then, I heard male voices and footsteps enter the room. More Nazis! I reached for my Weiss and leaped up, prepared for a final shootout.

"Jake, what happened? Your neighbor saw the SS and came running for us." It was Angel and five of our guys, with rifles ready.

"Thank God, it's you, Angel." The pounding in my chest eased a little as I explained.

"The two SS were probably on routine patrol and saw the footsteps in the snow," Angel said. "A regular roundup would've flooded this place with troops and surrounded the building. But there'll be a squad looking for these two, so we've got to move you to a new hideout."

"Rachel just delivered half an hour ago," I said. "A son."

"*Mazel tov*, Jake, and to you, Rachel. We'll rig up a stretcher or find a wheelchair for her. We've just prepared a new site at 30 Franciszkanska, a large bunker dug deep in the cellar of an old building. SS will never find it. The bunker's even got heat and electricity diverted from the Aryan side and a supply of food. You'll be safe there."

"My mama …" I pointed.

"I'm so sorry, Jake. We'll give her a proper burial next to your papa."

Angel went to Rachel's parents, who were huddled on the other side of the room with their three daughters. The girls had stopped crying, but their tear-stained faces still showed fright. The older two had their arms around their parents, while the youngest, a seven-year-old, had buried her face in her mama's dress.

"Quickly pack," Angel said. "The SS will raid this place any minute."

I went to Rachel, who had calmed the baby with her breast. My young son suckled like he was starving, and maybe he was; his cheeks were working overtime.

In the midst of tragedy, the scene—our newborn suckling so serenely at Rachel's breast—was beautiful, overpowering. I shook my head in wonder at new life entering the world and Mama leaving it.

I went to her body. Nadia had recovered and draped Mama with a blanket. I sat down on the floor beside her and whispered how sorry I was, that I hoped she was in a good place with Papa, and that we'd soon lay her in the ground next to him.

Guilt smothered me, and I felt like I'd never breathe again. This would live with me forever. I vowed to make the Nazis pay.

Finally, Angel broke the spell. "Get packing, Jake. We've got to leave now."

CHAPTER 36

Though we felt safe in our new bunker at Franciszkanska, we all suffered repercussions from the Nazi assault. It took weeks for Rachel's younger sisters to stop waking each night, screaming, from dreams about Nazis attacking them. Her parents had their hands full calming the girls' fears as well as their own. And since, once again, we shared a large room partitioned by hanging sheets, their nightly cries woke us as well.

We heard that Nadia had stopped doing midwifery and rarely left her bunker. I suffered my own private grief, mourning Mama. *If only I'd covered my footprints in the snow, she'd still be alive* played like a broken record in my head. I couldn't shake the image of her death.

I think Rachel was the most stable emotionally, probably because of little Ari taking up so much of her day—and night. He was the one bright spot for me also. We found a *mohel* in the ghetto to perform the ritual circumcision on the eighth day, and we celebrated Ari's bris with others in the bunker. As Angel had promised, we had food, and Rachel ate well enough to maintain a generous supply of breast milk for our little tot. He grew into a chubby miracle that helped keep us sane.

Deportations and roundups continued but less frequently than before. We had lookouts stationed all over the ghetto, and we ambushed Nazis whenever we could. The weather in March was bitter cold, which also cut down on patrols, but as April warmed, the Nazi presence increased.

We knew something was imminent when our spies told us the Nazis had brought in new leadership—Major General Jürgen Stroop. They spotted him sitting in the back seat of his car as he was driven through the ghetto, inspecting the German factories, even though he rarely wore his general's insignia—probably afraid we'd take a potshot at him. We weren't about to do that and bring the entire Nazi force down on us.

Our spies said he looked about fifty, a big guy who fit the arrogant Aryan mold perfectly with his Nordic features—blue eyes, blond hair, a straight nose, and a solid jaw. His SS uniform was flawlessly tailored, complete with gleaming boots polished as black as opals, brown leather gloves, and a matching leather crop that he snapped into the palm of his hand as they drove. When he barked an order, men raced to carry it out.

In mid-April, we sat down with Angel at a table in the central room of the bunker. This room—made up of a packed dirt floor and cinder block and stone-rubble walls, dug from the building ruins—was the principal meeting place. Multiple rooms, smaller but similar in appearance, branched off to house many families. Slashes of light appeared through cracks in the ceiling.

"I have news, some of it good but most of it bad," Angel said. His features were grim, dark; his voice soft. He was hard to read, but it didn't look good. "Which do you want first?"

"The good news," Rachel said with a smile, her tone upbeat. "Bad news won't spoil and can wait." She seemed determined to keep us in the best spirits; she was, by far, the happiest of us all.

Angel reached into his pocket and took out a chunk of chocolate. "Here's your good news. I know it's your favorite."

Rachel looked at him, eyebrows raised in surprise. "Thanks, but if that's all the good news, I don't want to hear the bad." She took the candy and bit into it. Her face wreathed in smiles. "Oh, the pleasure that this taste triggers—the memories of when I was a little girl, and we'd walk to the candy store and get a chocolate treat. Life was so wonderful back then, so simple and safe."

"Hold on to that memory," I said, watching Angel's face, "and take another bite. I don't think this is going to be fun."

Angel grunted a mirthless laugh. "Ready?"

We nodded.

"We have dependable information that the Nazis plan to wipe out the ghetto entirely—no one will be spared. First, they'll secure the ghetto, locking it up tighter than even now. They're bringing in more troops to search and secure every building, so it'll be impossible to hide or leave. Finally, every last Jewish man, woman, and child will be sent to Treblinka, workers included, or killed here. When the ghetto's empty, they'll repeat the process on the Aryan side to find Jews hiding there."

"When?" I asked, glancing at Rachel, knowing her thought was the same: *Ari.*

"Passover begins the evening of Monday, April 19, two days from now. My guess is they'll try to surprise us early that morning or the following morning. I've posted guards, and we've got spies listening, so we should know something in advance. I reached out to the Polish Home Army, but they refuse to join us, even though many of them think they're slated for Treblinka after us. They've sold us weapons, however—handguns, rifles, ammunition, one small machine gun, and components for Molotov cocktails and bombs. We've been smuggling the stuff in and preparing explosives during the last two weeks." His face remained grim; more bad news was coming.

"What else?"

"We transported Yitzhak Brachstein to London, where he told his Treblinka story to Churchill and the English Parliament." Angel looked pained.

"And?" Rachel prompted, a note of hope in her voice.

"They didn't believe him. 'Preposterous. No one, not even

the Nazis, would be so cruel as to exterminate an entire people. Besides, we don't want people to think we are in this war to save Jews,' they said. So, no outside help. We were hoping the Brits or the Americans would bomb the railroad lines to the camps after hearing that story—Treblinka is just one of several. That's not going to happen. Fortunately, international Jewry still sends money to Zegota. They're parachuting it into Poland with couriers, so we've got cash to buy food and arms and for bribes."

"That's it?" Rachel asked. Gone was her happy smile, replaced by a look that said she couldn't take much more.

"Almost. Take another bite of chocolate."

"I can't. It's all gone," Rachel said, with a helpless shrug and groan. She and I sat up straight and leaned toward Angel.

"The ZOB has decided to fight the Germans down to the last man and woman, knowing we'll eventually lose and be killed, but we need to make a statement to the world about what's happening here—that Jews would rather die fighting than passively accept Nazi brutality any longer."

"We've done that before," I said, remembering our stand against the Romans almost two thousand years ago at Masada. About a thousand Jews were trapped on a high plateau overlooking the Dead Sea in southern Israel. They fought to the death or committed suicide, rather than be captured.

I reached for Rachel's hand as she looked over at the crib where Ari slept. Her eyes filled with tears. Mine did too, thinking about what might lie ahead.

"And our son? What about him?" she asked Angel, a catch in her voice.

"He and the other children are our future. That's what Irena Sendler and her helpers have been working toward, as you know firsthand. The children *must* be saved, at all costs."

"Should we contact Irena about Ari?" Rachel asked, her voice breaking.

We'd been asking parents to give up their children for two years. Now, it was our turn. Could we do it? Maybe we could escape as a family. But how could we abandon our fellow Jews, even if we could get out? No, we had to stay, to fight to the last, but we had to save Ari.

"Irena's the final bit of bad news. Ready?"

We nodded and held our breaths as Angel's face—furrowed brow, pressed lips turned down, and sad eyes—said it all.

"She's been captured and is a prisoner in Pawiak Prison."

"Oh, shit!" I was so angry I couldn't sit still. I pushed back from the table and paced, wringing my hands in front of me, trying to get a grip on my emotions. How much more bad news could we take? "When?"

"Yesterday."

"What'll they do to her?" I stopped and looked at Angel.

He stared back, glum. "The Gestapo will let her stew in a jail cell for a day or two; then take her to their headquarters at 25 Szucha and torture her until she reveals the names of her accomplices. After that—if she's lucky—she'll get a bullet in the head or a rope around her neck to end her suffering. The Nazis have decreed anyone assisting a Jew to escape the ghetto will be killed. Irena and her organization have helped several thousand children escape. The Nazis will chase down her collaborators and shoot them."

Rachel gasped. "What about the children?" she asked, almost in a whisper.

"Irena kept a list of the names of all the Jewish children she smuggled out who are now posing as Catholics in monasteries, convents, churches, and private homes. She hid the list in a glass milk jar, buried in the backyard of her friend Jaga. If they break Irena, and she tells the Nazis about that list, they'll find and kill every child."

"No! We can't let that happen," I said, striking the table with the flat of my hand.

"I was counting on that response."

"What can we do?"

"I have a plan."

CHAPTER 37

A ngel's guess turned out to be correct, as usual. Our spies got word the Nazis planned a final *Aktion* on Monday, April 19, probably hoping to surprise us as we prepared for the Passover Seder that evening. As a diversion, the Germans held a huge outdoor party on the Aryan side of the wall on the eighteenth, ostensibly to celebrate Palm Sunday. They built a giant Ferris wheel next to the wall as part of the festivities, and people waited in line to take a ride and look over the wall into the ghetto.

Beginning around noon on Sunday, Angel sent the frail elderly and children into the safety of underground bunkers. Rachel and Ari stayed with her family in the bunker at 30 Franciszkanska Street. Rachel wanted to fight alongside me, but she was breastfeeding Ari, and we couldn't take the chance.

About two o'clock Monday morning, our scouts sent a message that the SS had mobilized and surrounded the ghetto. An emergency alarm went out for all troops to get ready. I met with Angel, Marek, and heads of the units in the ZOB headquarters at 29 Mila Street.

"The SS has sealed the ghetto into three sections, separated from each other," Angel said. "I think they'll attack section by section. We've got about 750 resistance fighters that we'll divide into three battalions, one to defend each section. We'll start as one group, since we don't know where they'll attack first. Most likely, it'll be the Nalewki Gate, so that's where we'll head now."

I watched faces as the ZOB fighters filtered out. Most were young—late teens or early twenties—and none had any real training as fighters, though some were expert with a gun. The very young—boys and girls fifteen or sixteen—should've been thinking about dating, not dying. But we were all in this together and had vowed death before surrender.

What struck me was that once we'd made up our minds that we were going to die, the fear of dying mostly disappeared. Unit leaders appeared more excited than worried. When death was your constant companion, it was no longer scary. It's when one of the young people was determined to live that he or she became afraid of dying. I could spot them with sweaty, pale faces and wide, fearful eyes.

Angel positioned units in doorways and alleys and on rooftops overlooking the gate. I waited with him and a group of ten fighters on a roof at the corner of Nalewki and Gensia Streets. Even though it was the middle of the night, we were so keyed up that sleep was impossible. We whispered to each other, checked and rechecked our weapons, and then fell silent as the hours passed. I thought about Rachel and Ari and prayed they'd be safe. I was prepared to die but hoped I'd live to see my family again.

Two hours later, the SS began infiltrating the ghetto in groups of four or five, which I guess was to avoid triggering suspicion of an invasion. We watched them form into platoons and companies. As the sun rose several hours later to warm the April day, we first heard and then saw motorized SS help arrive in the form of armored vehicles and tanks. The battle was about to begin, and we were eager to initiate our own Masada, to make our own deaths significant. I hoped someone would be left to tell the tale.

"Look at the sons of bitches," Angel whispered. "They're so confident that they're singing a marching fight song."

We could hear the off-key notes as they goose-stepped through the Nalewki Gate toward Gensia Street.

"Wait until the head of the column reaches the corner of Gensia and Franciszkanska," Angel hissed. Then he shouted, "Now!"

From the rooftop, I threw the first Molotov cocktail onto the marching column. I watched it explode, setting two SS on fire and triggering the onslaught.

Bedlam erupted. SS ran, screamed, and shouted orders, while our shooters on the ground and rooftops sprayed the column with deadly gunfire, making every precious bullet pierce German flesh. Homemade hand grenades and more Molotov cocktails poured down, and Nazi blood flowed like rainwater in the street.

The SS scattered to hide in doorways and slithered along building fronts to escape withering gunfire. They had only one option—to retreat in the direction they'd entered, leaving wounded comrades dying on the ground.

An SS officer bolted from under a balcony and shouted as he left, "*Unmöglich. Wie haben die Juden Waffen bekommen?*" Impossible. How did the Jews get weapons?

The revenge was sweet, even if my conscience was tweaked at the barbarism of it all.

"They're gone," Angel shouted, his voice charged with excitement. "Everybody into the street."

We raced down, hugged and kissed each other, and danced for joy.

"We did it! We did it! We kicked their asses and crushed the SS without losing a fighter. Well done!" Angel shouted. He grabbed me by the shoulders and whirled me around.

After the luxury of a brief celebration, we stripped the dead of their uniforms, guns, and ammunition and rushed to the next battle, several blocks away at the corner of Zamenhofa and Mila.

CHAPTER 38

A ngel positioned us at the four corners of the intersection as the SS column—this time led by two Jewish policemen as sacrificial lambs—passed by. We waited, as before, until Angel whispered, "Now!"

Marek Edelman threw a hand grenade that exploded in their midst. One of our shooters, Masha Glytman, fired from a window ledge across the street. An SS officer shouted, *"Scheisse! Sie haben sogar Frauen, die auf uns schiessen."* Shit! They even have women shooting at us.

I smiled to myself. For the macho SS to acknowledge that a Jewish woman was shooting at them was almost as good as a kill.

Another of our fighters, Eliezer Zuckerman, stood on a rooftop, aiming a Schmeisser submachine gun with deadly accuracy. I watched as he stood and sprayed the SS with bullets and then ducked back down under cover. But he got careless. The SS concentrated their return fire when he stood again, and he went down.

We routed the Nazis a second time, and they retreated, leaving many dead and wounded. This time, they came back with two armored cars and a tank.

I looked at Angel for instructions.

"Patience," was his calm response. "Just wait."

When the tank and cars passed beneath us on Mila, he gave the order, and we dropped our grenades and Molotov cocktails. The explosions set the tank and one car on fire. The tank crew scrambled to get out but were burned alive. The second car retreated.

Suddenly, artillery fire from outside the wall exploded all around us. The Nazis had called in heavy-arms support, the fearsome 88s.

Angel made a quick decision. "That's enough. Everybody out." We ran down the stairs of the apartment building, into the courtyard, and from there to an underground bunker that connected by tunnel to the ZOB headquarters.

Unit commanders regrouped and exchanged information. We'd hammered the Nazis a second time and were elated. Again, no fatalities, but Eliezer Zuckerman had been severely wounded. His comrades had carried him to headquarters, and he lay on a bunk with a bullet in his gut.

"Help me, please." He writhed in agony, holding his belly. "I can't stand the pain."

We tried to comfort him, but his pleas grew more urgent as his suffering increased. Over the next half hour, his screams became unbearable. We had no morphine, no cyanide, nothing to relieve his pain. What could we do? We looked to Angel for a decision.

He nodded at Zuckerman's unit leader, a big man named Guttman, and then back at Zuckerman.

Guttman shook his head. "I can't do it," he said. "No way."

Angel searched each face, but all eyes were downcast and avoided his. I could read the turmoil in his look as he struggled with the decision no one wanted to make.

Angel walked away from the group and paced several moments but came back when Zuckerman again screamed in pain. Finally, Angel drew his pistol and, with tears running down his cheeks, ended Zuckerman's anguish.

Angel moved off to sit by himself in a dark corner of the room, staring blankly at a wall. After several moments, I went to him, and we sat side by side, saying nothing.

I put an arm across his shoulders and broke the silence. "That was courageous. No one else had the guts. Thank you for all of us but especially for Zuckerman."

Angel stared back at me with sad, tearful eyes. "War is horrible," he said in a broken voice. "War is fucking horrible."

We'd been resting about an hour when a messenger arrived with bad news. The SS had regrouped with a vengeance. Supported by additional armored vehicles, tanks, and troops, they were charging through the Gensia-Zamenhofa gate, nearing Nalewki Street. They'd set up a barricade and were shooting machine guns and artillery, inflicting multiple ZOB casualties.

They'd exploded incendiary bombs that set 33 Nalewki on fire and trapped ten ZOB fighters inside. The messenger also told us the SS had established a second fighting front by barreling through the north gate and occupying Muranowski Square, cutting off the northern ghetto.

We were in big trouble. We had to save our people from the fire, as well as liberate the northern ghetto.

Angel gave the orders. "Jake, take five people and head to 33 Nalewki Street. Try to take them out through the tunnel to 6 Gensia. The rest of you come with me, half to Nalewki Gate and half to Muranowski Square. Grab your weapons."

My group slipped out of headquarters onto Mila and turned down Zamenhofa, hiding in the rubble of the buildings as we went. I had no idea what we'd find or how to proceed. Angel had showed confidence in me, but I wasn't certain I'd earned it.

We made it as far as the corner of Zamenhofa and Wolynska when we had to stop. A tank with a crew inside and seven SS crouching behind it was parked in the middle of the road, its turret with cannon and machine guns swiveling in a full circle, searching for prey.

This would be my first real test. I turned to my guys. "We can't get past them on the street. Let's head to the roofs."

The closest building was 16 Zamenhofa. I broke a window on the ground floor, climbed through, and sprinted up the stairs to the attic. From there, we scrambled to the roof.

Unfortunately, the next building sat at least a meter and a half away, with open space—six floors up—separating us. I hated heights, and as I peered over the edge of the roof, the distance looked enormous.

My men stopped and waited for me to decide.

"Check around for a board, a plank, anything we can lay across the gap."

We searched the roof but found nothing. If we were going to get to 33 Nalewki, we had no choice but to jump. And I had to lead. My head pounded, and my breathing quickened as I backed up for a running leap.

For some crazy reason, I thought of that amazing athlete Jesse Owens, winning the broad jump during the 1936 Berlin Summer Olympics.

"Anybody remember Jesse Owens?" I asked. There were nods from the older guys. "Remember how he pushed off with one foot, his arms and legs churning to give him forward momentum? That's what we've got to do."

I held that thought as I raced to the edge of the roof and leaped. My front foot landed just centimeters from the edge, and my momentum carried me forward, like Owens. I looked back in wonder as the rest repeated what I'd done.

Owens would never know his Olympic win got us across.

We jumped three more roofs in the same scary fashion until we were on the other side of the tank and the SS troops. I could see 33 Nalewki. It was a wooden building of seven floors. The third or fourth floor had taken an incendiary hit that'd set it on fire. We ran down the stairs of the closest building and into the courtyard. From there, we hid in the rubble and belly-crawled to 33 Nalewki.

The inside of the building was dark and smoky, and I didn't know where our people were trapped. We searched the first and second floors. Nothing. Flames had gutted the next three floors, but the concrete stairs remained intact.

"Up to the next floors," I said. "We've got to find them."

I darted up the stairs and reached the top-floor attic, where we found seven people huddled near a shattered window, trying to breathe. Three had already perished—probably from smoke inhalation—and lay unmoving on the floor.

"Praise God, you're here," one of them said, greeting us. "We thought we'd be burned alive. We've lost three already." He pointed.

"We'll lead you out. There's an escape tunnel to the next building somewhere. The opening's covered by wallpaper."

I pounded the wall facing 6 Gensia until I got a hollow response; then drove my fist through. I peeled back wallpaper to reveal the opening to the tunnel.

"Everybody ready?" I asked. I saw nods. "Nobody has claustrophobia?"

No one spoke, but it didn't matter. If they wanted to live, this was the only way out. Flames were licking at the stairs we'd run up just moments ago.

The tunnel was narrow, pitch-black, and filled with smoke. The low ceiling made me crouch and, at times, go to my hands and knees. We had no light, and breathing was almost impossible. The temperature must have been forty or forty-five degrees Celsius from a combination of the warm day and the flames below. My shirt was drenched, and sweat dripped down my forehead into my eyes.

Halfway across, I had to stop, wipe my face, and catch my breath. That part of the tunnel was so narrow that I had to wedge my shoulders against the sides to wiggle through. My eyes teared, my throat was raw and scratchy, and my hands and knees were hot as the flames drew closer. I breathed in smoke and started coughing. The person second in line stumbled into me in the dark and pushed me to move on.

It took us ten harrowing minutes to get through, but we finally made it to 6 Gensia and could breathe again.

We were in a small attic with a sloping ceiling and one window facing the front of the building. The floor was made of splintered, raw wooden planks that looked so worn I was afraid they might not hold our weight.

I went to the window and stared out. *Shit!* On the street was the same tank we'd seen at the corner of Zamenhofa and Wolynska. I guess we hadn't been so clever after all.

I sat our people on the floor and explained our situation. We had ten men and three women, all dressed in similar raggedy shirts and pants. Some wore hats; some had holsters on belts holding handguns or knives.

"Sorry we had to leave your comrades behind," I said. "There's no way we'd have gotten through the tunnel if we'd carried them."

Nods of agreement.

"What guns do we have?" I asked.

Ten held up handguns, and three had rifles.

"Molotov cocktails or hand grenades?"

One of each.

"Here's what we do." I stood so I could address them better. "We're thirteen. We split into two groups. The three with rifles and the two with the grenade and Molotov cocktail take roof positions outside this window. That leaves eight of us to go downstairs. The roof people drop the grenade and Molotov, and the rifle shooters open fire at the same time. That'll be our cue to come out shooting." I paused and looked at the group.

Nods all around.

"Anybody have a better plan?"

Silence.

"Okay, let's do it before this damn building catches fire." I turned to the roof people. "Give us, say, three minutes to get downstairs, and then you begin."

"How will we know when you're in position?" one of them asked.

"Good point," I said. "We'll just have to take the chance that we'll get to the street in three minutes. Should be plenty of time, unless we meet resistance on the way."

Everyone stood. We shook hands and separated, wishing each other good luck. The three women and four men followed me, and we crept down the stairs, keeping as quiet as we could.

As I turned to descend the last flight, I stopped cold and held up my hand to halt the others.

An SS officer was standing in the lobby of the building, facing a corner, urinating against the wall. I put my finger to my lips and motioned the group back up the stairs. As they went, somebody stumbled. The SS spun around, one hand still holding his pecker. If it wasn't so deadly serious, I would've laughed.

I flew down the remaining stairs and barreled into him, knocking him into the wall with my shoulder and clamping a hand over his mouth. Fortunately, he had only one free hand and offered little resistance.

Whoever was behind me unsheathed a knife and jammed it into the officer's throat, severing his vocal cords. Blood spurted from his neck as he slid down the wall with my hand still pressed over his mouth. He gurgled multiple times and breathed his last.

One of the women—actually, a young girl—stared at the SS. She bit her lip, her eyes wide and face white, as she slowly shook her head. "I can't believe I did that," she murmured.

"Thanks," I whispered. "What's your name?"

"Zivia."

I looked at her. She was a tiny girl, slim, with lots of guts. "How old are you?"

"Sixteen."

"Thank you, Zivia. You helped save my life." I shook her hand and gave her a hug. The rest of the group descended the stairs and gathered around. I didn't need to ask for silence. Everyone was too stunned to make any noise.

Suddenly, we heard two explosions, followed by the *tat-tat* of rifle fire. "Let's go, everyone. It's now or never."

We stormed through the lobby and out the front door. The tank was on fire, and two of the crew lay dead. The third was trying to operate the turret gun with one arm; his other arm hung bleeding at his side. Before he could act, someone from the roof shot him.

Two of the SS were on the ground, apparently dead. The others used the tank as their shield and returned fire at the people on the roof. When the SS saw us, they shifted and aimed for us. Zivia, beside me, got hit and went down with a bullet in her chest.

"Cover me!" I shouted. I scooped her into my arms, carried her back into the lobby, and laid her on the floor. The bullet had punctured the middle of her chest and probably had hit her heart. She was gasping for breath as she stared at me with unseeing eyes and died as I held her. I hoped she had family so I could tell them how brave she'd been.

"This one's for Zivia!" I shouted to the others as I rejoined the battle. "Kill the bastards."

The fight didn't last long. We had the SS in a crossfire. When they hid behind the tank from the shooters on the roof, they became exposed to us, and when they hid from us, the guys on the roof shot them. They hit another fighter from our group before we killed them all.

The roof people joined us, and we regrouped. I shook hands all around and patted backs. "You've done an amazing job. We've lost two people, but we knocked out a tank and killed its crew and seven others. Good work," I said. "Back to headquarters. This day is over, and we need to prepare for tomorrow."

The sun was fading fast. I knew the remaining SS would leave the ghetto, afraid to stay after dark. We collected the two bodies of our comrades—the three at 33 Nalewki had burned with the building—and headed back.

Angel was waiting for us.

"We drove the sons of bitches out!" Angel shouted as soon as we entered headquarters, his face flushed. "Fighters in the ZZW joined us, and we kicked their asses from Nalewki Gate and Muranowski Square but lost three."

ZZW was a separate underground Jewish resistance force that maintained independence from us but helped when they could. Angel had tried to coordinate the ZOB and ZZW before the uprising but had failed.

"Go back to your bunkers and celebrate the Passover Seder," he said, checking his watch. "You still have time. We'll regroup tomorrow morning at six to hear what's scheduled for day two. It's

April 20, Hitler's birthday—the evil son of a bitch'll be fifty-four—and I'm sure the SS have big plans in store."

I'd started to leave when Angel caught my eye and motioned me to stay. When we were alone, he said, "Come early tomorrow morning—say, five thirty. We're going to free Irena."

CHAPTER 39

"Thank God you're okay." Rachel rushed to greet me with a relieved smile, holding Ari in her arms. We hugged and kissed, with the little guy between us.

Ari stared at me with a big-eyed look that seemed to ask, "Who are you?" I took him from Rachel, and the warmth and smell of his body displaced the fatigue and emotional strain of the day.

"Hey, little guy, I'm your papa. Remember?" He was a week shy of two months. I didn't expect an answer, but I did get a crooked smile—and then a milk spit-up from his last feeding.

"Come; wash up for the Passover Seder," Rachel said, taking Ari and handing me a towel. She pointed to the table in the middle of the room, set with the traditional Seder plate, candles, and—*wherever did they find it?*—matzos and red wine. There even was a copy of the Haggadah, the text that told of our release from slavery in Egypt over two thousand years ago and that provided a ritual road map for the Seder dinner celebrating that freedom.

Rachel's mother held her arms out to welcome me, and her father followed. Her sisters were seated at the table, hungry to begin eating.

I washed and sat down.

As the Seder began, Rachel's youngest sister asked the first of four questions that Jews throughout the world would be asking that night.

"Ma nishtana ha lyla ha zeh mikkol hallaylot?" How is this night different from all other nights? The answer, of course, was that we'd been unchained from ancient Egypt's yoke and could eat, drink, and recline as free people.

But I was a mass of conflicting emotions. That freedom—true in the past—had been ripped from us. We were celebrating a Jewish holiday over two thousand years old, while sitting at a dinner table in the middle of a hidden underground ghetto bunker with stone walls and a dirt floor, surrounded by Nazis who'd murdered hundreds of thousands of us and would continue to massacre more. We'd killed a few hundred of them today, and tomorrow I certainly would attempt to kill more as I tried to free the most generous Christian I'd ever known. Irena Sendler was prepared to give her life to save Jewish children, as I was prepared to give mine to save hers.

Santayana's teaching came to mind: *Those who cannot remember the past are condemned to repeat it.* When would humankind ever learn to abandon war and destruction? How many times did we need to free ourselves from being held captive? How many times to rebuild lives? To rebuild civilizations?

If we were indeed the Chosen People of the Old Testament, it would be nice if God chose someone else once in a while.

Later, as I lay with my arms around my wife in the quiet of the night—though I suspected our lovemaking earlier hadn't been so quiet—we whispered about the next day and the future.

"What's going to happen to us, especially to Ari?" Rachel asked, her lips against my ear. "After you free Irena, should we ask her to smuggle him out of the ghetto? Would he be placed in a Catholic sanctuary? I don't know if I can handle that, Jake." Her voice trembled.

I felt warm teardrops on my arm. I hugged her close. "I know, but if he stays in the ghetto, his chances of survival are not good. Our chances of survival are not good. The Nazis plan to empty every building and deport us all to Treblinka. If they can't do that, they'll wipe out the entire ghetto—and us along with it."

She knew this but still gasped. "How long will it take the Nazis to … to … to kill us all?" she asked, wiping away a tear.

"Depends on how much firepower they decide to throw at us. Today was a good day because we surprised them, and we'd stored up a bunch of explosives they were not prepared for. Hopefully, tomorrow will be good also. But after that, the fighting will get tougher because they'll bring in planes and bombs, artillery, tanks, armored cars, and several thousand men. They'll also begin to realize that fighting us at a distance improves their odds."

"Why?"

"Reduces the effectiveness of handguns, our major weapon. We've only a few rifles and a machine gun or two, and we're running low on grenades and Molotov cocktails. We do have one or two surprises left, but that's about it," I said.

"Any hope of the ZZW joining forces? Or the Polish Home Army?"

"ZZW is fighting independently, and that helps. They're more experienced fighters than we are and better armed. They accomplished a gutsy move yesterday when they hoisted Zionist and Polish flags over their headquarters on 7 Muranowska Street. That really has to piss off the SS."

"The Polish flag should make the Polish Home Army happy."

"Probably, but they aren't doing a whole lot so far. They praise us for fighting and give us a few rifles, but only a handful actually fight."

I rose on one elbow and looked down at my wife. Pregnancy had made her even more beautiful—her luxuriant auburn hair cascaded to her shoulders, her blue eyes shimmered, and her curvaceous lips always were upturned in a smile. "Tomorrow's going to be more dangerous because we'll attack Pawiak Prison. If anything happens to me, I want you to know I love you and Ari more than anything in the world, but I have to do what I'm doing."

"I know you do, Jake. I understand, and I'd help if I could. I love you too."

I kissed her tenderly on the lips. "I've got to get some sleep, darling. Angel wants to meet at five thirty. Good night, my sweet. Good night."

CHAPTER 40

We met in the underground bunker headquarters at 29 Mila. Angel had coffee ready, along with a slice of dark bread on a table in the middle of the room.

"Jake, today's a big day. It's already started."

"What's happened?"

"The Nazis tried to overrun ZZW headquarters to remove the two flags. The word is that they're furious, particularly General Stroop, that ZZW had the guts to fly them. ZZW was ready for the attack and drove them off using the two machine guns they'd gotten from the Home Army. I wish we had such firepower."

"We did okay yesterday without machine guns."

"We did, and you did a great job saving our people from the fire."

"Thanks. Today, it's Save Irena Day."

"Yes, it is. First we've got to deal with several hundred SS troops gathering near the Krasinski Gardens outside the wall at the corner of 6 Walowa and 32 Swientojerska."

"Trying to overrun the ghetto?"

"That's what they're planning. But we're going to give them a big surprise and save Irena at the same time."

∽

About fifty of us were positioned at the gate near the Krasinski Gardens in the northeast corner of the ghetto. The gardens were bright and beautiful, bursting with spring blooms in reds, golds, purples, and whites. Flower fragrances sweetened the air. That splendor contrasted with the dirty, gray ghetto streets, littered with rubble from bombed-out buildings, collapsed storefronts, and smelly dead bodies.

"Hope this one works better than yesterday," Angel said.

"What happened?" I asked, as we watched from a building rooftop overlooking the gate.

"Our guys had chased about thirty SS troops to Smocza Street near Nowolipie, where we'd planted a roadside bomb. SS were standing right next to the bomb, but the damn thing didn't explode."

"What went wrong?"

"It'd rained. The engineer who built it said a wet wire shorted. They still killed a bunch but nowhere near what a bomb would've done."

"Get it fixed?"

"We did. That'll be your entrée to Pawiak. You got Zegota's envelope?"

I nodded and patted my jacket. "Thirty-five thousand."

"Careful with it. They want her out before the SS force any names from her." Angel called over two young men who were standing near a bomb detonator. "Hanoch and Simcha, come and meet Jakob Holmberg. You three are going to save Irena."

We shook hands. Hanoch Kowalski and his friend Simcha Nowak were broad-shouldered and athletic-looking with Aryan features; they looked a bit younger than I.

"Like our uniforms?" Simcha asked, performing a mock goose-step in his SS officer's clothes. "These got us close enough to the prison to plant the bomb."

"No more wet wires?" I said, looking from one to the other.

"Not to worry." Hanoch gave me a reassuring smile. "It'll work."

Angel silenced the conversation as we watched SS troops strut across the Krasinski Gardens and stream through the gate.

"Hanoch, you ready?"

"More than ready. The fuckers wiped out my family. This is payback."

I focused on Hanoch's face as he waited for the SS troops to enter the gate. He wore a look of anticipation and beamed as he depressed the plunger.

Kaboom!

The intersection of the two streets exploded. Rocks, cement, glass, blood, and body parts blasted into blinding, swirling clouds of debris. The air filled with screams and cries for help as the SS column was blown to nothingness. Grenades, Molotov cocktails, and bullets followed to finish off anyone who'd survived the blast.

We'd scored big. At least a hundred SS lay dead or wounded; the rest were driven out of the gate and back into the gardens.

"Yes!" Angel shouted, his eyes sparkling. "The engineer got it right this time. Okay, Jake, that's your cue. I'm sure the guards at Pawiak Prison heard this blast and will come running to help. You guys get out of here."

Simcha handed me an SS officer's uniform. "Quick—put it on."

I dressed in seconds.

"Good luck," Angel said. "Bring Irena back."

We walked fast to Zamenhofa and turned west on Dzielna Street. The sidewalks were busy with Nazi troops running toward the explosion. Three men disguised as SS officers, traveling in the opposite direction, drew no attention.

We reached 24 Dzielna Street in five or six minutes. The Pawiak Prison was a rectangular building with two turrets, surrounded by a stone wall. The main building of four stories opened with an arch to the entrance and housed male prisoners. The women's prison was smaller, with three stories.

"No guard at the gate," Hanoch said.

"Good," Simcha replied. "Probably all left to help at the explosion."

"Wait here." Hanoch ran to the gate, bent near the arch for a few seconds, and ran back, trailing a long wire that he connected to a detonator.

"Want to do it?" he asked, smiling as he handed me the detonator.

"With pleasure." I'm sure my face had the same expectant look that his did at the gardens.

He nodded, and I pressed the plunger. The bomb wasn't nearly as powerful as the one at the Krasinski Gardens, but it was big enough to blow a hole in the entrance.

We ran through a long hallway of gray-stone walls that Rachel had described after she'd been brought there to clean toilets. We took the first corridor to the right that led to "Serbia," the name given to the women's prison.

Hans Burkl, deputy commander of Pawiak, was standing at the entrance to Serbia, hands on hips, booted feet wide apart—a don't-fuck-with-me stance. He wore a Gruppenführer SS uniform and had a Luger strapped to his belt. Medium height, with an oval, fat, pitted face and mean-looking shadowy eyes, he was a sadistic killer who enjoyed torturing prisoners before executing them, women especially.

"You made it," he said by way of greeting. His eyes flared as he took in our uniforms.

"Yes, as arranged," I said.

"You have my fifty thousand zlotys?"

"Zegota told us you agreed to thirty-five thousand." I reached into my shirt for the envelope.

"I changed my mind. Fifty." He snatched the envelope. "Come back when you have the other fifteen." He turned his back on us and began to walk away.

"Hey, wait a fucking minute!" Hanoch shouted, hurrying after Burkl. He grabbed him by the shoulder. "We had a deal. Free Irena Sendler. Now."

Burkl whirled, his hand on the gun in his belt. "Back off, Jew, or you're a dead man."

I stepped in front of Hanoch and faced Burkl. "Gruppenführer, we had an agreement." I did my best to keep my temper in check.

"You heard me. Another fifteen thousand."

"Okay, but free Irena now, and we'll get you the money tomorrow."

He laughed in my face. "You think I'm crazy? Trust you once you have her? *Nein!* Get the money today."

"And if we do, how do I know you won't want another fifteen when I return?"

"You don't."

"Enough of this bullshit." Hanoch reached for his gun, but Burkl was too quick. A shot rang out, and Hanoch collapsed to the floor, clutching his head.

Simcha and I charged Burkl. I seized his wrist and pointed the gun at the ceiling as he pulled the trigger. Simcha wrestled him around the neck, and together, we dragged him to the ground. I pried his fingers loose and yanked the Luger from his hand.

Simcha had him in a stranglehold.

"Don't kill him. We need him to find Irena."

Simcha loosened his grip, and Burkl stood. I kept the Luger aimed at him as Simcha ran to Hanoch. He bent down and held his friend in his arms. Hanoch's scalp was spurting blood, and he was not moving.

Tears flowed over Simcha's cheeks. "He's dead. My best friend is dead." He rocked Hanoch back and forth, a dazed look on his face.

We heard a groan. "My head—my fucking head hurts." Hanoch tried to sit up. He wasn't dead! The bullet had just creased his skull and knocked him unconscious.

Simcha flew at Burkl and crashed his fist into Burkl's jaw. Burkl went down on one knee, reeling from the blow, his mouth and nose bleeding. "That's for almost killing my best friend, you bastard."

"Fuck you, Jew," Burkl said, wiping his face and standing back up, a haughty look in place.

"Where is she?" I said, aiming the gun at Burkl.

"You can both go to hell. My guards will be back any minute, and we'll make you permanent guests of Pawiak." He rubbed his chin.

"You've got ten seconds to lead us to Irena, or you're a dead man." When he didn't move, I shot him in the foot.

He collapsed, screaming. He clutched his foot as blood oozed through a hole in his boot.

"Du verdammter Hurensohn," he yelled. *"Bist du verrückt?"* You fucking son of a bitch. Are you crazy?

"I don't know what that means," I said, keeping my voice calm, "but in another ten seconds, the next bullet is between your eyes if you don't lead us to Irena."

"I can't walk," he shrieked. "My foot! You shot my foot!"

"I promise your head will be next. Stand up and lean on me. Where is she?"

He led us, limping, down another corridor flanked by cells on both sides. Cries and moans filtered out from behind closed doors. Burkl stopped at number 35, a squat metal door with a small, barred window at the top. He unhitched a small key ring from his belt, selected one of two keys, and unlocked the door.

I propped him on the floor, and he groaned as he leaned against the wall. He removed his boot and sock and gaped at the bloody hole where his big toe had been.

"Scheiss!" he moaned.

Irena's cell was barely large enough for a person to stand upright, even one as short as she. She could touch both stone walls while standing in the middle of the room. There was no furniture. A smelly bucket served as the toilet.

Irena lay in a fetal position on the dirt floor, her face bloodied, and her right leg angled in an unnatural position. She seemed barely conscious. I bent down and raised her head in my hands.

"I haven't told them anything," she whispered. "Nothing. The lists are safe."

"We're taking you out. Can you walk?" I asked.

"Thank God," she said, bursting into tears. "I thought I would die here. My name's on the execution list for tomorrow."

"Won't happen. Not while we're here. Can you walk?" I repeated.

"With help. They broke my leg."

I took one arm, Simcha took the other, and we lifted her from the floor. She draped an arm across my shoulders to support her right leg. She bit her lip to keep from crying out. We had no crutch and no wheels. She'd have to do the best she could. We'd carry her if we had to, but that would attract attention.

"What are we going to do with him?" Simcha asked, head tipped toward Burkl, who was clutching his foot. "I'd like to shoot the bastard right now."

"I would too, but we may still need him."

"I could strangle him."

"I'm sure you could. How about we lock him in Irena's cell?" I said.

"You can't leave me here. Please—my foot's bleeding. They'll never find me."

"Yeah, they will. When they come to get Irena tomorrow morning," I said. "Be happy we're letting you live."

We dragged Burkl into Irena's cell and slammed the door shut.

As we helped Irena walk, she stopped. "Can we free some others?" she asked, looking from me to Simcha. "I have friends in here."

"We're going to do more than that, Irena. We're going to free the whole damn prison. I think the guards are going to be busy near the garden for quite a while." I opened Burkl's key ring, kept the one he'd used to open Irena's cell, and gave the other to Hanoch. "Run to the men's prison. Free as many as you can. I'll do the same here. If the guards return, shoot the bastards. They won't be able to stop all of us."

I sat Irena down in the hallway, her back leaning against the wall. "Wait for me. I won't be long."

It took me half an hour to open all the doors on the three floors. Shouts of joy, *thank God*, and *I can't believe it* greeted me at each cell. The women hugged me, kissed me, and cried on my shoulder when I opened their cell doors and told them they were free. They slowed me down so much that I had to push some away so I could get to the other cells. I worried about the returning guards.

But the elation I experienced in thinking of these women rejoining husbands, children, and families was worth any risk. The hallways were soon crowded with men and women, laughing, embracing, and jumping for the sheer bliss of being free.

When I returned to Irena, I found her surrounded by friends, wishing her luck and offering to carry her out. Someone had rigged up a brace using a broom handle for her leg.

The door to Irena's cell was open. Burkl lay on the floor, dead, executed with a bullet to the back of his head. I didn't know who'd killed him and didn't care. I'm sure many had a score to settle.

I knelt beside the body and searched his pockets for my envelope. It was gone! Someone had stolen the thirty-five thousand zlotys.

I jumped up, open-mouthed, as Simcha walked over, grinning. "Looking for this?" he asked, waving the envelope at me.

CHAPTER 41

I t had been a good day. Actually, more than just a good day—a blessed day.

And it might be our last for a while.

The next day, Wednesday, April 21, General Stroop issued a decree that he would not tolerate any more insurrection. He planned to eliminate *every* building in the ghetto. Even the factories that still produced Nazi goods, along with the workers in them, would be destroyed. Those people hiding could volunteer to relocate to work camps in Lublin or be shot.

We had until noon to give ourselves up.

We knew relocation was a lie. Most people had burrowed deeper into attics, underground bunkers, abandoned storage sheds—any place they could find. Only several hundred crept into the street. The SS rounded them up and marched them to the Umschlagplatz.

"I smell smoke," Rachel said. It was just past noon on Wednesday.

I slipped from our bunker at 30 Franciszkanska, keeping hidden in the ruins, and checked the neighborhood.

The Nazis had placed large drums of gasoline in front of the buildings along the street and set them on fire. The old wood-framed houses were easy prey. Entire blocks would become blazing infernos—and so would the people inside. The house that shielded our bunker was just starting to smolder as flames from next door licked at the roof. A neighbor ran by, yelling that the houses on Walowa and Swientojerska Streets, just north of the Krasinski Gardens, were ablaze.

Burning us out was smart. Safe for them, and death traps for us. We had no water and would soon have no place to hide.

People began to surge out of doors and windows—coughing, gasping for air, and swatting at smoldering clothing. Those surrounded by flames jumped from second- and third-story windows. The Nazis used them as target practice.

I ran back inside to warn everyone before the fires trapped us. Though we were underground, the floors above would soon come crashing down as burning beams gave way.

"Rachel, start packing whatever you can carry. Help your folks. We need to make it to ZOB headquarters at 29 Mila." The HQ was well ventilated and, hopefully, protected from flames. I prayed they had room for us.

I tried to calm everyone, but Rachel's sisters became hysterical. There wasn't much I could say. The reality was horrendous—the SS would eventually kill us all by fire or bullets. But we weren't dead yet and would die fighting—and take some of them with us. I made sure my Karabiner had ten bullets in the clip and my Luger was tucked in my belt, and I grabbed my last hand grenade.

We poked our heads out, ran west on Franciszkanska away from the fires, and then turned north on Zamenhofa. I carried little Ari, asleep, in one arm and a pillowcase filled with essentials in the other.

Black soot and smoke hung in the air like fog. We inhaled it, along with the acrid smell of burning wood and scorching flesh. The reduced visibility and building ruins offered some protection from roving SS squads searching ghetto streets in tanks. Armored vehicles spewed lead at anything that moved.

As we neared Wolynska, we heard gunshots close by. I turned

to see a tank rumbling north on Zamenhofa toward us, shooting at Jews fleeing burning buildings.

"Hurry," I urged our small group. "We've got to reach headquarters before they get close."

"We're trying, Jake," Rachel's father said, breathless, "but the little ones can't move any faster." Rachel's youngest two sisters, seven and nine, were so frightened they could barely walk; their mother half-dragged them along, holding each by a hand. Rachel's father and her twelve-year-old sister carried supplies and clothes they'd packed.

The tank was gaining. "Let's duck onto Wolynska instead. Maybe they'll pass by."

We turned west onto Wolynska and hid among the ruins of a bombed-out building about ten meters from the corner.

"Everyone flat on the ground. Don't make a sound."

The girls were crying and wouldn't stop, despite the parents' efforts. This was not going well.

The tank reached the intersection, halted, and silenced the motor. A head popped up in the turret and examined the area with a pair of binoculars. The girls were so petrified they'd become mute.

Suddenly, Ari woke and started whimpering. Rachel quickly unbuttoned her blouse and thrust her nipple into his mouth, but he wasn't interested. He twisted and squirmed and began crying. His wails pierced the silence. The binoculars swung in our direction.

"Down," I whispered to Rachel. "Down flat with Ari."

She lay back on the ground and held him to her chest.

I heard the gunshot a fraction of a second before a bullet ricocheted off the cement pillar in front of us. "We're too close to the others," I said. I fired a precious bullet at the SS, and when he ducked down into the tank, I grabbed Ari and ran, hunched over as low as I could, dodging through the rubble to a spot ten meters away. Rachel followed close behind. We dropped behind several boulders. Rachel took Ari from me, and this time, he was eager to suckle.

The gunshots had frightened Rachel's sisters into crying once again. The guy in the tank stood and aimed the binoculars at the new sound. The tank motor rumbled back to life. The 70mm cannon swung in that direction and began firing.

"Stay here," I told Rachel.

I darted from boulder to boulder toward the tank. When I was five meters away, I took careful aim and shot the SS in the chest. He slumped over the rim of the turret.

The cannon swung toward me. I ran to the back of the tank, tossed my grenade into the open turret, and ducked to the ground.

After the grenade exploded, I climbed onto the turret. Two SS troopers were dead, and the tank was disabled.

"All clear!" I shouted to Rachel and ran to where her family had been hiding.

I gasped. They were all dead, blown to pieces, body parts scattered in the rubble around them.

Rachel approached. I tried to block her from the scene, but I was too late.

"Oh my God! No! No!" she screamed as she tottered and began to collapse. I caught her and Ari as she crumpled to the ground. She crawled on her hands and knees to the remnants of her family.

She gagged when she reached their remains and began to vomit. Not much came up but dry heaves continued. After several minutes, she took a deep, shuddering breath. She sat back on her heels, her face pale, and buried her head in her hands, sobbing.

I went to her and hugged her to me. There were no words. Her world had literally exploded. I just held her in my arms.

"My father—my mother—my sisters—my whole family. All gone. All gone." She stared at me wide-eyed, mouth agape.

Ari, rolled up in blankets on the ground, began to cry. That sound penetrated her consciousness. She picked him up and gave him her breast.

In the distance, I saw another tank rumbling up Zamenhofa.

"Rachel, honey, we have to go. Now."

"I can't just leave. What about—" She swept her hand around.

"It's horrific, but we have no choice. Look." I pointed to the approaching tank.

She nodded. I pulled her to her feet. Silently, we gathered what we could, grabbed Ari, and raced to ZOB headquarters.

We arrived to see people pouring out of the bunker. Our headquarters, 29 Mila, was on fire.

CHAPTER 42

Angel was the last to leave, the captain finally abandoning ship. "What happened?" I asked, helping him carry out some boxes that were still smoldering.

He shook his head. His frown cut deep craters across his forehead. "The Nazis are getting real smart, Jake. They're using dogs and sound-detecting equipment to find our bunkers. They give little kids candy to spy on us, capture those in hiding, and march them to the Umschlagplatz or shoot them if they try to run."

"The barbarism never stops," I said. "Just serves as fuel for more."

"Bastards found the entrance to 29 Mila this morning, poured in petrol, and set it on fire. Then they waited in the basement across the street"—he pointed—"for the smoke and flames to drive us out. Shot six of our fighters before we killed them with a grenade."

"They burned us out too, Angel." I briefed him on what'd happened.

He went to Rachel and hugged her. "I'm so very sorry. I wish I could offer more than words, but I'm afraid it's going to get worse. We've lost the element of surprise, along with many of our brave fighters, and we're low on ammunition."

Rachel was silent; she stared at the ground and passively accepted his embrace. I'm not sure she even heard what he said. She hadn't spoken three words since the shooting.

Angel turned back to me. "The new head, Stroop, is no dummy. We've ambushed his men so many times that they avoid the ghetto, especially at night, unless they come in tanks and armored vehicles."

"They know fire will eventually beat us and at the least cost to him," I said.

Angel nodded. "Stroop doesn't care about these buildings. They've even started dropping incendiary bombs to burn us out. Unfortunately, we can't hold out much longer."

Rachel looked up, and our eyes locked. No words, but we were both thinking about how we'd get Ari out while there was still time.

"Where do we go now?" I asked.

"Do you remember Shmuel Asher?"

"No, should I?"

"No reason, I guess. He was a big-time thief, the head of an underworld consortium in Warsaw before the war. Controlled crime in half the city. Made a lot of money."

"Sounds like a good man to know."

We both laughed.

"Turns out when you emptied Pawiak Prison two days ago, you saved his brother-in-law, a guy named Hershel Zucker. Zucker was scheduled for execution with Irena the day after your raid. Shmuel's invited us to share his bunker at 18 Mila Street. That's where we're headed."

Shmuel Asher sent a young boy to lead us through a series of hidden passages, accessible only by a whispered password to a guard at each entrance. We finally descended a steep tunnel to 18 Mila, an underground labyrinth five meters beneath abandoned ruins created by German bombs in 1939.

"Welcome to the largest and most luxurious underground bunker in the ghetto," boomed Shmuel Asher as we reached the ground floor. "We are three hundred already—my family, friends, and business associates—but you are welcome to share whatever we have. My home is your home, my food is your food, and my men are your men." He grasped each of our hands in a vigorous shake.

Shmuel Asher was a big man, tall, ruddy-faced, and thick-necked. A bulging belly hung over his belt, and his shiny bald head reflected pink in the overhead light. He wore a clean white shirt, open at the neck. A wide black belt with a pistol on each hip held up blue pants stretched taut, like an inflated balloon. Black boots, shined to a mirror finish, completed the image of an outsized host.

"I'm so glad to welcome all of you, to be able to thank you personally for saving Hershel. Who is Jakob?" he asked, smiling.

I tipped my head.

"Thank you so much, Jakob," Shmuel said, shaking my hand again. He called over his brother-in-law, a man half his size but wiry and resilient. "Hershel, this is the man who saved you. We need to drink to his health."

Hershel took my hand and, despite his size, crunched my knuckles before giving me a bear hug and a kiss on each cheek.

Several men with trays of wine glasses passed among us. We all took a glass, raised it for a toast, and listened to Shmuel.

"I pledge to you our total support. You'll find our skills unmatched and invaluable. We know the sewers like our own home. We know how to move silently and unnoticed through secret passages in the ghetto and slip through cracks in the wall. We can open any lock, rob any store, and kill without leaving any trace. Anything you want, we can get." He raised his glass. "To your health, Jakob and Angel, and to all of our new friends."

He drained his glass, and we followed.

We soon learned that Shmuel Asher was a benevolent dictator. He ran the huge bunker according to his rules, on his schedule and his demands. No one entered or left without his permission. He planned the daily menus, activities, and interactions. His word was law and was also his bond. When he told us that what was his was ours, he meant it. There *was* honor among thieves—or at least this thief.

His men had excavated this huge bunker as a hideout beneath

the rubble and courtyards of what had been three large adjoining buildings. They'd fashioned individual rooms, a catacomb for the men and their families, including a large central meeting room, a kitchen and well-stocked pantry, and a reading and recreation room. Electricity smuggled from the Aryan side powered this underground city, and a well had been dug for water.

Shmuel found an empty cubicle for Rachel, Ari, and me. Angel refused to permit his men to displace any of Shmuel's gang, so he had the fighters extend the bunker another ten meters by digging additional space for them and their families.

Shmuel ordered our group to eat dinner first tonight. Angel's protests were ignored, and we all shuffled through the kitchen to fill our plates with some sort of roasted meat—goat, I think— freshly baked bread, and a vegetable dish called *cholent*, a mixture of potatoes, beans, and grains. This was better than we'd eaten in weeks and helped to lift our spirits.

Except for Rachel.

"Rachel, I know how terrible the day's been, but you have to eat, darling. Ari needs milk, and you have to eat to be able to give it to him."

My beautiful wife looked at me with the saddest pale-blue eyes still filled with tears and a brow wrinkled with sorrow. "I'm not hungry, Jake. I can't shake the image—" She stifled a sob.

I leaned over, put my arms around her, and kissed her cheek. "I know. I felt the same when they killed Papa and then Mama. But we have to go on; we have to live long enough for Ari to ..." I left the sentence unfinished.

"Not now," she said, raising her voice in a tone that drew looks from people eating near us. She pushed me away. "I can't handle losing him too."

I let the subject drop and went back to my dinner. Rachel was too upset to talk, but we both knew we'd have to face it—and very soon. We'd lucked out with Shmuel. I was sure I could count on him and his men to help smuggle Ari out of the ghetto.

Irena had been taken in by her Aryan friends. She would remain

199

in hiding and out of commission as her leg healed. I could use her network, but I'd have to get Ari out of the ghetto myself. And it would have to be in the next several days. Even though we were well hidden in this underground fortress, it was only a matter of time before the Nazis found it and burned us out.

We spent a restless night in our new quarters and went to bed without further words. Ari seemed upset to have been moved again and fussed for several hours, despite diaper changes and feeding.

Finally, toward morning, the three of us fell asleep, only to be wakened by someone knocking on the wall of our cubbyhole, yelling, "Breakfast! Everyone, now. Breakfast. To the kitchen, if you please."

Although jarred from sleep, at least we were going to be fed.

CHAPTER 43

Afternoon several days in the bunker, I hoped fresh air might perk up Rachel's spirits. She still hadn't come to grips with giving up Ari and wouldn't let him out of her sight.

I explained it all to Shmuel.

"Sure, go topside—but stay hidden, and keep a careful lookout for Nazis. They come mostly by tank or car, but some SS like to sneak up on foot patrols to shoot any Jew caught in the open."

I held Ari and took Rachel's hand as we left the bunker. It was the morning of Easter Sunday, April 25, bright and sunny—a beautiful, warm day with a light, cool breeze stirring the new leaves. The air smelled of spring and early summer flowers and of green grass we could only imagine.

We could hear Poles across the wall, laughing and shouting, going to church, riding the musical carousel and the Ferris wheel. At the top of the Ferris wheel arc, they peered over the wall to watch the fires burn and the slaughters occur. They pointed excitedly when one of us got shot or was engulfed in flames or jumped from the window ledge of a burning building.

They were dressed in Easter finery—bright, colorful hats and dresses—sharing the Ferris wheel cars with their children and eating and drinking as if they were watching a movie, not the death of Jews fighting for their lives.

One particular family—the woman in an apple-green dress with matching flowered hat and the man in a dark-blue suit and light-blue shirt—caught Rachel's attention. The mother held a baby wrapped in a pink blanket tightly against her chest. The baby's face nuzzled the mother's neck. Each time they rose high enough in the rotating Ferris wheel to be seen above the wall, Rachel stopped and stared at them. Her eyes misted, and she hugged Ari even closer, mimicking the lady she was watching.

When the ride ended and the passengers off-loaded, Rachel remained staring at the vacant cars. She seemed mesmerized by their emptiness until the Ferris wheel started again, once more filled with laughing, shouting people.

She handed Ari to me. "It's time, Jake; it's time. We need to talk to Shmuel."

∽

"Of course I'll help," Shmuel said when I approached him. "In fact, my brother-in-law Hershel is the most experienced sewer man we have. He'll lead you to the other side like a walk in the park. I presume you'll want to leave little Ari with the nuns at Father Boduen's Children's Home."

"Yes, if we can," I said.

"I'm sure we can arrange that. We'll have to forge papers with a new Polish name. That'll take a few days." He looked at Rachel, serious and concerned. "You do know he'll be baptized and raised as a Catholic."

"We do," Rachel answered with a resigned expression. "But he's so young; we're hoping the war will end soon, and he won't remember anything about it."

I met Shmuel's eyes and shook my head the tiniest amount. The odds that we'd survive and collect Ari at the end of the war were not too good, but that was the only way Rachel could process what we were doing.

"We certainly hope so," Shmuel answered. "Meanwhile, why

don't you go have some lunch, and I'll get someone started on the forgeries and other arrangements. We'll have to find the name of a Polish baby who has just died and not been reported. Let's plan for you to leave in a couple of nights. I'll tell Hershel."

∽

I held Rachel in my arms in bed that night and tried to comfort her as Ari slept, peacefully unaware that he was on the threshold of a new existence, to be raised as a Catholic orphan.

"Darling, we have no choice. We've been over this so many times. Literally thousands of other Jewish mothers and fathers in this godforsaken time and place have had to do the same thing. It's heart-wrenching, but hopefully, we'll survive—and most importantly, Ari will. We'll come for him when this madness ends."

She squirmed out of my arms, lay on her back, and stared at the ceiling. "Suppose he doesn't know us when we come for him? Suppose he doesn't want to leave with us? Suppose he doesn't remember he's Jewish and wants to stay Catholic. Suppose—"

I propped myself on an elbow and looked at her. "Rachel, you can suppose and suppose and suppose. I don't have answers except that the biggest *suppose* is, suppose the Nazis discover 18 Mila tomorrow or the next day and burn it with us trapped inside or shoot us as we try to escape."

She wiped her eyes as tears slipped down her cheeks.

"We're blessed that we found each other to love—for however long; that together we've created a new life we love—also for however long. And now we have to do all we can to preserve that new life. I don't know what else to say or do."

She was silent, eyes fixed at the ceiling.

I tried to humor her. "You know the story of the old Jew on his deathbed?"

She looked at me doubtfully and shook her head.

"He'd been a faithful Jew all his life—kept a kosher home, went to pray at the synagogue regularly, and obeyed all the Jewish laws.

With only hours to live, he calls in his entire family, and they gather around his bed. '*Kinder*,' he says. 'Children. I want to become a Catholic.' They're stunned. The oldest son says, 'Papa, how can that be? You've been a pious Jew all your life. Now, on your deathbed, you want to become a Catholic. That's crazy.'

"'I've made up my mind. I want to convert, to become a Catholic.'

"'Why, Papa? Why would you want to become a Catholic, now of all times?'

"'Better one of them should die.'"

Rachel laughed, the first happy sound I'd heard from her since we'd left Franciszkanska days ago. "Thank you, Jake. Thank you for being you, for being there for me. I know you're right."

She kissed me on the lips and rolled over, and I soon heard the regular, slow breathing of sleep.

CHAPTER 44

"Aleksander Goerner. That's Ari's new name," Shmuel announced two evenings later. "The real infant died a few days ago, unreported."

Hershel handed us Ari's new papers; then stood and adjusted his backpack. "Ready for the sewers?" he asked with a grin.

We nodded.

"Wait, before you go," Shmuel said, "I have a present for the new Aleksander." Beaming, he reached under the table and brought out a white cardboard box that he handed to Rachel. "This is a special gift from all of us at 18 Mila to a Jewish boy who will become a Catholic, so he doesn't forget his roots—when and where he came from and who he was." Shmuel wore a look of happy expectation.

Rachel opened the box and lifted out a baptism gown. She spread it on the table and then held it up in front of her. It was a white silk lace coat with an undergown and silk cap. The hem was made of doubled-over heavy silk that matched the silk sash tied in the back and the lace booties.

Her eyes lit up, and her smile was broad. "It's ... it's ... it's stunning, Shmuel. Where did you ever get it? How can we thank you?" She turned to me. "How can we thank him for all he's done?" A tiny tear slid down her cheek.

"We can't; we—"

"Yes, you can," Shmuel interrupted with a wave of his hand. "First, you already have by saving Hershel." He flashed his brother-in-law a warm smile. "Second, what you can do now is save a life for our future." His demeanor was serious, his eyes focused on Rachel, his lips firm.

"Whether Ari's raised as a Catholic or not, he'll always be a Jew in the eyes of God and our Jewish faith because you, his mother, are a Jew." He held up a forefinger, professorial-like. "According to Judaic law, the child inherits the religion of the mother, as you know." Shmuel's features softened, and he smiled. "Now, go with God's blessing. Be safe; take this little one to Father Boduen's Children's Home. They'll see to it that he has a wonderful baptism in a brand-new gown. It will always remind him of who he is, and where he came from." Shmuel's eyes twinkled. "Return safely to us. I'm sure Angel has plans for the two of you when you get back."

The head of this den of thieves at 18 Mila stood, belly quivering. He embraced Rachel, tenderly kissed Ari on the forehead, and shook my hand. "Go with God," he said, raising his hands in blessing, "and come back soon." He turned and left the room.

Rachel held up the gown once more and ran her fingers over the luminous silk, admiring its satiny, creamy finish. "It's so beautiful." She shook her head as if she couldn't believe what she was holding.

"We—um—sort of found it in a very fancy store on the Aryan side," Hershel said, grinning, including us in his conspiracy. "The price was right—a real bargain." He chuckled. "Okay, enough. Time to go."

I collected our things, including the baptism gown, into a backpack that I flipped over my shoulders. I tucked the Luger I'd taken from Burkl in my belt, along with a spare clip, and draped my Karabiner over my shoulder.

Rachel snuggled Ari securely in a cloth rucksack bound to her chest and placed a blue baby bonnet on his head. The bonnet had little rabbit ears sticking up. She kissed his head through the bonnet as we followed Herschel out the tunnel. A few drops of Luminal kept Ari asleep, despite the jouncing.

When we reached outside, it was almost midnight. I looked around as my eyes adjusted to the night. The area appeared deserted.

"You okay?" I whispered to Rachel.

She seemed short of breath but nodded. "Yes."

I was breathing fast, both from the effort and the excitement. "Want me to carry Ari?"

"No."

The air had cooled, and the night was dark, with clouds obscuring the moon's glow. For us, that was perfect. We planned to return while it was still dark.

We walked quickly to the corner of Franciskanska and Nalewki Streets, where a manhole cover protected the sewer entrance.

Hershel gave us last-minute instructions. "You said you were in the sewers before so this will be no different. When I take off the cover, you'll find iron rungs embedded in the side wall to use as a ladder. The rungs can be wet and slippery, so hold on tight, and go slowly. I'll lead. Wait here until I tell you to come—Rachel first, so Jake can slide the manhole cover back in place."

Hershel lifted the metal plate and slid it to the side. He flicked on his flashlight to illuminate the rungs and descended. Fumes of excrement floated up and drove us back several steps.

"Holy shit," Hershel exclaimed and climbed back to the top.

"What's going on?" I asked.

"It's like a traffic jam down there. People are all over the damn place—some sitting, some standing, and others walking. Some even are lying down in the filthy water, either passed out or dead. I think the whole ghetto's trying to escape tonight." He frowned.

"Do we have a choice? Another route?" I asked.

"No. We've arranged our contact to meet us at the sewer exit next to the Children's Home, so let's get on with it. We'll just have to push through the crowd. It's going to take us longer than we'd planned." His long sigh signaled reluctant acceptance.

Hershel climbed back down, and Rachel followed. I dragged the manhole cover back in place and descended.

Hershel had not exaggerated. The smelly tube was crowded with people walking crouched over, waddling around bodies in their way, and ignoring the cries and screams of others who were blocking the passage. There was no way to save any of them, so we plowed on with our mission, pushing and elbowing to get through. The channel narrowed at some places so that only one person at a time could squeeze past.

Four hours later, on a trip that should have taken half that time, we climbed out of the sewer and waited near a group of trees in a small park. It was four thirty and still pitch-black. We gulped in the clean, fragrant air, relieved to stand straight, without reeking bodies pressing against us.

"Who are we meeting?" Rachel asked, hugging Ari close and stroking the back of his head. The baby still slept soundly.

"One of the caretakers, a woman named Wladyslawa Marynowska." He smiled. "She's a wonderful lady; worked with Irena Sendler. She should've been here by now. I hope she didn't give up because we're so late."

Hershel searched the park. "Oh, there she is," he said and pointed to an attractive young woman with short, curly blonde hair who was walking briskly in our direction. She had a dark cape draped over her shoulders, and her hand was outstretched. Her wide smile radiated warmth and friendliness.

Hershel introduced us and explained why we were late.

"I was getting worried," she said, greeting us—a brief hug for Hershel and a handshake for us. "So many people are trying to use the sewers now. They've become very dangerous. The Nazis are flooding some sections with water and piping acetone into others." She paused, took a step away, and wrinkled her nose. "You guys sure do carry a special bouquet."

We all laughed.

Ari—I mean, *Aleks*—began to stir.

"He's hungry," Rachel said. "Can we go to the Home before he wakes fully and gets fussy?" she asked. Her eyebrows peaked as she looked at Wladyslawa. "We need to get him someplace where I can nurse."

Wladyslawa stared at Hershel with a questioning look. "I thought you were just going to hand him over so you could get back into the sewer while it was still dark. Has that plan changed?"

I read panic in Rachel's face. This was going to be difficult.

"No!" Rachel said with a head shake. "No. I must feed him now."

"Honey, it would be safer if—"

In the dim light I could see her lips flatten and her eyes narrow. I knew that look. She wasn't about to give in.

"Then you go," she said, her tone angry and her eyes fiery. "I plan to stay and feed my son. I'll come back when I'm finished—alone, if I have to."

"I won't leave you, Rachel. You know I'll stay," I said. This was a battle I had no chance of winning.

"If you stay, so will I," Hershel said. "You need me to guide you back in the sewer. Wladyslawa, please let's go to the Home. We'll take our chances later."

Wladyslawa shrugged. "If that's what you want, okay. I don't think it's wise, though. Too risky." Her tone became cheerier. "But follow me, and let's get this little one a dry diaper and some breakfast. What's his name?"

"Ari," Rachel said, at the same time as I said, "Aleks."

Wladyslawa smiled and nodded. "I've been through this before with parents. You need to practice saying his new name, so you get accustomed using it. Ari or Aleks? Which?"

"Aleks," Rachel said in a small, uncertain voice. "It's Aleks," she repeated with more conviction. "Aleks Goerner."

We followed Wladyslawa several blocks to Father Boduen's Children's Home. It hadn't changed since our last visit, still an imposing two-story building with a cathedral-like brick entrance set behind a metal fence and brick wall.

Wladyslawa pulled a handle on the side of a brick column that opened the gate. "A secret. Used by unwed mothers who drop off their children anonymously," she said, smiling.

She unlocked the front door and took us inside. We sat in a small room just off the entrance. It had a changing table in the middle, several easy chairs set back against the light-blue and yellow wallpaper, and a window that faced onto a small garden near the front entrance.

Wladyslawa disappeared for a moment and returned with a fresh diaper, a small basin of water, soap, a washcloth, and a towel. Aleks woke, gurgling and happy. Rachel changed, washed, and dried him and began nursing. When she finished, it was after six o'clock, and he fell asleep with a full belly.

That's when we heard the crunch of tires on gravel in the driveway. An armored car, bright headlights glaring and red lights flashing, came to a screeching stop in front of the building.

Wladyslawa drew back the corner of the curtain and peaked out. Her face blanched, and she crossed herself. "Oh, dear God. It's the Gestapo."

CHAPTER 45

ershel and I bolted from our chairs, and Rachel pressed Aleks to her chest, eyes wide with fear. Wladyslawa pulled a shade across the window. I checked the Luger in my belt and grabbed the rifle I'd propped against the wall.

"Surprise inspection. We've been taking in more children than usual, and the Gestapo suspect they're Jews from the ghetto." She sounded breathless.

"We should've left when we had the chance," Hershel muttered, his face red with anger.

"There's a hidden panel in the wall behind you." Wladyslawa pushed a lever concealed by a curtain, and a seam in the wallpaper became a door that swung open to a tiny crawlspace. "Get in, and don't make a sound." She put her finger to her lips.

Our loud voices woke Aleks, and he began to cry. Rachel tried to soothe him back to sleep, but the pounding on the front door increased his wail.

"Give him to me," Wladyslawa ordered. "Leave his papers on the table. The three of you get into the hiding space—now!" In a loud voice, she shouted, "I'm coming! I'm coming. Just changing a diaper. Hold on for a minute."

We squeezed into the tiny space, and Wladyslawa shut the door.

We stood scrunched together, bodies stiff and straight. We could barely breathe.

We heard Wladyslawa walk out of the room, open the front door, and return, followed by the stomp of boots on the wooden floor. It was hard to make out how many people came into the room, but there had to be at least two and probably three.

Aleks was now screaming at the top of his lungs.

A man shouted, *"Was machst du so früh auf? Warum war das Licht in diesem Raum an?"* What are you doing up so early? Why was the light on in this room?

"Ich spreche kein Deutsch. Bitte sprechen Sie Polnisch," Wladyslawa replied in halting German. I don't speak German. Please speak Polish.

"Who is this baby?" the man demanded.

"He is a newborn, sir, just dropped off yesterday."

"Er stinkt," another voice said. He stinks.

"Alle Juden stinken. Sie riechen nach Kanalisation," the first man snickered. All Jews stink. They smell like the sewer.

They all laughed.

We heard Wladyslawa's heels click. "Here are his papers. As you can see, his name is Aleksander Goerner, a nice Polish boy."

"Who are his parents? Where are they?"

"I don't know. He was just left at our door. That happens frequently."

"Why were you up so early?"

"Babies don't tell time, sir. He was hungry and had a dirty diaper, so I fed him, cleaned him, and changed his diaper."

Oh Christ, I thought. The diaper stuff was in the room, but there was no bottle to show he'd been feeding. I wondered if they'd pick up on that.

"How do I know he's not a Jew with false papers? Take off his diaper," the man ordered.

"Are you sure you really want me to do that?" Wladyslawa asked. I could hear the panic in her voice.

"Absolut. Mach es jetzt," he ordered, his voice stern. Absolutely. Do it now.

Shit! They would be shot. Rachel's fingers dug into my arm. I took the Luger from my belt and held it up for Hershel to see. He waved his pistol in reply.

I was about to charge out the door when Wladyslawa asked a question.

"Have you had your typhus vaccination?" Her voice sounded innocent, inquiring.

"Nein, warum?" No, why? I could hear the suspicion in his voice.

"This little boy has typhus. That's why he was up so early to have his diaper changed. Lots of diarrhea."

Aleks continued to cry.

"See, he's upset with terrible stomach cramps. He's been spreading germs around, and I'm sure he's going to make the other children sick too. I wouldn't want you to catch it."

I heard mumbling in the background; then a loud, "Make sure you don't hide any Jews here" and the stomp of boots fading in the distance. The front door opened and slammed shut.

I sucked in a deep breath, let it out through clenched teeth, and slipped the Luger back in my belt.

The door to our hideaway opened. Wladyslawa stood there, her face a mix of fright and relief. She handed Aleks to Rachel, and he stopped crying.

But Wladyslawa started. She collapsed into a chair, buried her face in trembling hands, and sobbed.

CHAPTER 46

We showered, thankfully, slept four hours, and spent the rest of the day focused on Aleks—holding him, talking to him, playing with him, and Rachel nursing him.

I etched in memory a farewell picture of my precious wife, sitting in a chair, holding our son to her breast, gently stroking strands of his hair—blond like mine but just wisps of fuzz. I went to her, kissed them both, and sighed, my heart breaking.

When it finally came time to tuck him in for the night, Rachel descended deep into a fog of depression. She toyed with her food at dinner and barely said two words. Her eyes constantly filled with tears. She seemed to have aged years in a day.

Wladyslawa was a bedrock of understanding and comfort. She refused to be rebuffed by Rachel's attitude and seemed to know exactly what to say and when to say it. I'm not certain her upbeat outlook helped Rachel, but it sure did me.

When the night grew dark and it was time to leave, I pulled her aside to give her my thanks and tell her we were going to survive the war and return for Aleks.

"Please take good care of our son. He's just on loan."

She smiled, but I was serious.

The sewer was dark and filthy and filled with cold water. We were up to our waists in swirling debris and floating bodies. A benefit was that much of the human waste had been swept away. Another was that the human tide had been reduced to a handful of people, so we made good time, except when we had to walk against the current.

We arrived where we had started in two and a half hours and climbed out of the sewer at the corner of Franciskanska and Nalewki. The streets were empty, and we headed straight to 18 Mila.

"Damn, I can't wait to get clean," I said, walking quickly along Mila, wiping my hands on my pants. "That sewer smell is horrific."

Hershel laughed. "The Nazis hate it also. That's why we can still use them as long as the Nazis don't flood them too much or pump in too much gas. The good thing is that whatever they do doesn't last long—the sewers were built to transport everything in them to the Vistula."

When we got back to 18 Mila, we found it crowded with many more people. The Nazis had successfully flushed Jews from multiple bunkers in the short time we were gone, and survivors were forced to seek new shelters. Word had spread about the refuge at 18 Mila, one of the few safe sites left.

Shmuel and Angel turned no one away. It was too dangerous for anyone to remain on the streets. Also, they feared that anyone rebuffed could be captured and reveal Mila's location in exchange for their lives.

Despite law and order kept by Shmuel and Angel, the large bunker could not easily accommodate the excess number of new inhabitants. As Rachel and I walked back to our cubicle, tired and dirty and smelly, we passed rooms built to hold eight that were filled with thirty.

And we had four new guests in our room. Privacy was a thing of the past.

The bath I'd been looking forward to was impossible. The bathroom in the bunker had generated lines too long for impatient users and had led to accidents in the halls. Odors that reminded me of the sewer permeated the bunker and added to the heat generated by the warm spring, too many bodies, and poor ventilation. Our oasis had become a pigsty.

We had to wait on a slow line for lunch. Nightly forages by Shmuel and his men had turned up less food, and rations had dwindled. Also, to hide telltale kitchen smoke, the kitchen crew could only cook at night, insufficient time to feed the large crowd.

So in just a day, paradise had become purgatory.

CHAPTER 47

At dinner, Shmuel and Angel welcomed us back with a warm hug and a "thank God you're home safe." Rachel remained silent and didn't eat.

Angel noticed.

"Rachel, now that you're no longer nursing, I could use you in the field. Are you ready for some Nazi payback? When we first met, Jake told me you were fearless. Still true?" His manner, as always, was calm, nonthreatening, and understanding.

Rachel frowned; she looked up at Angel and then at me. Her fingers twisted a loose lock of hair. "Doing what?"

"Going out on patrol with Jake and me, maybe taking a few shots at the SS, ambushing a tank or two, or dropping a Molotov on their heads. You know, just routine life-and-death stuff," he said with twinkling eyes and a dry laugh.

I watched her, studying her features, and tried to crawl inside her head. My attempts to help her deal with her grief had failed. Jews had a saying when someone died: *May his memory be a blessing.* It was meant to fill the void, to relieve some of the heartache. Reminding Rachel of the wonderful memories of her family and our son wasn't enough.

Angel's approach was the opposite—to jolt Rachel into the present, to remind her why we were here and what we were trying to accomplish. To do something about it, not just sit in a corner and mope. I hoped his method worked better than mine.

I thought I detected a glimmer of light in her eyes, the spark of a response.

She cut a slice off the slab of meat on her plate, took a bite, and chewed without saying anything. I watched her swallow and sip her water. I could almost see the wheels turning in her brain as she wrestled with Angel's call to action.

Several moments passed before she looked at Angel and answered, "Okay. When?"

"Tomorrow night, after dark."

"What're we going to do?"

"Rachel, before we go into that, let me make myself perfectly clear." Angel leaned back from the table, crossed his legs, and folded his arms across his chest. He fixed his gaze on her and spoke in his usual unemotional tone. "I'm prepared to die and expect to before this war's over. But while I'm still alive, I want to kill the German bastards who've done such horrific things to our people. I want to show the world that we did not go meekly like lambs to slaughter, that we fought to the last drop of our blood. And we did this against overwhelming odds, with little or no help from the rest of the planet that turned a blind eye to our suffering."

He delivered this last sentence with increasing volume and slammed a fist on the table, making the dishes rattle. I'd never seen him so angry.

"We're with you, Angel," I said, "but let me make a suggestion." I pushed forward, my elbows on the table. "It's getting harder to kill Nazis. They keep their distance, attack in armored cars and tanks, and burn us out, day by day. Their strategy is to let the fires beat us, and it's been effective."

He nodded. "So?"

I turned both palms up and shrugged. "Suppose we let them have the goddamned ghetto—or what's left after they burn everything down. We try to find a way out, maybe through the sewers, and then join partisan resistance fighters in the Lomianki

Forest. We could team up with ZZW and the Polish Home Army, if they ever get into the fight, and really do some damage, more than what we're doing now. Especially since we know the land and the Nazis don't."

He smiled, agreeing with me. "I've had similar thoughts, Jake. To do that, though, we need to find safe passage out of the ghetto, not just for the fighters but for everyone who's left. Lots of old folks won't be able to navigate the sewers. We can't just abandon them."

"What do you have in mind?" I asked.

He tipped his head back, stared at the ceiling as if searching for an answer in the rocks overhead, and stroked his chin. He looked from me to Rachel and dropped his voice. "We've discovered an abandoned tunnel at 7 Muranowska Street."

"The former ZZW headquarters?"

"Yeah. It's a big tunnel, and it may go under the wall to reach the Aryan side."

"*May* reach the Aryan side? You don't know?" I asked.

"We don't." He shook his head and pursed his lips. "ZZW built it when they carved out their headquarters, but when the Nazis destroyed that site, they may have destroyed the tunnel as well. That's where we're going tomorrow night—to find the entrance to the tunnel and explore where it leads. Could be the escape route we're looking for that could lead us out of the ghetto."

"Count me in," I said. "Rachel, you in?" I searched her face.

"Yeah, me too." Her eyes misted. She rubbed them impatiently. "I'm hurting, Angel, but what you said resonated. I'm hurting because of them, those sons of bitches who killed my family and forced me to give up my son. If my life has any purpose left, any meaning at all, it's to hurt them as much as they've hurt me. I'm ready. Let's do it." Her flattened lips, narrowed eye, and furrowed brow left no doubt about her decision.

CHAPTER 48

We met in the central room at ten the next night—eight of us, all in black. Rachel had covered her hair with a black scarf, and the rest of us wore dark hats.

She held some sort of cloth to her face, inhaling its scent, putting her lips to the material. I walked over to look at it. It was Aleks's little blue bonnet with the rabbit ears.

"For luck?"

She nodded. "And memory."

Angel had foraged handguns for everyone. I gave Rachel a quick lesson, loaded the clip, and chambered a round for her. All she had to do was point and pull the trigger.

"No problem," she said. Angel's approach seemed to be working.

"We'll split into two groups," Angel said, pacing in front of us. "I'll lead one, and Marek Edelman will lead the other." He pointed at me. "Jake, you and Rachel come with me. Everybody keep close to the ruins along Mila. Spread out so we can help each other if someone gets ambushed. At Zamenhofa, we turn onto Muranowska. I spoke with one of the ZZW fighters, so I have a good idea where the tunnel entrance is. Any questions?"

He paused and searched each face. "Okay, then, we're off. Good luck to each of you. Let's all come back in one piece. I have a bottle of schnapps waiting if we're successful, courtesy of our

Aryan neighbors who were relieved of their decadence by the light-fingered skill of Shmuel's men."

That triggered a round of laughs as we climbed out of the bunker.

A silver sliver of moonlight cast eerie shadows as we crept along fallen brick, stone, and cement remnants of bombed-out buildings. Rags tied to the soles of our shoes muffled the crunch of walking on stones and debris, so the only sound was heavy breathing.

The air was dense with the stink of decomposing bodies. There'd been no time to collect our fallen comrades, and no place to bury them. We walked carefully to avoid tripping over arms and legs. Leaving them exposed without proper burial was a sin, but we had no choice. Rats the size of small cats slunk out of our way as we disturbed their feeding.

We hadn't gotten very far when Angel held up his hand to stop us. Not more than twenty meters ahead, three German soldiers stood with their backs to us next to an armored car, talking in low voices. Foolishly, they were smoking, the tiny red dots of their cigarettes glowing in the dark.

Angel pointed to me, Marek, and himself and then to the Germans, and he drew his forefinger across his neck. Marek and I nodded, understanding. The three of us crept forward, keeping low to the ground to avoid loose stones. I unsheathed the knife Zivia had used on the SS officer who'd urinated in the building lobby.

Though the night air was cool, I broke into a sweat, and my pulse raced. I'd killed before, but this was going to be up close and messy.

As we approached, Angel stopped and again gestured, pointing first to the German on the left and then to Marek; then to me and the middle German; and, finally, to himself for the last one.

Then he held up three fingers, gazed at us to be sure we saw them and understood, and collapsed his hand. Then he held up first one finger, then two, and on the third finger, we raced to the targets, with the rest of our group trailing as backups.

I zeroed in on the middle guy, who was about my size and

221

wearing the green uniform of an SS Oberführer. I tried to grab a fistful of hair, intending to yank his head back and slash, but his wide-brimmed hat deflected my hand. He whirled and wrapped his fingers around my throat as I plunged the blade into his chest. Despite the knife, he tightened his grip until—

Bang!

His head exploded brains and blood, and he dropped to the ground. I turned to see Rachel, still pointing her handgun at where his head had been. Her eyes were wide, excited, and her lips were firmed into a victorious scowl.

"Serves him right," she muttered and wiped traces of blood off her face. "That felt good."

I rubbed my neck. "Thanks." I had been saved twice by a woman and wondered if there'd be a third.

I checked to see if Angel and Marek needed help. They didn't.

We regrouped around them.

"Well done, everybody," Angel said. "Three less Nazis to worry about. Grab their guns, ammo, and uniforms, and check out the car. See if there's anything we can use. Then, we've got to get moving. When these three don't report back, they'll send search parties."

Half an hour later, we were combing the ruins at 7 Muranowska Street. It didn't take Angel long to find the tunnel entrance, cleverly hidden beneath a thick slab of concrete covered by loose rock and dirt. Angel had brought three folding shovels, and we set to work digging away a mountain of rubble to gain access.

After ten minutes of excavation, we had an opening, slipped through, and entered a tunnel spacious enough for two adults to stand upright side by side. We flipped on flashlights.

ZZW had done a good job. Reinforced timbers prevented the sides and top from collapsing, though some areas had given way and littered the ground with dirt and stones. The tunnel was long and snaked into the darkness. We followed for several hundred meters with no exit in sight. I couldn't tell for sure, but it seemed we were angling north, perhaps under Niska Street and beneath the ghetto wall.

We emerged in the cellar of a bombed-out building and cautiously climbed the stairs to the ground floor. I looked out the window. We were in 6 Muranowska, on the Aryan side of the wall.

We'd found an escape route!

Maybe we'll beat the Nazis yet, I thought.

"You wait here," Angel said in a low voice. "Marek and I are going to explore a little farther up the street while it's still dark. We need to find a safe house on Stawki or Muranowska, where friends on the Aryan side could hide weapons and food to smuggle in through the tunnel. That way, we can fight a few more days as we smuggle people out."

"Need security backup?" Rachel asked, her voice eager. "We'll come with you." She looked at me for confirmation.

Angel turned to Marek. "What do you think?"

"Can't hurt. But keep to the shadows. Remember, this is the Aryan side, and we're pretty conspicuous."

"I could pass for an Aryan," Rachel said, grinning and primping her hair.

Angel scoffed. "Sure, as dirty and skinny as we all are and wearing such fine raggedy clothes and needing haircuts, maybe we all can pass as Aryan beggars."

The group laughed. It lightened the moment.

"Why don't the rest of you start back to headquarters," Angel said. "We'll be fine, and we'll join you in a half hour or so. We don't want to get caught out here at daybreak. Just leave a little schnapps for us." He chuckled. "Make sure you hide the tunnel entrance like it was before."

CHAPTER 49

Angel and Marek led the way along Stawki Street. Rachel and I hung back fifty meters or so, prowling among the ruins for any abandoned weapons or SS bodies not yet picked clean. We needed guns and ammunition badly.

I heard the growls before I saw the pack of dogs clustered around a corpse. The body had been stripped of clothes and the animals were tearing off hunks of flesh. Unhappy at being disturbed, they growled and barked, even as we detoured around them.

"Not good," I whispered. "We need to get out of here fast."

We tried to walk quickly, but in the dark amid rubble, we both stumbled repeatedly.

"Wer geht dahin?" someone shouted from the building to our right. Who goes there?

We froze. I knew enough German to understand what he'd said. I hoped Angel and Marek had also heard the shout. I couldn't tell where they were or whether they'd already passed where the German soldier was hiding.

"Halt an und komm mit erhobenen Händen auf die Strasse," he ordered. Halt, and come into the street with your hands up.

"What do we do?" Rachel whispered, her voice high-pitched and nervous. "If Angel and Marek didn't hear him, they could be walking into a trap."

"We've got to find the German before he finds them."

"How?" Rachel asked.

"I'll do as he ordered—walk into the street—and you take the shot when he comes out."

"No way. I'll go into the street, and you shoot."

"I'm not letting you—"

"Two solid reasons," she whispered, cutting me off. "First, I can barely hit something one meter away, never mind ten and in the dark. Second, he'll shoot as soon as you walk out. If he sees a woman, he's likely to pause at least for a couple of seconds in surprise, and that'll give you time to nail him."

"Suppose there's more than one."

She shrugged. "Shoot twice."

Rachel undid her scarf and shook her head to loosen the curls that fell around her shoulders. She took out Aleks's baby bonnet, put it to her lips, and then tucked it back into her pocket with the scarf. She turned and kissed me. "Ready. I love you. Try not to miss."

"I'll do my best."

Rachel walked toward the street. "Coming out," she said in a loud voice. "Coming out with my hands up."

She carefully picked her path through the rubble to Stawki Street. I stayed a few meters behind, keeping low and timing my steps to match hers.

When she reached the open street, a man slipped out of the shadows and moved toward her, a gun in his hand.

As he got close, he exclaimed, *Eine Frau? Wie kann das sein?* A woman? How can that be? He paused a fraction, aimed his handgun at her, and—

I fired. I hit him in the shoulder before he got off a round that dug into the dirt. Rachel finished him with a chest shot.

My third save by a woman, twice in one night and by the same one. I ran to her and held her in my arms. She was trembling but her expression was exultant, like she'd just won a race.

"What's going on?" I heard Angel yell in the distance. "You two okay?"

"Yeah," I said, "but I think we'd better get out of here. The gunshots are going to bring reinforcements."

Marek and Angel appeared out of the gloom. I briefed them as we walked to the tunnel. They said they'd found a safe hiding place.

"We'll let our contacts know," Angel said, "to smuggle stuff in as we smuggle people out."

∽

The bottle of schnapps was half empty by the time we returned, and our comrades were feeling no pain. They congratulated Rachel and me and filled our glasses to the rim.

"To fearless Rachel," they toasted, "and to her husband—what's his name?"

We slugged the alcohol down in a single gulp and went for seconds. The warmth set fire to my stomach and spread like a slow heat wave through my arms and legs. It was a perfect ending to an exciting mission.

Rachel and I wobbled a bit as we walked back to our room. I had my fingers crossed that—yes, we were alone!

I took her into my arms. "You're a brave lady, and I love you—not just for that but for lots of things."

"Name them all," she said with a smile, nuzzling my neck. "I like to hear you say them." She pressed her body against me, brushed my lips with hers, and teased me with her tongue.

"You're smart," I said and unbuttoned her blouse.

"And?"

"You're beautiful." I smiled and unzipped her skirt.

"Keep going."

"You're a wonderful mother." I undid her bra and kissed each nipple.

"Uh, oh. This last one better be good."

"You're my soul mate," I said, as I slipped off her panties.

"You win," she whispered and collapsed against me.

CHAPTER 50

I slept late. It was May 8, twenty days since we'd started the uprising. Rachel was still asleep, and I propped myself on an elbow and just watched her. She was so beautiful, so serene in sleep. I hoped her dreams matched her tranquil appearance.

Her blanket had drifted down, exposing her breasts. I was tempted but, instead, covered her and let her sleep. She needed her rest. Maybe later that night, if I was lucky.

I dressed quietly and left the room, thinking about how much I loved her and wondering what the future held for us and our son.

Walking to the kitchen, I passed a mound of decomposing bodies in the hallway from deaths during the night. It had become too risky to venture out in the daylight. The SS patrols had gotten bolder as our defenses had weakened. We'd bring the bodies topside and leave them on the street when it got dark.

Other fighters lay on the floor, exhausted. The swelling population and lack of fresh supplies made food and water even more scarce. I hoped the tunnel would reverse all that.

When I arrived at the kitchen for coffee and a slice of bread, I found Shmuel pacing up and down, hands clasped behind his back, muttering to himself. He'd lost weight, doing without to feed his guests. His cheeks hung in wrinkled folds, his underarms were skinny flabs, and his belly draped his belt like a deflated balloon.

"Shit, fuck it, *goddamn it!*" he exploded when he saw me, his normally jovial spirit gone. "We've little food left, electricity's cut off, the well's almost dry, it's hot as hell, and people are dying right here in the best bunker in the ghetto."

Shmuel cornered Angel as he entered the kitchen. "What are we going to do, Angel? We need food and water today—now—or more are going to die. Weapons and ammunition after that. Can we use the tunnel?"

Angel hesitated. "I just got word from our scouts." He spoke in a low tone, without enthusiasm. "The Germans found the dead SS and then the tunnel. They've stationed men to guard its ghetto entrance at 7 Muranowska and the Aryan exit at 6 Muranowska. We're cut off from the other side and any supplies. The tunnel's as dead as the guy we killed."

"Fuck!" Shmuel yelled. He pounded the kitchen table with his fist. "Fuck! Fuck! Fuck! We're fucking doomed."

"Then why stay any longer?" I asked, getting up from the table and walking over to face Angel. "We've made our point. We've survived their most brutal attacks for three weeks. We can't fight the fires. And without bullets and guns, we can't fight the Germans. So, like I said before, let's give them the goddamn ghetto and get the hell out."

"And the thousands still here, still hiding and trying to survive in the ghetto? They aren't fighters. What happens to them, Jake?" Angel asked, taking a sip of his coffee.

"We bring out as many as we can," I said. "They're all going to die here anyway. We can at least try to lead some out."

Angel looked defeated for the first time; his expression was filled with despair. "And once we're on the other side of the wall, Jake—let's say we make it out through the sewers—how do we cross the city to reach the forests and safety? It's not like we can disguise ourselves as Aryans."

He was right. That would present a big problem.

He continued. "Our scouts have told us the streets are filled with *szmalcowniki* looking to catch and blackmail anyone with Jewish features or turn them over to the Gestapo for a reward."

Our voices rose as we argued over whether to stay and fight or try to escape.

Suddenly, Angel put his finger to his lips. "Shush," he whispered, quieting us, and pointed to the ceiling.

I could hear it, a pounding overhead, followed by a drilling sound.

"Germans," Angel said. "I thought I heard it for an hour or so yesterday but couldn't be sure. This morning, it's pretty clear. They've found us; they've found 18 Mila. They've made the decision for us. There's no escaping."

CHAPTER 51

"Take your stations immediately," Angel ordered the fighters assigned to guard the five hidden entrances. "This is no test. We are under attack."

Angel whispered to his girlfriend, Mira Fuchrer, "Go check on them. Make sure they cover each entrance and that they have enough bullets."

The civilians in the bunker began to panic—crying, shouting, and running aimlessly from room to room. Shmuel tried to quiet them.

He spoke in a soft voice to a large group gathered in the central room. "You must be quiet. Yes, the Nazis may have discovered our bunker, but they don't know for sure if anyone is here. They must not hear you. Go back to your rooms. Hide, if you want. Get guns if you have them. And let's wait and see what happens. Maybe they'll move on if they think no one's here."

The drilling stopped after about two hours. The tension did not. The quiet and uncertainty were as unnerving as the noise.

Some prayed. "Dear God, please make the Germans think the bunker is empty and leave us alone. I don't want to die."

Footsteps at the main entrance told us their prayers had not been answered. A voice shouted in Yiddish, *"Aoyb ir kumen aoys itst ir vet zeyn zikher aun vern geshikt tsu a arbet lager. Aoyb ir antkegnshteln*

230

zikh, ir vet shtarbn." If you come out now, you will be safe and be sent to a work camp. If you resist, you will die.

One of our own had betrayed us—probably to save his own life or his family's. The Nazis knew we were here.

"Baren ir, ferreter," one of our fighters guarding an entrance replied. Fuck you, traitor. He fired several rounds. Nazi grenades followed, tossed into each bunker entrance, where they exploded and killed the fighters on guard.

I saw a Nazi start down the tunnel into our bunker and reached for my Luger. Before I could fire, Angel shot and killed him.

"Protect the entrances," Angel yelled. "May be more on the way."

Rachel came running up, waving a gun in her hand. "Are you okay?"

"Careful with that," I said and guided her hand toward the floor. "I'm fine." I pointed at the dead German. "Stay ready. He may just be the first."

We waited for additional attacks, but none came. The Nazis must have known it was suicidal to advance because our narrow entrances admitted only one person at a time. As long as our bullets lasted, we could fend them off.

It wasn't long before the drilling began again and showered us in dirt and dust. Shiny metal drill bits penetrated the earthen ceiling overhead and created big round holes that let sunbeams light up the bunker.

That's when I smelled it.

Gas!

The Nazis were pumping gas through the holes. That's why they'd stopped sending in troops. Why waste soldiers? Let the gas kill us.

We'd evaded Treblinka's gas chambers, only to be caught in one of our own.

The same risk for the Germans entering now applied to us exiting. They'd shoot us, one by one. We had no escape.

But to remain was to die from poison gas.

Panic in the bunker escalated to total bedlam. Civilians and fighters shouted, clashed with each other, screamed, and wept. The noise level grew so loud and chaos so frenzied that it was impossible to think.

Angel tried to restore order. He stood on a chair in the center of the room, waved his arms, clapped his hands, and shouted for us to be quiet and listen. When people calmed, he spoke in somber tones.

"We've done all we could," he said, his voice choked with emotion, "all we set out to do. Our enemy has been humiliated, and we have redeemed Jewish honor. Now, it is our time to die with that same honor. We must perform this function like warriors, like brave men and women, in a manner that will be told and retold to our children, our grandchildren, and generations after—like the tales of Masada—and will make all Jews proud of us and our heroism."

A noise at the entrance interrupted him. The Jewish traitor repeated in Yiddish the appeal to surrender and stay alive to join a workforce.

Shmuel broke from the group, placed a chair alongside Angel's, and stood on it. "I disagree. We are still alive and should not give up and die. God has created miracles before, and He may make one now. I intend to surrender to the Germans and go to a work camp so I can live. Who wants to leave with me?" He pointed at the ceiling that was belching gas. "We must go quickly." He took out a white handkerchief and raised it over his head. "Follow me if you wish life over death."

"Wait," I said, walking toward him as he climbed down from the chair.

"You want to leave with me, Jake?" he said, smiling.

"No." I extended my hand. "I want to thank you on behalf of myself and Rachel and Ari"—I looked around—"and all of us here for letting us share your bunker and making us welcome."

He brushed aside my hand and gave me a big hug. "Go with God," he said.

He entered the tunnel and waved, and about a hundred civilians followed.

After they left, Angel resumed. "The rest of us will not be captured alive. You have choices on how to die. You can try to escape and maybe shoot one or two Nazis before they kill you, if you're lucky. If you're not lucky, they'll capture you. That would be most unfortunate because you'll be interrogated at 25 Szucha and then shot or hanged."

He looked around to see if there were any takers. All were silent, waiting for him to continue.

"You can breathe the gas and die." He pointed to the ceiling. "Or you can take your own lives. Whatever your choice, perform it with dignity. That will be our last revenge."

"How do we kill ourselves? What can we do?" someone shouted.

"We have a limited supply of cyanide capsules. Or you can use a gun. A bullet will be a lot quicker and less painful. Or wait for the gas." Angel spread his arms out over our heads like a rabbi performing a benediction. "We should all be proud. A battle we hoped would last a day has stretched to twenty and could have been thirty, were it not for the fires and lack of ammunition. God bless you, and maybe we'll meet again somewhere. Now, it's time to say goodbye. Kiss your loved ones and hold them tight. May your deaths be as quick and painless as possible."

He stepped off the chair into Mira's arms. They hugged and kissed. I turned to Rachel and did the same. Throughout the room, people said their last goodbyes, hugging and kissing.

A subdued gloom settled over us that replaced the panic and bedlam. Most of those who remained were gathered in this central room, about 120 fighters and 80 civilians. A few hid in the back rooms of the bunker.

Many wandered about in a tearful daze, sobbing, sharing final partings with friends with handshakes, tender pats on the back, and hugs. Others were resigned and just stared at the ceiling. Some davened, kippahs in place and bodies rocking in prayer.

I watched one old man with a long gray beard shake his fist at the gas enveloping him and shout, *"Gay avek, Tayvl, lozn mir aleyn."* Go away, Devil. Leave me alone.

The first gunshot jarred our senses. A second one followed immediately. I spun around and saw a man and woman lying together on the floor, off in a corner, both dead from bullets to the head. He still held the gun in his hand.

The effects of the gas increased as the toxic cloud from the ceiling settled lower and lower. People breathed faster and coughed in dry, hacking spasms, clutching their chests. Some were retching; others wobbled unsteadily on their feet, holding on to the wall, a piece of furniture, or each other. Groans and gasps replaced screams and cries, as people grew weaker and more short of breath and tried to conserve air.

Additional gunshots rang out, and people crashed to the floor, blood spraying.

I helped one elderly woman steady the gun to her head after seven self-inflicted gunshots failed to kill her, and she cried out for someone to help finish the job. Another asked for the same relief after the cyanide capsule left her in excruciating abdominal agony.

Rachel and I clasped wet cloths over our faces to delay the gas effects. Soon, we began to cough too, and I felt an overwhelming nausea and fatigue. We no longer had the strength to stand, and we crumpled to the floor in each other's arms. Our coughing increased, along with an agonizing hunger for air. Each breath required superhuman strength and triggered lightning bolts of chest pain. My vision blurred, and the room began to spin in crazy circles.

It was over. We couldn't fight any longer. "I love you," I whispered, lying down beside her.

"I love you too." Rachel gasped, clinging to me with fading strength. "Take care of Ari," she said, taking his blue bonnet from her pocket and handing it to me.

I stroked her cheek and kissed her lips as my beloved took her last breath.

CHAPTER 52

The pain each time I inhaled was excruciating, like fire burning through my chest and into my throat and mouth. Even my gums and teeth hurt. I coughed nonstop, spitting blood into a rag someone had placed over my mouth. I tried to sit up, but a hand pressed me down, and a voice said, "Easy now. Just lie quietly and concentrate on your breathing."

I wanted to say, *What the fuck do you think I'm doing? Trying to breathe is all I'm thinking about,* but I didn't have the strength. I opened my eyes and strained to look around but couldn't move my head.

"Where am I?" I mumbled.

"You're in a bunker at 22 Franciskanska," a familiar voice replied.

"Where's Rachel? Where's my wife?"

There was silence.

I repeated the question.

"I'm so sorry, Jake, but she didn't make it. She's dead."

My brain went blank, and I stopped trying to breathe.

I felt a cold cloth on my forehead. It was annoying since it forced me to leave wherever my brain had been hiding. I tried to push it off, to sit up to breathe, but I still didn't have the strength. My brain retreated again someplace safe, a sanctuary, and I fell asleep.

When I woke, my coughing had faded, and my breathing had become easier, less painful. Some strength returned. This time, someone helped me sit up with a steady hand pressed against my back. I stared into the face of Marek Edelman.

"What happened? I only remember dying. How did I live?"

Marek handed me a glass of water. I drank it in one gulp and asked for another.

"I'm not sure, Jake," he said, refilling my glass. "What do you remember?"

"Collapsing with Rachel in my arms."

Saying the words made it real. Tears ran down my cheeks. Half of me had died, leaving the other half raw and bleeding, hemorrhaging, dying also. I sobbed, spilling the water down my shirt. Marek wiped me dry and waited until I regained control.

"What about Angel and Mira?"

He shook his head. "Dead also, along with all the others. Only a handful survived."

"What happened?" I asked again.

"From what we've learned, the Nazis pumped in the gas, dynamited the five exits closed, and left. But there was a sixth exit no one knew existed—not even Angel. Maybe Shmuel Asher created it when he originally built the hideaway. Three fighters in the back rooms of the bunker stumbled onto it and managed to crawl out. They came to 22 Franciskanska—we'd arrived here two days ago—and we immediately went to search for survivors. By that time, the gas had seeped out through the holes in the roof. We found you and two others still alive. Rachel had pressed her body over your face, which probably prevented you from breathing in all that gas."

Even when she was dying, she saved me.

"What did you do with the bodies?" I shuddered, thinking of my poor Rachel lying on the cold ground of the bunker, all alone. I fought back a sob.

"Nothing, Jake. They're sealed in that tomb, probably forever. That'll be their grave, their final resting place. No one will ever disturb them."

Marek's face was troubled as he handed me the silver ring from Irena that I'd given to Rachel. "I hope I did the right thing, taking this off her finger."

I drew in a sharp breath and nodded. "Thank you." I brought the ring to my lips and then slipped it on my pinky. "What happens now?"

"We've run out of options, Jake. We have no food, little water, and no ammunition. Nothing's left. There's barely a building standing. Anybody still alive is hiding underground. Stroop's determined to find and kill every last Jew here. It's time to leave the ghetto."

"Who's going?"

"As many as we can take, civilians and fighters."

"Through the sewers?"

He nodded.

I remembered what Angel had said. "How're we going to get out of Warsaw?"

"We're trying to arrange buses to meet us in the city at the intersection of Prosta and Twarda Streets and carry us to the forest. You with us?"

"What choice do I have?"

We lifted the manhole cover at the intersection of Zamenhofa and Stawki, and fifty of us descended into the putrid, murky depths. The Nazis had flooded the sewer, and the water was waist high and cold, with dead bodies and excrement floating past our noses. The few of us who'd survived 18 Mila were in the worst shape—hungry and thirsty and exhausted.

We walked single file, the strongest positioned at the head and rear of the column. The height of the sewer forced us to walk in a crouch. We stopped to rest every few minutes to accommodate the weakest. Progress was slow.

"No one will be left behind," Marek, our new leader, promised the procession of ragged followers. "If you have a heartbeat, you will continue to put one foot in front of the other, breathe this foul air, and escape the ghetto."

The Nazis had laid booby traps in the sewer—wires and ropes on the bottom that entangled us and further hindered our progress.

"Do not touch any foreign objects," Marek warned. "You might trigger an attached grenade."

As we walked beneath manhole covers on busy streets, we heard voices, children's laughter, footsteps, and the wheels and horns of passing cars. It was a cruel reminder that a three-meter wall less than a kilometer away separated the death and destruction we'd just vacated from Poles living ordinary lives. God truly had abandoned us.

When we reached the manhole cover at Prosta Street, one of our group, Filip Kaminski, a slim, dark-haired young fighter with handsome Aryan features, slipped out to arrange transportation. He'd worn rubber boots and brought a change of clothes for that purpose.

The rest of us waited in the sewer. Some experienced sewer travelers carried short wooden boards which, when placed horizontally and wedged against each side of the sewer, served as a platform to sit on and get out of the water.

I heard a church bell toll noon and wondered who in their right mind had arranged for the escape of fifty smelly Jews in the middle of the day in downtown Warsaw.

I needn't have worried. A contact slipped a note to Marek through the slots of the manhole cover with bad news. The buses would not be here before nightfall. We had to endure another eight hours without food or water, standing half submerged in cold water, bent over at the waist, before we'd be freed.

"Listen carefully," Marek shouted for attention. "I'm concerned about all of us bunched under this one manhole cover for another eight hours. A single grenade dropped into the sewer would kill a lot of us. I need fifteen or twenty volunteers to spread out down the passages and reconvene in eight hours. Anything changes, I'll send for you."

Nightfall came, and still no word. Finally, we heard footsteps and saw a note drop into the sewer. Marek read it and told us that the police, possibly suspecting something, had congregated on the surrounding streets. "Rescue impossible now. Wait until morning."

I couldn't hold out much longer. I was cold, hungry, thirsty, and cramped, and my chest hurt with each breath. I thought it must be even worse for the older folks—the civilians counting on us to lead them to safety.

Moans and grumbles echoed through the closed space and confirmed my feelings. We were going to lose people if we didn't get out soon.

A sudden rap on the manhole cover scared us before someone said the password and opened the cover. The aroma of food seeped in as two people topside handed down buckets of hot soup and lemonade and baskets of sausages and bread, enough to carry us for at least a few more hours.

That night was one of the worst in my life. The only good thing was that most of the water had flowed out of the sewer and into the Vistula River, and we could sit at the bottom with the water only up to our chins. Sleep was impossible, but if I had slept, I'd probably have drowned.

No one spoke; most just concentrated on staying alive. I thought about Rachel and Ari—it was still hard to remember to call him Aleks—and what might have been and what might be in the future.

The rabbis were right. Rachel's memory was a blessing, but how I missed my loving, lovely, courageous other half. I tried to hold back, but the tears rolled out anyway. My heart ached. It was broken and would never heal. I longed for her so terribly that I had real, physical chest pain.

I didn't know when I'd be able to get Aleks, assuming I survived. I hoped I didn't have to wait until the war ended, but who knew what the future held, fighting with the resistance forces?

CHAPTER 53

I tried to stay awake but fell asleep with my head propped against the wall of the sewer. I didn't drown but woke sputtering as my head drifted to the side, and rancid water ran into my mouth. I spit, stood as best I could, stretched, and looked around.

Sunlight filtered through the holes in the manhole cover onto a slightly elevated mound, where Marek was pacing in circles, shaking his head. I went to him as a note fluttered down from the manhole cover. I read it over his shoulder. Filip had not been able to arrange the buses. We'd have to wait until nightfall, a total of thirty-six hours in the sewer.

Marek turned the note over and wrote a response. "No! Absolutely not. People will die. Get transportation *now*!" He passed it back through the cover. A hand above snatched it.

Several hours passed before we heard a knock overhead, then the password. Blinding light flooded the sewer when Marek opened the cover. We hadn't seen the sun in twenty-four hours.

Filip Kaminski stood above, waving his hand for us to come out. "Hurry. I've got us a ride. We have very little time."

People pushed and shoved to scramble up the iron rungs.

"I need a volunteer to bring back those fighters I dispersed yesterday. Who'll go?" Marek asked.

There was complete silence. No one wanted to risk being left behind. Finally, I volunteered.

"Thanks, Jake. Everyone let him through. Step back so he can pass." He handed me a flashlight. "Be quick."

I pressed through the horde crowding the opening. I shouted and flashed the light as I walked. I found a group of three and sent them scurrying to the Prosta Street manhole.

I came to a fork in the sewer and didn't know which to take. I chose left, walked about fifty meters, and found another five guys. They told me the rest of the group had taken the other fork. I reversed direction.

That's when I got caught. I tripped a snare at the bottom of the sewer and couldn't free my foot. The more I struggled, the tighter the noose became around my ankle.

I reached down and fumbled blindly, but the rope was too tight. I pulled out Zivia's knife to cut the rope. My hands were cold and my fingers stiff, and the blade slipped into the water.

I began to panic. No matter how long Marek might want to wait for me and the others, he'd have no choice but to move on. It was too dangerous to remain in the middle of downtown Warsaw.

I had to get free. Repulsive as it was, I held my breath, ducked my head into the slime, and searched for the knife. I surfaced after the first attempt, spit, wiped my lips, and prayed I hadn't swallowed enough germs to kill me. Finally, on the fifth try, I found the knife and managed to cut the binding.

Freed, I hurried down the passage, shouting for the others. After several hundred meters, I found them, trying to prevent one of their dead from floating away. I convinced them to let him go. There was no more time.

"There's another group of four or five farther down the tunnel," one of them said.

"How far?"

"I don't know. We've lost contact."

I wrestled with an agonizing decision. That damn snare had

consumed precious minutes, and time was running out. I couldn't jeopardize this group by not returning immediately.

"You guys go back. I'll look for the others. Tell Marek to hold the bus as long as he can." I took off down the tunnel as fast as I could in the swirling water.

After a hundred meters of shouting and flashing my light, I got no response. Further delay was too risky, and I had to turn back. It might already be too late.

The water slowed me down. When I finally reached the Prosta manhole, no one was left. The cover was still off, so I charged up the iron rungs to the street and daylight. The sun was a blinding but welcome sight. I stood on the top rung for a moment, savoring the warmth that penetrated my chilled bones.

I stepped out of the hole into a small area protected from the rest of the street by a wooden fence. I peered at a group of Polish faces that gaped at me over the top of the fence. I couldn't blame them. I was dressed in rags, smelled like shit, and was dripping wet.

A truck with a canvas cover was pulling away. There was no other vehicle in sight, certainly no bus. I was too late.

"Hey, you," one of the Poles shouted. "You a cat coming out of the sewer?"

Oh, fuck. My stomach lurched. The guy was tall, brawny, unshaven, and wearing a green cap and the green shirt of the Gestapo.

"I think maybe we got us a Jew here," he sneered. "Meow for us, Jew." He put one leg over the fence.

My only thought was, *I didn't survive the ghetto only to die on the Aryan side.*

I reached for my knife. I had one bullet left that I'd saved for myself, but the Luger was soaking wet and would probably misfire.

Suddenly, the truck careened back to where I was standing. Marek shouted from the passenger window, "Get in, Jake! Get in!" Someone lifted a corner of the canvas in the back, and I dove in. The truck roared away.

Bodies were packed sardine-like in the back of the truck and covered by a large, dirty, gray canvas sheet. I burrowed beneath the tarp and wedged myself between people.

Filip smiled at me as my face came to rest next to his. "Hello, Jake. Well done. We waited as long as we could. The Poles got wise to the fence we built and came over for a look."

"It was close—too close." I explained what'd happened. I wiggled my shoulders to get more space. "I thought you were going to get buses for us."

"Ha! Be happy we got wheels at all. Never forget this day, Jake— Monday, May 10, 1943, the day this old truck saved your ass from the ghetto. Getting it was a last-ditch effort."

"What happened?"

"Belongs to a construction company. I posed as a builder and told them I needed a truck to pick up a load of bricks for a foundation I was constructing. They rented me this rattletrap and driver. We drove to the Prosta Twarda street corner, and I ordered him to pull to the curb and wait. When he saw Marek and the others emerge, he threatened to drive off. My gun to his head convinced him to take on a load of people instead of bricks, wait a bit, and drive us to Lomianki Forest. That's where we're headed."

Maybe God was still in Warsaw.

It took us an hour to travel the eight kilometers to Lomianki Forest because we had to zigzag and double back so many times to avoid German patrols and sentries.

When we finally arrived, ghetto survivors who'd escaped over a week ago greeted us with open arms—literally—hugging us, despite our smelly, filthy appearance. They fed us. The air was fresh, the sun was shining, and the forest green was soothing. It felt good to be alive.

But I couldn't stop thinking about the people I'd left in the sewer. Their survival chances were slim, either to escape the sewer like we did or return to the ghetto. Guilt festered in my gut, and when night came and they still hadn't arrived, I told Marek I had to go back to try to save them.

Since I could pass for an Aryan—albeit a skinny one—I cleaned up, changed clothes, and boarded a streetcar to Warsaw. As it approached the intersection of Prosta and Twarda, I saw that a large crowd had gathered. I jumped off and made my way toward them.

Our four fighters lay on the ground, dead. I wanted to cry out, to kill, to do anything to avenge their deaths.

A Pole standing next to me pointed at the bodies. "Earlier today, a bunch of cats crawled out of the sewer and escaped in a truck. Gestapo caught these four this evening. Got what they deserved."

Marek had promised that no one would be left behind, but I had let him down. I felt the same agony deep inside as when my footprints had led to Mama's death.

"Well, guess who's back," I heard a man in the crowd shout. I looked up to see the green cap and shirt of the guy who'd spotted me leaving the sewer.

"We do got us a Jew boy," he shouted. "Let's get this cat."

CHAPTER 54

I broke from the crowd and ran down Prosta Street with Green Shirt and two others chasing me. As I turned the corner on Twarda, I heard a gunshot and felt a searing pain in my side. I pressed my hand against the agony, and it came away bloody.

Another gun shot rang out. I heard the bullet strike a passing car. I left the street and ran on the sidewalk. Dodging late-night pedestrians slowed me but made me a more difficult target and would also slow Green Shirt and his friends.

The pain was incessant, and I was tiring, but I had another kilometer to go. I crossed Sienna and continued down Twarda. Brakes squealed behind me, and I hoped one of them got hit.

I paused to catch my breath. I did not see or hear anyone so maybe I'd lost them. I couldn't suppress a groan as I shifted positions. A searing pain shot through my side.

A shot pinged off the road near my feet and sent me running again. I crossed two more streets and then made a right onto Nowogrodzka—the street was dark, thank God—and I stopped in front of the gate at number 75. It was locked, but I remembered the hidden lever used by mothers abandoning children. I opened the gate and collapsed behind the brick wall at Father Boduen's Children's Home.

I hunkered down as footsteps on the pavement drew closer. The gate handle rattled, and I held my breath.

"Gate's locked so he couldn't have gotten in," Green Shirt said. "C'mon, he can't be far."

I waited another twenty minutes, pressed against the wall. I was weakening from blood loss, and I had to risk seeking help inside.

I stood with difficulty, stumbled to the entrance, and rang the bell several times, leaning against the building for support. I didn't know the time, but it was probably near midnight. After a while, a light flicked on, and the front door opened.

I collapsed into the arms of Wladyslawa Marynowska.

I struggled to open my eyes and sit up but immediately lay down again, as the room spun in circles and spasms of pain shot up my side.

I looked around from my bed. The room had three more beds, dressers, and a large window letting in the sun. The walls were painted light blue. A faded picture of Jesus on the cross hung on one wall and one of the Virgin Mary on another. A large crucifix dangled on the wall over each bed.

Heels clicked on the wooden floor, and Wladyslawa Marynowska entered the room. "Hello, Jake," she said. "Nice to see you again."

"Hello, Wladyslawa."

"Feeling better?"

"No, I feel like s—" I caught myself in time. "Not very good, like I've been shot," I said, trying unsuccessfully to joke. "Weak and dizzy. Where's Ari—I mean, Aleks?"

"One thing at a time." She smiled, and her kindly face lit up the room. "You've lost a lot of blood, but the bleeding's stopped; your wound was cleaned and stitched. With God's help, you should recover soon."

"Where's my son? I want to see Aleks."

"He's not here." She pressed her lips together. Her cheeks flushed.

"What? Where is he?" I half rose and then fell back, weak and dizzy.

"We placed him with the Franciscan Sisters of the Family of Mary in Pludy. Mother Superior Matylda Getta is looking after him. He's in good hands. They've taken in a number of our youngsters."

"Why?"

"We try to locate the babies in a more permanent place than here, Jake. I thought you knew that. We're more a temporary home. Also, it's probably a lot safer than being in Warsaw."

"Can I see him?"

"Of course. He's still your son. But not now. You're much too weak, and it's too dangerous to travel. We had to smuggle him hidden in a carpenter's box with workmen who were repairing the chapel in Pludy."

"How far away is Pludy?"

"About 120 kilometers east."

"How long have I been here?"

"Almost four days. You were in pretty bad shape when you arrived. What happened?" After I told her, she asked, "Will you rejoin your friends in the forest? It may be too risky to leave for a while."

"Why?"

"The people you ran from were Gestapo, and they've been here searching for you. We hid you, and they haven't been back, but I notice them often patrolling on Nowogrodzka Street in front of the Home. They said bloodstains on the sidewalk stopped at our gate. Fortunately, it rained two days ago. You should stay until you're fully recovered."

"That's kind of you. Thanks." I couldn't stop the tears. She'd saved my son and now me at great personal risk. "There's no way I can ever repay your kindness."

"I'll let the good Lord handle that," she said, smiling. "We've prepared a new set of papers, a new Kennkarte."

She handed it to me. It was gray, the color for a Polish citizen, not yellow for a Jew or stamped with the big J or Jude. I read the name.

"So, I'm Josef Goerner now?"

"Yes, I hope you like the name Josef. I do; that's why I picked it. The surname Goerner was necessary to match Aleks's papers."

⧢

I settled into life at Boduen's Children's Home, helping out wherever I could and generally staying out of the way. I thought a lot about the events of the last year and decided that I'd killed enough and nearly been killed enough to last a lifetime. The only thing I wanted was to join my son and keep him safe. I was anxious to give him the blue bonnet. Even though he was only three months old, I hoped it might connect him to a memory of his mother.

I tried to send word to Marek by one of the Polish workers at the Home, but I'm not sure he ever got it. He probably figured I was killed along with the other fighters coming out of the sewer.

Wladyslawa provided follow-up information about the ghetto from German sources she had in Warsaw. The Nazis bragged they'd killed or sent over three hundred thousand ghetto Jews to the Treblinka gas chambers, plus more than fifty-six thousand captured or killed during the uprising. A handful of Jews were left.

On May 16, 1943, at 8:15 p.m. the Nazis blew up the national symbol of Polish Jewry, the Great Synagogue of Warsaw, located on Tlomackie Square, just outside the ghetto wall, and declared the ghetto uprising officially over.

But that wasn't the last building standing, nor the last of Polish Jewry. They left untouched the Nozyk Synagogue, located right in the middle of the ghetto, not out of compassion but because they were using it as a horse stable.

The Gestapo searched for me several more times at the Home, but by this time, my bullet wound had healed, and I was the good Catholic, Josef Goerner. I could recite the Lord's Prayer and the catechism and knew the difference between matins and vespers, and my forged Kennkarte looked authentic.

It was easier—and safer—being Josef Goerner, the Catholic, than Jakob Holmberg, the Jew. I planned to leave the Children's Home, find Aleks, and remain with him in Pludy until the war ended. Then we'd immigrate to the United States as Josef Goerner and son, Aleks. Jakob and Ari Holmberg were gone, at least for now.

I began writing this memoir as Jakob Holmberg and have ended it as Josef Goerner. Only time will tell which one will survive, the Jew or the Catholic.

PART III

CHAPTER 55

I printed out a copy of Jakob's memoir and sat down to read. Once I started, I couldn't stop, and I read through the night. I had trouble with the name, though. Jakob was Grandpa Josef to me. I guess he had trouble too, since he was uncertain which one would survive.

Whichever, the memoir held the key to where I came from, who I was. It made me whole, as everything fell into place: the wedding ring with Irena Sendler's name inscribed in it; the Kennkarten and its addresses; the little blue bonnet with the rabbit ears; and, of course, the baptism gown and silver spoon that triggered my journey. The memoir contained no explanation of how Ari's spoon got engraved and was sewn into my father's baptism gown, but I'm sure it was a gift from Shmuel Asher. It *had* to be. Where else could it have come from? However, the truth would remain buried with him.

I wrestled with the fact that my whole family was Jewish, from Great-Grandpa Solomon to Grandpa Josef and my father, Alex. What was I to do? Could I suddenly stop being a Catholic and become a Jew? Did I really want to? Grandpa Josef was right when he said it was easier and safer being a Catholic.

I had felt something—I don't know what it was, some connection—when I visited Rabbi Kleinman at the Nozyk Synagogue. But changing religions would be a huge step—and not just for me.

The horrors my family and other Jews lived through were

incredible, unimaginable. Nazi cruelty reached a scale unfathomable by any rational individual, and although genocide atrocities still occurred in many places, I doubted they attained the systematic, organized level of killing perpetrated by the Nazis.

How any reasonable persons could call themselves neo-Nazis today or brand others as Nazis, wear a Nazi uniform, even in jest, or have a swastika tattooed into their skin or sewn on their clothes was beyond me.

And it was impossible to imagine that the average German during World War II—cultured, educated, contributors to music, art, literature, science, and law—could have accepted and, in many cases, abetted the Nazis' Final Solution to wipe out all Jews, as decided at the Wannsee Conference.

Wars revealed the most disturbing truth of all—that ordinary people had a darkness in their hearts and could turn vicious and cruel, like Brachstein in Treblinka or American troops in My Lai during the Vietnam War. Wars also created heroes, like Irena Sendler, Mordechai Anielewicz, and Marek Edelman. Wars didn't change people; they only brought to the surface that which lay beneath. Choices made when nothing was at risk meant little. Choices under pressure meant everything, revealed true character, and exposed a person's core—who they really were. I wondered whether all of us or just some had a cruelty gene that could be exposed under the right circumstances.

I gave Cassie a blow-by-blow summary as I prepared dinner the next night. She'd fed Zoey and put her to bed. We talked without interruption.

"Oh, wow. That's a shocker. Jewish." She pointed to the Christmas tree in the living room as she placed a bowl of salad on the table. "What do we do with that and the ornaments, especially the cross on top and the Nativity scene below? And remember, we have Christmas dinner next week that my father planned for your parents and us. I think he's finally forgiven us for becoming pregnant. Do your parents know any of this?"

I scooped out fresh lettuce and diced veggies and added balsamic vinegar and olive oil for the salad. "Whoa. One question at a time. I doubt my parents are aware of anything. They've been churchgoers for as long as I can remember, and Mom's been active in the church choir and on committees. Grandpa Josef most likely told them nothing."

"Have you discussed this with them?"

I shook my head. "I want to do it in person when they come for dinner. My father is the key to what happened, but his memory is unreliable."

We finished the salad; I cleared the plates and brought over the salmon filet I'd grilled, along with fresh asparagus and baked yams.

Cassie bit into the fish. "Umm. Delicious. You operate as well as you grill?"

"Better." I couldn't resist—"Don't talk with your mouth full."

She looked at me with a startled expression. I burst out laughing and described the scene from the memoir.

She laughed, chewed in silence, and then asked, "So what do we do?"

"The reality is that the Christmas stuff—tree, ornaments, Nativity scene—are just that: stuff. Accoutrements. The truth is much more profound."

"Yes and no." Her tone grew more serious. She stopped eating, her fork suspended between her plate and her mouth. "The accoutrements, as you call them, represent our faith in Jesus as our Savior, the Son of God. They're not just for decoration but a declaration of our faith. I'm sure Jews have similar accoutrements, like their six-pointed star and menorah."

I sipped my wine, a Cakebread sauvignon blanc. "Good point. But the real issue is how we live our lives going forward. How do we raise Zoey? Jewish or Catholic? Or nothing, and let her decide when she's old enough? Do we leave the church and join a synagogue? Or do I but not you and become an interfaith family? Or do we just say screw all religions and go about our lives as if nothing's changed?"

"Slow down. Let's not get ahead of ourselves." Her face was stern, lips pressed together, brow creased—*that* look. "How do we know the memoir's legit, that this isn't just a bunch of made-up stories sent by email, making you out to be Jewish?"

We both stopped eating as the discussion grew heated.

"That's ridiculous. Who would do that, and why? And bury it in a Jewish cemetery, mixed in with prayer books and Torahs? That makes no sense. You're not challenging the reality of the Holocaust, are you?"

"No, of course not. That's fact, but how do we know what you found in the cedar chest really is a part of *your* family—*our* family?"

"The names, Cassie. The names all fit; the history and timelines fit with Jakob's memoir. Why would someone lie? And how did all the stuff like the bonnet and the smelly blouse get preserved in the first place in the cedar chest if it wasn't part of my family? That chest was very special to Grandpa—objects he'd saved since the war."

She picked at her food. "I don't know. But this is so life-changing that I want absolute proof before any one of us considers becoming Jewish. Absolute proof, Gabe. I fell in love with and married a Polish Catholic, not a Polish Jew."

"Cassie, I love you, and you love me." I looked at her for confirmation, but she was staring at her plate. I reached over, took her hand, and brought it to my lips. "I'm your husband. I'm still the same person I was before I went to Poland."

She looked at me and shook her head. "No, you're not. You're different if you're Jewish."

"How so?"

"You just are. Jews are different."

"How? They believe in God. So do we."

That look again—it said, *you can't convince me.*

"Jews don't believe in the Trinity—the Father, the Son, and the Holy Spirit—like we do. They don't believe Jesus Christ is the Son of God, our Savior, God in the flesh, who came to earth and died for our sins. They don't believe in original sin, in heaven and hell, in the power of the confessional, or the New Testament. There are so many things that are a part of who we are that we'd have to give up. It would be a huge change, a commitment to a totally new lifestyle."

"Like what?"

"Like not having confession."

"When was the last time you went?" I couldn't help the grin.

She thought for a moment and tried to suppress a smile. "You win. It's been a while."

"I think many Catholics use confession as a Get Out of Hell Free card."

She laughed. "True, but that doesn't change all the differences between Jews and us."

"Yes, but you don't have to switch religions, even if I do." I sipped the wine and debated whether to ask the next question. I looked away for a moment and then back at her. "Would you not have married me if you believed I was Jewish?"

"I don't know. You're not, so it doesn't matter." She finished eating and pushed her plate away. "There's a lot of anti-Semitism today—killings, beatings, and temple desecrations. How would that affect us, but especially Zoey growing up? It's not safe being a Jew."

"And if I stay a Catholic but might really be Jewish, will that make it different?"

She didn't answer. There was no arguing with her, and we were silent as we finished dinner.

The following day, Cassie read Jakob's memoir. Even when he said it was easier and safer for him and Ari to live as Catholics failed to convince her that this was my family.

"I want absolute, unequivocal proof that what was in the cedar chest represents your—and now my—family, not just hearsay from something written seventy-five years ago. And written under a great deal of duress, I might add."

"The Bible was written centuries after the actual events took place. And that was hearsay. You believe those words."

"That's different."

"Cassie, there's nobody left to testify. How can I get absolute proof? You just don't want to accept the obvious reality."

"The reality, as far as I'm concerned, is that your parents, you, and Zoey are Catholics. And I'm Catholic, and there's no need to make any changes."

She was not being rational, but I couldn't convince her otherwise. I believed what Jakob—I kept stumbling over the name; it was Grandpa Josef—had said in his memoir. We were Jewish and had become Catholic by an arbitrary decision he made to save him and my father. Hundreds, if not thousands, of other Jewish parents in the ghetto had made the same decision for the same reasons.

But I had to get absolute proof if I was going to keep my marriage intact and this family together. I thought I knew how.

CHAPTER 56

The week limped along. Cassie remained upset. Even though she'd decided we were all still Catholic, I think she'd made up her mind that I was Jewish. She told her father about the memoir, and his mellowing hardened.

Zoey was my solace. Her unqualified love was for her daddy, me—Jewish or Catholic, it didn't matter.

I came home in the early afternoon on Christmas Eve day—a cold, snowy day with pewter-colored winter skies—and hoped to find Cassie in a good mood. Our interactions had been tense, and I wanted to attend the dinner party on better terms.

My parents had flown in the day before and had opted to stay at a nearby hotel to avoid the frenzy we'd had during their last visit, when four adults shared two bedrooms and a bath in our small apartment. They planned to meet us at Jim McManning's house at eight that night.

The trip took a lot out of them, especially my father, who was becoming even more frail. In fact, my mom talked about moving to Indy to avoid the travel and live close to us. I had a realtor scouting for a condo or small house.

"Cassie, I'm home," I announced, walking into our bedroom. My timing was perfect, as she exited her shower wrapped in only a towel.

She sashayed her hips and sauntered toward me. She stopped, her face inches from mine. "Miss me?" She stood on tiptoes and kissed me lightly on the lips. "I've missed you, Jew or Catholic." She handed me a corner of the towel with a grin. "Want this? For sale, cheap."

I tugged, gawked at my gorgeous girl, and then drew her to me, one hand on each soft, rounded, beautiful buttock. "More than you know. Jew or Catholic, I totally love my wife."

"Prove it." She undid my belt, let my pants slide down, and brushed her hand over my growing bulge.

∽

Christmas Eve got colder with heavier snow, and we bundled up to go to my father-in-law's house. We left Zoey sound asleep, still too young to be excited about Santa Claus or Christmas presents in the morning. Our sitter was one of the OR nurses, hired to give our live-in nanny the night off.

When we reached McManning's house, my parents' rental car was already parked in front, no doubt driven by my mother.

The chef's assistant answered the door, took our coats, and ushered us into the living room.

My parents were sitting together on the sofa, each holding a fluted glass of something white and bubbly. Jim McManning sat in a nearby overstuffed armchair, and he and Mom were engaged in conversation. My dad just nodded, more like an uninvolved passenger as the talk rolled past him.

"Here comes the rest of the family," McManning said, rising to greet us. I shook his hand—his handshake seemed cold—and he hugged Cassie. "How's my granddaughter?"

"Sleeping when we left," Cassie said.

I squeezed between my parents on the couch and put an arm around each.

"So, fill us in about the spoon and Warsaw. What did you find out?" Mom asked, excited, kissing my cheek.

"How about a glass of Macallan first?" Jim asked.

"Scotch is fine for me, but I think Cassie'd like a glass of white—sauvignon blanc, if you have it."

We sipped and toasted, and I launched into a brief summary of my trip. I'd brought a duplicate copy of the memoir and read Grandpa Josef's last lines out loud. I handed the pages to my mother. She studied them without saying anything, and her eyes traveled to the last page several times.

The room was dead silent as she scanned the printout. No one even drank.

I searched each face for clues. McManning's look was predictable—a dark, angry scowl. For whatever reason, he didn't like Jews and people of color and didn't hide it. Mom's face just showed surprise and seemed neutral. Cassie was shaking her head in disbelief and mouthing, "Proof. I want proof."

Dad was the biggest surprise. Tears trickled down his cheeks. He'd been born in '43 and came to the States in '45 or '46, so at most, he would've been three years old when he left Poland. I tried to trigger a memory.

"Dad, what do you remember? Maybe Pludy? The Sisters? The monastery?"

He hesitated. He squeezed his eyes shut tight in concentration. "M-Mo-Mother Superior Matylda," he stuttered. "Nice lady. Made pancakes Sunday after mass. Good." His features relaxed into a smile.

"See?" Cassie said, her look triumphant. "Your father was Catholic. This stuff"—she jabbed a finger at the pile of papers Mom held in her lap—"is not your family. Jakob was Jewish and couldn't be your grandfather Josef." Her mouth was set in that unchanging resolute line.

I looked at my father for a reaction, but whatever fog had lifted briefly resettled, and he was merely a passenger again.

"Cassie, you're wrong, darling. I'm sorry, but you're wrong. Jakob Holmberg was my grandfather and changed his name to Josef Goerner. Ari Holmberg is my father, whose name was changed to Alex, just like Jakob says in the memoir." I thought I saw a flash of recognition in my father's face, but if it was there, it flared out just as fast.

Cassie chugged her glass, held out the empty to her father for a refill, and gulped some more. She smacked her glass down on the table, crossed her arms, and then flipped one leg over the other. "I know what Jakob's memoir says, but it's not proof. I bet a lawyer would call it hearsay or circumstantial evidence or something like that. So prove it or forget it. I can't handle this anymore. We're talking about losing our immortal souls—eternal life as Catholics versus eternal damnation if we switch."

I reached into my jacket pocket and extracted a white envelope. "Cassie, first of all, the issue is about me switching, not you. You can remain a Catholic and save your soul. That's totally your decision, and I'll love you, whichever way you choose. Second, you want absolute proof. I have it." I stood in front of her, opened the envelope, and held up several pieces of paper. "I don't know what you remember from genetics in medical school. I forgot a lot and had to be reeducated to understand this."

"What is it?" she asked, brow bunched in surprise.

"The genetic profile of Jakob and Ari Holmberg."

"Impossible after seventy-five years," McManning muttered, pouring more Macallan.

"Not so. The genetics lab at the university was able to find microscopic skin cells adhered to the inside of the silver ring Grandpa Josef wore." I held up my hand to show them the ring on my pinky. "This ring initially belonged to a woman named Irena Sendler. According to Jakob's memoir, she gave it to Grandpa Jakob, and he gave it to Grandma Rachel when they got engaged. He got it back after she died and wore it more than seventy years, until he died. The genetic analysis of these cells matches mine and proves unequivocally that he was my grandfather."

Cassie's arms unfolded. Her severe look softened. "Oh, my. And Ari?" she asked more gently, looking at my dad.

I took out one last item from my pocket and handed it to my dad. Tears flowed down his cheeks in a steady stream as he held it against his face, smoothing the material like petting a puppy. He mumbled something to it, but I couldn't understand.

"Baby hairs from this blue bonnet with the rabbit ears show genes identical to those of my father, Alex, which naturally also match mine. There's your proof, Cassie. Jakob is Grandpa Josef, and Ari is my father, Alex."

Cassie uncrossed her legs and nodded slowly, a resigned look on her face.

Mom now also had tears in her eyes. She kissed Dad and hugged him. This wasn't going to change their lives—certainly not like it would change mine.

McManning, silent until now, jumped up. He took a slug from his scotch. "Not so fast. When Cassie told me about all this sh—" He caught himself—"stuff, I did some research too. Even if the genetic analysis is real, there's still a major problem. Two, actually." He took another drink. "What do you know about the Congregation for the Doctrine of the Faith?"

"Nothing," I said.

"Anybody?"

Silence.

McManning took center stage, a professor lecturing us. "That church doctrine says that once a child is baptized, whether or not the parents were Catholic, the baptism is considered valid, and church doctrine must be followed to ensure Jewish children do not create the mortal sin of apostasy, renouncing Catholicism by returning to their Jewish faith."

"That may be true if you believe in church doctrine. But what if you don't believe anymore?" I asked.

"Doesn't matter what you believe. It's what the church believes. That's what's important," McManning retorted. His face was getting red.

I needed to defuse this, but I couldn't stop myself. "You surprise me, Jim. Indiana University doctrine—to use your phrasing—stated surgeons had to stop operating at age sixty-five, but you refused and threatened to join Saint Vincent's staff if they didn't extend yours by five years. How's that any different than this?"

"One's from God; the other's from man."

"Or one you agree with and one you don't."

His eyes were dilated. I could picture his blood pressure climbing, with all that booze helping to fuel his anger. "You should've been a lawyer instead of a surgeon," he said.

"It's not too late," my mother said.

McManning flashed her a brief smile as he gulped the remaining Macallan.

The sous chef entered the room. "Dinner is served."

CHAPTER 57

Conversation at dinner began low-key and skirted religion. The chef's delicious roast turkey kept us too busy to talk. The mood seemed one of forced cheerfulness, even though alcohol had lubricated our tongues, if not our dispositions. Finally, during coffee and dessert, McManning broke the unspoken truce.

"Why do you need to become a Jew? What's wrong with being a Catholic?"

"Nothing's wrong, but being Jewish is the right thing to do because that's who I am."

"Your grandfather changed that."

"Not really."

"So three generations of men living as Catholics, with two baptisms—three, including Zoey's—don't count for anything?"

"It counted for keeping my grandfather and father alive seventy-five years ago, but once they came to the States, there was no reason to perpetuate the lie."

"You call it a lie?" McManning said.

"What would you call it?" I took a sip of wine.

"Voluntarily switching religions."

"Okay, then, I'm voluntarily switching back," I said, trying to keep the conversation light.

"You can't do that."

"Why not?"

"It's against the law. I quoted you the doctrine."

"I don't accept the doctrine, and besides, I don't even know if it still exists. Maybe the church altered its position. We can't have been the only family with this experience."

"I said there was a second reason."

"What, Jim?" I asked.

"I found out that, according to Jewish law, the child takes the mother's religion. You can't always tell who the father was, but you always know the mother." McManning looked at my mom. "Molly, you're Catholic, right?"

She nodded.

"Then so is your son, even if Alex is Jewish." His eyes sought Cassie. "And so is Zoey."

I'd read that in Jakob's memoir but chose to disregard it.

The difference was that I *felt* Jewish because of what Jakob and Rachel had lived through, which eventually gave life to my father and me. *Their* history was *my* history, who I was. I *owed* them to be Jewish. Jakob's new way of living—he'd adapted rather than perish—was fine for him and Ari then, not now. And not for my daughter. I needed Zoey to help keep Judaism alive.

"A technicality, Jim. I'm Jewish, and that's all there is to this."

McManning was red-faced, his anger flaring again. He shoved his dessert plate back, finished his coffee in a gulp, and stood. He walked to my side of the table and leaned over me. "I don't think I can handle this, Gabe."

I ignored the threat, took a forkful of the blueberry pie, and chewed slowly. I could feel his breath on my neck.

Finally, I rose and faced him. "There's nothing you need to handle, Jim. You're not becoming Jewish; I am."

He poked a finger in the center of my chest. I had to remind myself who he was and that he was sixty-eight years old. "You're changing my life as well as yours, and *that* I won't accept."

"How am I doing that?"

"You're taking my daughter and granddaughter from me; that's how."

"Wait a minute. Slow down. We've made no definite decisions about Zoey, and Cassie hasn't said what she's going to do. She has a mind of her own. And even if they convert to Judaism, I'm not taking them from you. They'll still be your daughter and granddaughter, Jewish or Catholic."

"You also know there's a helluva lot more anti-Semitism around than anti-Catholicism."

"That may be the first thing you and I can agree on."

"A good reason to stay Catholic and keep my daughter and granddaughter safe."

"I've thought about that a lot, Jim. But traveling to Poland and talking to Jewish survivors of the war, reading Jakob's memoir, and finding out who my family was have all changed me. I think that the presence of anti-Semitism is even a better reason for me to become a Jew, so I can help fight it. Silence in the face of evil encourages more evil."

"Gentlemen." Cassie came and stood between us. "Gabe and Dad, cool it. That's enough. Let's finish our Christmas Eve dinner and go to midnight mass. Okay?"

"Maybe your Jewish husband doesn't want to go to church."

"Cassie's right, Jim," I said. "Let it rest for now. We've plenty of time to fight in the future. Let's go to midnight mass so we can celebrate the birthday of the Jew, Jesus."

We were late entering Saint Luke and had to be seated in the only remaining empty pew, right under the pulpit of Reverend Monsignor James H. Sparkle. Cassie wedged herself between Jim and me. My father and mother, too tired to come, had driven back to their hotel. I'd see them in the morning.

The dais was beautifully decorated. On one side stood a large manger scene with full-size figures of Mary and Joseph, bending over infant Jesus in swaddling clothes, lying on a bed of straw. On the other side of the dais, three large Christmas trees glowed, with bright ornaments hanging from every limb. In the center was a luminous white-marble table with a dozen lighted candles, surrounding miniature porcelain figurines of saints. A huge statue of Jesus, white robed, haloed, hands outstretched in benediction, was suspended from the back wall and appeared to be blessing the entire proceedings.

We arrived as Monsignor Sparkle was ending his homily about a God of love and forgiveness, a God of human kindness, a God who sacrificed His only Son for the benefit of humankind.

"The Father and His Son, Jesus, will always be with you, for you, guiding you, protecting you, making you whole. We are here tonight to celebrate the birth of our Savior, to be a part of His kingdom, to bathe in His radiant light, and to enjoy its peace forever. Amen."

"Where was He seventy-five years ago," I stage-whispered to Cassie, "when the Nazis massacred six million Jews, along with five million others, and the world needed a savior, a redeemer, a protector? How could He let a Holocaust happen if He's a caring, just, and omnipotent God?"

"It served you Jews right," McManning shot back. "You brought it on yourselves."

"What're you talking about?"

"Jews don't believe in Jesus. In fact, you killed Him. That's another reason I don't like Jews and why you're different. Jews got what they deserved."

Cassie put one hand over my mouth and one over her father's as Monsignor Sparkle stopped speaking and looked down at us from behind his lectern.

She mouthed *sorry* to him.

Sparkle adjusted his glasses, strode to the center of the dais, and addressed the congregation. "I would like to add an addendum to my homily. I've been overhearing a discussion among Goerner family members"—he nodded at us—"who celebrated their daughter's baptism at Saint Luke not too long ago. The discussion—as I've listened to it just now—raised the question of where God was during

World War II and the attempt by the Nazis to exterminate the Jewish race. It's a relevant question, particularly at this time of year, and one with which the church has wrestled as well."

Cassie's face turned red. McManning shifted in his seat, crossing and uncrossing his legs. I was taken by Sparkle's honesty, even if it focused unwanted attention on us.

"I think it's safe to say that Pope Pius XII, our Catholic Church, and many members stand rightly accused of unacceptable silence during the war, when they knew of the brutality being inflicted by the Nazis on the Jews and did little to stop it. In fact, Pope John Paul II confessed to this offensive behavior, asked God for forgiveness, and pledged a commitment for brotherhood with Jews going forward. When he visited the Auschwitz death camp in 1979, John Paul said that the very people who had received God's commandment, 'Thou shalt not kill,' were themselves the recipients of that brutal killing.

"In 2000, in front of Yad Vashem, the memorial in Jerusalem to the Jews killed in the Holocaust, John Paul said any displays by Christians of hatred toward Jews and anti-Semitism saddened the Catholic Church, and he hoped for a new relationship between Christians and Jews." Sparkle looked directly at us. "I recommit our church to the pope's wish for peace and love between all Christians and Jews and hope you enjoy a wonderful Christmas season together. Amen."

Cassie grabbed my hand, squeezed, and brought it to her lips. Her eyes brimmed with tears. She whispered, "He's right. I love you, my husband, the Jew," and leaned over and kissed me.

McManning flashed me a malevolent look, devoid of the peace and love that Sparkle had preached. He stormed out of the church without a backward glance or a goodbye to Cassie. I didn't expect one, but I thought he'd at least say good night to his daughter on Christmas Eve.

CHAPTER 58

Surgical admissions to the hospital slowed after Christmas and into January, which gave me the opportunity to attend several Friday-night services at the Indianapolis synagogue, Temple Beth El Zedeck. I got to know the rabbi and some of the congregants as I delved more deeply into Judaism. I felt comfortable; I felt I belonged.

Admissions picked up again in February, putting me back in the OR full time. Fortunately, I was well along in my training and was becoming more independent when operating, often performing a major part of the heart surgery while under the watchful eye of a senior surgeon.

Tempers waned, and McManning and I once again became professionally cordial in the hospital but avoided personal issues. He often asked me to assist him, especially as my technical skills increased and his decreased.

McManning briefed me before our pre-op meeting with a new patient, Michelle Dabro.

"Her husband, Stan Dabro, is one of the richest men in Indiana. Real name is Stanislaw Dabrowski, a nice Catholic Polack—what you really are or used to be." He held up his hand to stop my retort. "Dabro started as a lawyer—defended some very high-level bad guys and got them off. He now builds shopping centers all over the world. He divorced two wives and married his third—this patient—after she popped out of his fifty-fifth birthday cake wearing nothing but a G-string."

I laughed, imagining that scene.

We met them in McManning's office. Everything about her screamed *trophy wife*, from the gold Rolex on her wrist and the walnut-sized diamond on her finger to the double strands of pearls hugging her neck. Her blonde hair, parted in the middle, cascaded in thick waves to her shoulders. Blue eyes, slightly almond-shaped and outlined with smoky blue eyeliner and shadow, hinted at an Asian forebear. She reminded me of a porcelain doll—a Japanese geisha. I could understand why Stan Dabro would marry this beautiful woman, who was probably half his age.

But there was a fragility about her beauty that I couldn't place, as if the porcelain was threatening to crack. Her eyes flitted about the room. She fidgeted on her chair, and her breathing was fast. She was stressed, scared.

Her husband looked many years her senior—balding with gray hair, droopy eyelids, large ears, and a scraggly gray beard of several days' growth. Despite his unkempt, homeless-like appearance, he spoke with a tough authority, as someone used to issuing commands that were promptly obeyed.

"Dr. McManning, we've shopped around for the best surgeon, and it seems you're it. Michelle's brother died suddenly in his sleep—he was only twenty-five—and we're concerned Michelle has the same problem, Marfan syndrome."

Marfan syndrome, an inherited disorder of defective connective tissue, could weaken blood vessels, especially the wall of the body's main artery, the aorta, and cause it to rupture. Replacing the aorta with a Dacron graft was high-level, very demanding surgery, well past the skill set of many cardiovascular surgeons.

"Yes, I'm certain she has it," McManning said. "I reviewed the x-rays and other information her referring doctor sent. The CT scan shows her aorta is already dilated to 6.2 centimeters—way too big. Aortic rupture probably killed her brother and threatens her. I'll have to replace the entire first half of the aorta. That's high-risk surgery."

"Do I have a choice?" Michelle asked, voice quivering.

"No, I'm afraid you don't."

"Then schedule it as soon as possible," Dabro said, standing. He checked his iPhone. "Tomorrow or the next day fits my schedule."

"Tomorrow. Until then, Mrs. Dabro, no stressful activity. Just relax, lie around, and don't exert yourself."

"I'm good at that," she joked.

∞

A few hours later, as I lay sleeping, the ring of the phone jarred me awake. I groped for it and glanced at the clock: one a.m. "Hello."

"Dr. Goerner, this is the university operator. Please hold for Dr. McManning."

"Gabe, get your ass in here. Michelle Dabro's aorta ruptured tonight during sex. Her husband called 911, and she's in an ambulance on her way to the hospital. I've notified the OR."

"Blood bank ready?" I asked.

"Five units on hand. Another ten in reserve."

I gave Cassie a quick summary, dressed, jumped into my car, and sped to the hospital. I reached the emergency room as the ambulance off-loaded Michelle Dabro from a stretcher; she was unconscious, her eyes open but not seeing. Her face, as pale as the sheet covering her, was distorted by a red breathing tube in her nose. An IV trickled fluid into a thin plastic tube in her neck, and another dripped blood into an arm vein.

I hurried to the surgeon's lounge, changed into OR scrubs, and started washing at the sink.

McManning joined me as I stifled a yawn. "Wake up, boy. You want to be a cardiovascular surgeon, or you want to have a good night's sleep? You can't have both."

"I'll be ready whenever you are."

We finished scrubbing and entered the operating room. Virginia Strozky handed us sterile towels and helped us into sterile gowns and gloves.

"Prep her for a median sternotomy," McManning said, pointing at Michelle Dabro on the OR bed in the center of the room. She was still unconscious.

McManning turned to Brad Singleton, the anesthesiologist and longtime colleague. "Keep her as light as you can and still anesthetized. Maintain a low normal blood pressure. We'll take her down to twenty-eight degrees. This surgery's going to be very stressful."

"Will do, Jim." Brad hung up another unit of blood to keep up with her leaking aorta.

We studied the films. "No question about the diagnosis. Ascending aortic root dissection right there," McManning said, pointing at the CT scan. "You can see the tear in the aortic wall. I'll try to save the valve."

I looked over his shoulder and nodded. Every fiber in my body tingled. This was why I was put on earth and trained to do—complex cardiovascular surgery in patients who were in life-or-death situations. The drama of the moment was mesmerizing. McManning had once compared the life-or-death excitement in the OR to the drama portrayed in many operas, but this was bel canto opera on steroids.

Almost any kind of emergency surgery was fraught with risk but particularly one with this degree of complexity. Surgical mortality for ascending aortic dissection could be as high as one in ten, and the risk of a serious complication, like a heart attack or stroke, was double that.

Also, starting in the middle of the night, when many key players had slept just a few hours after completing a ten- or twelve-hour workday increased the chance of a slipup. Complex surgical procedures performed on evenings, weekends, or over holidays incurred a higher risk. But the mantra by which surgeons—especially heart surgeons—lived was, *never show fatigue, never tire, and never quit.*

"We'll begin by cannulating for cardiopulmonary bypass from her groin and open her chest through a median sternotomy. I'll replace her aorta with a Dacron graft and reimplant her original aortic valve. Should take us five or six hours—seven, tops—assuming no complications. Any questions?"

There were none. I glanced at the wall clock. Two a.m.

∾

Six hours later, the adrenaline high was fading, and I was tired. I stood across from McManning and watched his eyes. They were cloudy, and his hand movements were beginning to slow. He was more than thirty years my senior. If I was fatigued, he must've been exhausted.

Larry Finn, the scrub nurse, successfully predicted each instrument McManning would use next and had it waiting for his outstretched hand. I tried to do the same by anticipating his next move and doing what I could do to help. But each time, he'd slap my hand away and perform the procedure himself.

We were reaching a critical point. McManning had removed a section of the damaged aorta and sewn the Dacron graft in place— like replacing a curved four-inch piece of a garden hose with a new plastic tube and then turning on the water faucet.

"Going off cardiopulmonary bypass—now," McManning said, funneling the patient's blood from the heart lung bypass machine through the new conduit.

I saw it first. The ends of the graft began to leak, an ooze that increased in seconds to a brisk dribble.

"Dr. McManning—sir." I pointed. "The graft—"

"Shut up, Gabe. I see it. I'll—"

The dribble exploded into a red geyser as sutures under pressure tore loose from weakened aortic tissue. Blood showered the air and flooded the operating field in a crimson river, obscuring our vision. Virginia frantically wiped blood from the lenses of the magnifying glasses we wore and from our faces.

"Blood pressure unobtainable," Singleton shouted. "Infusing two more units under pressure. Only eight more in reserve."

McManning seemed frozen in place. The surgical mask obscured his face. I couldn't tell whether his look was one of shock and bewilderment or anger and scorn. Whatever it was, he was motionless. I needed to take over before this disaster got worse.

"Back on bypass," I ordered. I rechanneled the patient's blood through the heart-lung machine, bypassing the leaking aorta. The move slowed the red tide. I'd partially turned off the faucet. McManning glared at me, eyes squinted, but said nothing.

"Can you suck up this blood, Dr. McManning?"

He hesitated. In slow motion, he took the metal sucker I held out. Again, I couldn't tell whether he was confused or just noncooperative. I wondered if he'd stroked.

"Larry," I said to the scrub nurse, "get me 4.0 propylene sutures on a needle holder. I'm going to reinforce the anastomoses with pledgeted felt mattress sutures. Her aortic wall is like butter."

"Yes, Dr. Goerner." He turned to the circulating nurse. "Virginia, I need 4.0 propylene sutures and felt pads, stat."

Virginia hurried to a side cabinet, pulled out the sutures, opened the sterile pack, and deposited them on Larry's tray.

I spent the next hour buttressing the sutures to secure the ends of the Dacron graft to an aortic wall weakened by Marfan syndrome. McManning assisted me, as I had him. After I was sure I had all the leaks plugged, I gave the order for partial bypass. We all stared at the suture lines as blood began to flow through the graft. There were no leaks.

"Come off bypass fully."

The connections held.

"We'll wait fifteen minutes to be sure." It was now past nine o'clock. I wanted to wait longer, but she'd been under anesthesia for almost eight hours, and I didn't want to take the risk. All looked good.

"Dr. McManning, if you agree, sir, we're done, and I'll close her chest."

He nodded, turned from the table, and left the OR. I finished the operation.

⁓

I sought out Stan Dabro in the surgical waiting room. He was sitting at a table, tearing through a magazine.

"You damn near killed my wife!" he shouted and jumped up, red-faced and steaming as I walked in. "McManning told me the sutures you sewed tore loose, and she had no blood pressure until he resewed them. She fucking better pull through, or I'm going to sue your ass."

"Wait a minute, sir, I—"

He walked over and shook his finger in my face. "Don't you 'wait a minute' me. I heard what you did, and you'd better pray she recovers. If she doesn't, one way or another, you're finished as a surgeon. I mean that. You won't be able to operate on a fucking mouse when I'm through."

"Are you threatening me?"

"You bet your fucking ass I am."

He stomped out of the room and slammed the door.

CHAPTER 59

At dinner that night, I told Cassie what had happened. I moved food around my plate, not hungry and barely containing my anger. But this was my wife's father, a world-renowned surgeon, and I held my temper.

"What did you do to piss him off?"

"Became a Jew." I sipped my wine.

"No, really."

"Really, that's it. He's been angry since midnight mass two months ago."

"But he wouldn't lie to a patient about what happened in the OR."

"He did, damn it. He pinned his error on his Jewish son-in-law. He not only lied to Stan Dabro, but the entire hospital is buzzing about Goerner's mistake—*my* mistake! Several doctors asked me what happened, and when I gave them my version, they looked at me like I was from Mars. How could the great Iron Balls make such a mistake?"

"How did the patient do?"

"Not well. I checked on her just before I came home, and she's not regained consciousness. She had no blood pressure for less than two or three minutes when she bled in the OR—I switched her to bypass circulation as soon as I took over—so I doubt that caused any permanent damage. I don't know how long it took her husband to call

911 and get her to the hospital, but I'd bet that's when she developed brain damage."

"What're you going to do?"

"If she recovers, it'll all probably blow over."

"If not?"

I finished my glass and poured another. "Get a lawyer. Stan Dabro's going to sue."

∽

Michelle Dabro never regained consciousness and died four days later.

∽

A lawyer from the university's Risk Management office called me at home, early the next morning. We met in his office before I started operating, and I explained what'd happened.

"That's not how Dr. McManning tells it. The scrub nurse, Larry Finn, and the anesthesiologist, Brad Singleton, support McManning's version."

"They what?" I'm sure my look showed the surprise I felt. I couldn't believe they'd lie.

"Both backed him."

"Did you check with Virginia Strozky? She'll tell the truth."

"I did." He stared at me from behind his desk, fingers interlocked church-like and resting in front of him.

"And?" I stared back.

"She supported your story, but I know she and McManning have some past issues and don't get along." He unlaced his fingers and drummed on the desktop, seemingly impatient to be done with this.

"So you believe McManning's buddies instead of her?"

His delayed response confirmed my suspicion. Iron Balls was chief of surgery, and I was only a resident in training. I could be replaced; he couldn't.

278

"What're the next steps?" I rose from the chair, paced in front of his desk, and prepared to leave. This guy didn't give a damn about saving my ass, only McManning's.

"I'm trying to head off a lawsuit, Doctor. Please sit back down." He shuffled some papers on his desk and continued. "We have persuaded Stan Dabro to attend a hearing by Indiana University's Grievance Committee. That'll be followed by an adjudication from an independent three-panel Medical Review Board. If they decide you've committed malpractice, we go to court. If not, we call it an unavoidable complication and move on."

"Who's on the review board?"

"Three people you won't know. A non-IU surgeon, an ethicist, and a lawyer."

"When?"

"The Grievance Committee meets tomorrow morning, the Medical Review Board in the afternoon."

"Glad you gave me all this warning. Thanks." I stormed out.

CHAPTER 60

The next morning, we met in the university's board room, a pine-paneled chamber with a large oval mahogany table in the center that sat fifteen. Adam Cherney, MD, JD, a slim, gray-haired middle-aged man with a narrow mustache and trimmed goatee, occupied the black-leather high-backed chair at the head of the table. He looked more lawyer than physician, wearing a trim blue suit and matching vest with a white shirt and red bowtie.

"I call this Grievance Committee meeting to order. We're here to discuss the unfortunate death of Michelle Dabro, who underwent surgery for a ruptured ascending aorta five days ago. Mr. Dabro"—Cherney looked up from his notes—"I want to convey the condolences of all of us here. We all regret the passing of your wife."

Dabro nodded.

"This committee meeting will be recorded." Cherney pointed to a stenographer sitting behind him. "We'll begin by going around the table and having each person state his or her name and position. I'll start."

The attendees included the people in the OR and three members of the Medical Review Board.

"I will now read into the record the statements prepared by the surgeons Drs. McManning and Goerner; the anesthesiologist, Dr.

Brad Singleton; the scrub nurse, Larry Finn; and the head circulating nurse, Virginia Strozky."

When Cherney finished, he asked each of us for additions or corrections to our personal statements. There were none.

"It's clear the recollections of the participants differ, and we'll discuss that in a moment. I want to stress that this meeting is not like a trial with cross-examination by lawyers. It is fact-finding, and we're just going to hear statements from the participants. If this case goes to trial, there'll be plenty of time for questions. Any issues with that?"

Silence.

"Now we'll hear the autopsy report of Michelle Dabro, prepared by the head of pathology, Dr. Pamela Page, which was not available until this morning. Dr. Page, the floor is yours."

Pam Page was a grandmotherly-looking lady with a bun of gray hair gathered at the back of her head. She wore a physician's white coat, brightened by a pink-and-yellow scarf around her neck. She projected PowerPoint slides while describing the pathology of the aortic graft that had torn loose and that was then securely sewn in place. She also showed images of Michelle's brain, with changes indicating lack of blood flow. She made no mention of blame.

I watched Stan Dabro's face during the presentation. He showed no emotion. I didn't think I could have watched pictures of Cassie's organs without displaying feelings of grief or anger or both.

"It seems we're at somewhat of an impasse," Cherney said. "The autopsy confirms that sutures of the initial graft placement tore loose but doesn't identify who did that placement. Dr. McManning, Dr. Singleton, and Nurse Finn state it was Dr. Goerner, while Dr. Goerner and Nurse Strozky maintain it was Dr. McManning. Comments from anyone?"

I needed to prove McManning and friends were lying. "Can we see the slides again, please?"

Pam Page flashed them on the screen.

I carefully studied the picture of the graft. "Dr. Cherney, may I ask Larry Finn a question?"

"Certainly."

"Larry, what sutures did Dr. McManning use to—as you claim—repair my mistake?"

"He used 3.0 propylene, as he always does in such a repair," Finn answered.

"And what did I use?"

"You asked for 4.0 propylene and felt pledgets," Virginia Strozky interrupted from her seat. "I remember because they were not on the operative tray, and I got them for you, at Larry's request."

"That's true," Finn confirmed.

I turned to the pathologist. "Dr. Page, can you distinguish 3.0 from 4.0 sutures at autopsy?"

"Yes."

"What's the difference?"

"The suture number indicates suture size. As the number increases, suture diameter decreases," Page replied.

"So 4.0 has a smaller diameter than 3.0, correct?"

"Yes."

"And the smaller the size, the less tensile strength, correct?"

"Yes."

"And the tensile strength should be as strong as the tissue into which the suture is sewn so that the suture doesn't tear through the tissue, correct?"

"Yes."

"Dr. Page, what are felt pledgets?"

"They are tiny squares of synthetic material placed between the suture and the tissue to prevent the suture from tearing through the tissue."

I turned back to Larry. "So, Larry, is it possible that the 3.0 sutures Dr. McManning used tore through the weakened aortic wall, while the 4.0 sutures supported by the felt pledgets did not?"

"That's possible, but it's also possible that the 4.0 sutures you used weren't strong enough to—"

I cut him off and fixed my gaze on Pam Page. "Dr. Page, the sutures used to repair the tear should overlie the first set of sutures that caused it, correct?"

A big smile lit Page's face as she saw where I was going. "Yes."

"Please examine the slide, and tell me which sutures were placed first, causing the tear, and which were placed second."

"From the picture, it is clear to me that the 3.0 sutures were first, and the 4.0 with the felt pledgets were placed on top of them."

"Thank you." I sat down.

"Dr. McManning, from that, it would appear you performed the initial suturing that led to the tear. Any response?" Cherney asked, sounding like a prosecutor, despite his opening statement that this inquiry was not to be a trial.

McManning pushed back from the table and stood with such force that his chair bounced with a loud thump off the wall behind him. His face was dark, eyes squinty, and bloodless lips formed a flat gash across his face. "Show those slides again," he said, striding to the screen.

When they appeared, he bent his head close to the picture and studied the image of the graft. Finally, he stood and faced the group.

"There's no way from these images that you can know, to a reasonable degree of medical certainty, which set of sutures was sewn first or second. Dr. Page, you're influenced because you saw the actual heart. I'd need to study the heart myself to be sure. I assume you preserved it."

She gave a sheepish headshake. "Actually, no, I did not. I was told that the deceased must be buried as she entered the world, with all her organs. So the heart went with the body."

All eyes turned to Stan Dabro, who nodded.

"Can the body be exhumed?" McManning asked.

"She was cremated."

"Then, I would offer, as Dr. Cherney said earlier, that we are at an impasse, and, lacking the opportunity to study the organ in question, the issue cannot be resolved." McManning sat back down with a satisfied look.

"How long has it been since your last physical, Dr. McManning?" Cherney asked.

"Many months. Why?"

"You pushed the Credentials Committee to extend your operative privileges beyond the age-sixty-five cutoff. It is reasonable for this committee to consider whether your age could have impaired your judgment as to the choice of suture or, if not that, could have affected your technical skills."

"I object to that question; it implies that I was the one who performed the initial improper repair. I maintain it was Dr. Goerner."

The room fell silent. Cherney studied his notes, and Dabro sat expressionless, hands folded in his lap, thumbs twitching.

"May I say a few words, Dr. Cherney?" I asked.

"Certainly."

I stood and walked to the head of the table. The sentiments of Pope John Paul II, echoed by Monsignor Sparkle, ran through my mind about a wish for peace and love between Christians and Jews.

I rested my fingertips on the table's edge, leaned forward to engage the group, and looked at each person for a moment as I spoke.

"I've known Dr. McManning for almost two years and, as many of you are aware, I'm married to his daughter, Cassie. So you might think my remarks are out of support for him because he's my father-in-law. That is not true. In our private lives, we disagree about some major issues, and he has strong—shall we say, unenthusiastic—personal feelings about me. However, those disagreements are exactly that—intense but personal.

"I want to separate the person from the surgeon to speak about his surgical skills and his care of his patients. There is no surgeon at the university—or any I met during my four years in the army—better skilled, mentally or technically, and no one who places his patients' needs before his own more than he does. A famous physician said many years ago that the proper care *of* the patient is caring *for* the patient. Dr. McManning epitomizes that physician role model, and we would all do well to emulate him as a surgeon.

"Having said that, I think he made an error in judgment during the Dabro surgery—he chose the 3.0 sutures, but it was something any one of us could have done, thinking the aortic tissue was more normal and stronger than it was. We've all made a bad call in the

OR at some time or other. I was fortunate to have profited from his decision and chose the thinner suture, 4.0. Had I been the surgeon in charge, I would have likely called for the 3.0 suture initially also."

I looked around the room. "But I don't think that's what caused Mrs. Dabro's death." I focused on Pam Page. "Dr. Page, you described significant brain changes at autopsy from lack of blood flow. How long would flow to the brain need to be stopped for those changes to occur?"

"Brain cells are extremely sensitive to lack of blood. They begin to die in four to five minutes. Her changes were so extensive I would think she had no blood flow to her brain for at least ten to fifteen minutes."

"Thank you. Dr. Singleton, you monitored her blood pressure during surgery. How long was her pressure at zero?"

"About two minutes," Singleton said.

"Thank you. So the brain damage found at autopsy could not have resulted from the graft pulling loose."

I was tempted to ask Stan Dabro how long it took him to call 911, but my gut said not to go there. If he'd been having sex with her when her aorta ruptured, he probably had enough guilt without my adding fuel. McManning had warned her to refrain from any stressful activity until surgery. She'd even joked about it. I could imagine Dabro coercing her into having sex one last time before her operation. He'd have to live with that.

I looked at him. "Mr. Dabro, nothing I say can ever replace your loss, but I firmly believe one of us made an unfortunate—but understandable—error in judgment that was quickly corrected and was not a cause of her death. She died because of aortic rupture prior to—not during—surgery."

We locked eyes. His dark, crinkly brow, compacted lips, and fists clenching and unclenching on the table in front of him left no doubt about his feelings, but it was clear in my own mind that if he sued, he'd lose. I hoped, as a lawyer, he realized that also.

Dr. Cherney stood, gently nudged me aside, and addressed the group. "I think we're done here, unless anyone has anything to say."

He took a deep breath and looked at each face. No one said anything. "Let's adjourn and leave this room to the Medical Review Board for their deliberations, which, I understand, will be held in private."

I anticipated McManning saying something to me after the meeting, but he departed with Dabro. I trailed behind them and overheard Dabro mutter, "That fucking Jew. He killed Michelle. He's not going to get away with it."

I expected McManning to defend me, as I had him, but instead, he patted Dabro on the back in a comforting "there, there" gesture, and they walked out.

CHAPTER 61

I was seething. This paragon of a surgeon was an anti-Semitic bastard. I'd tried to keep his bigoted beliefs from influencing my respect for him as a surgeon. After all, I still listened to *Lohengrin* and *The Ring Cycle*, even though Wagner was an anti-Semite. And I applauded Lindbergh's solo flight across the Atlantic, even though he'd been a staunch Hitler supporter. But McManning's anti-Semitism was too personal, and I shouldn't have defended him.

I recounted the day's events for Cassie over a Beefeater gin martini before dinner. I rarely drank gin, but I was not on call and needed that to calm down.

"Thanks for what you said about Dad as a surgeon. I guess he thought the same of you since he wanted you to operate with him, despite being upset that you've become Jewish."

"Yeah, great. He respects me as a surgeon so much that he told Dabro I killed his wife and then said nothing when Dabro threatened that he was not going to let me get away with it. Your dad's an anti-Semite, Cassie. You know that. He and Dabro are a pair."

Cassie's look was pained, as if I'd just slapped her.

"Sorry, honey, but I regret defending him. My tribute obviously doesn't extend to the man."

"You know the National Academy of Surgeons?" she asked.

"Of course. It's the Hall of Fame for surgeons."

"Dad was nominated for membership years ago. Didn't get accepted. He said there was a Jewish member who blackballed him, and that kept him out. I don't know if it's true, but he's had a problem with Jews ever since."

"Weak excuse."

Cassie shrugged. "Any word from the Medical Review Board?" she asked, changing the subject.

"No, but I'm sure they'll find no evidence of malpractice and recommend against a lawsuit."

"Will that stop Dabro?"

"Not necessarily. If he and his wife were having sex when her aorta ruptured, he's got to feel guilty as hell, a good reason to shift the blame to me. But he knows any good defense attorney will take him apart in court."

The phone's ring interrupted us. Cassie checked the receiver; then looked at me. "It's Dr. Cherney."

My gut constricted, and I took in a deep breath. "Good evening, Dr. Cherney."

"Evening, Gabe. Congratulations. The Medical Review Board decided this was an unfortunate complication, not malpractice, and recommended no further action. Stan Dabro was livid but accepted that decision, so you're off the hook."

Even though I knew Dabro could not win, a huge weight lifted from my chest, and I breathed a deep sigh of relief. "That's great." I pumped a victory fist in the air. "Thanks for your help."

"Keep up your good work. You're on track to become an outstanding heart surgeon. I've heard rumors you're going to be asked to be chief surgical resident for next year. That's quite an honor."

"Thank you, sir, and thanks again for helping with this case."

I hugged and kissed my wife. "Thank you for believing in me, Cassie. I know it's hard being estranged from your dad. I didn't mean to put you in such an uncomfortable position."

"It has been difficult," Cassie said. "How about dinner with Dad to work things out between us? He's my only family, other than you and Zoey. I don't want to lose that."

CHAPTER 62

I was driving to work at five the next morning for early rounds when Cassie called. She'd been sound asleep when I left. Something was wrong.

"What's up, Cassie?"

"It's your dad, Gabe." Her voice broke into sobs. "He died during sleep last night. Your mom just called. She didn't want to call you in case you were operating."

"Oh, my God." Tears flooded my eyes and blurred my vision. "Wait a minute."

I pulled off the road at the next intersection and breathed fast to regain control. While his health had been dwindling, when death finally came it was always a shock.

I turned off the motor. "What did Mom say, Cassie?"

"Just that when she woke this morning, he was dead. He died peacefully sometime during the night."

"I'll call her right now. You okay?"

"I am. Be careful driving."

I sat for a moment, thinking about my dad, about Grandpa Jakob's memoir, and about what he, my father, and Great-Grandfather Solomon had lived through. I remembered what Jakob had written about Janusz Korczak and his orphanage. One of Korczak's dreams had been that the children would grow up to live normal lives, despite the horror around them. My father came pretty close to doing that, thanks to the sacrifices of so many.

I calmed down and called my mother.

"Mom? How are you? I'm so sorry. I'll catch the next flight out."

Her voice was soft, subdued, sad. She sounded tired, probably all cried out. "I'm okay, I guess; feeling empty. He was not doing well, especially after our last trip to see you. The last two days were the worst. He didn't know who I was or where he was. I dreaded thinking he might die a lingering death. Thank God, he went quickly and didn't suffer. I can't ask for more than that."

"I'm so sorry." I fought back more tears. I was afraid if I started crying, so would she. "I'll fly out—"

"No. I don't want you to come here, Gabe. I'm going to fly to Indy later today with Dad's coffin, as soon as they get him ready. If I buried him here and then moved to Indy, I'd never get to visit him."

"True. Stay with us until you find a place of your own."

"I think he'd like to be buried as a Jew in a Jewish cemetery. There's one in Indianapolis called Beth-El Zedeck South Cemetery."

"Yeah. I've been going to services at Beth-El synagogue. How can I help?"

"Arrange things with the cemetery and meet us at the airport. We'll arrive tonight at eight thirty."

"Will do." My voice choked. "I loved him."

"I know you did, Gabe. I did, too. He lived a good life. He was one of the lucky ones; one of the survivors."

We buried Dad the next day at Beth-El Zedeck Cemetery. It was just Cassie, Mom, me, the rabbi, and a couple of friends from the hospital. Following the burial, we returned to our house to sit shiva, the seven days of mourning, according to Jewish tradition. It was a time for spiritual and emotional healing, to share memories, and to have a bite of food or a drink with friends and relatives. Some brought a little remembrance of the deceased, or a plate of food, or a bottle of wine.

As much as I wanted to be alone with just Mom and Cassie, visitors were a welcome distraction.

The first few evenings drew the most people, and we had a steady stream of hospital folks paying their respects, including Virginia Strozky, Larry Finn, and Brad Singleton. No one discussed the Dabro disaster. We reminisced and told happy stories about Dad, about the family. The memories *were* a blessing.

I stayed up late on the final shiva night, long after the last person had left, hoping Jim McManning might still show. Cassie and my mom went upstairs to bed. I was sitting alone, drinking a Macallan, when the doorbell rang. I hurried to answer it, thinking it might be McManning.

I opened the door. A tall, broad-shouldered man wearing a white mask held a gun pointed at my chest.

CHAPTER 63

"Hands high," he said, "where I can see them."

I tried to slam the door, but he wedged his shoulder against it and forced his way in.

"Who are you? What do you want?" I took a second look at the mask. A black swastika had been crudely crayoned on each side. In a flash, I was transported to the Warsaw ghetto. I half expected him to shout, *"Raus, Jude."*

He pushed forward, with the gun barrel jammed in my stomach, forcing me back into the room. "Sit down," he ordered. "Do as I say, and maybe I'll let you live."

He motioned to the dining room table, and I sat down. My pulse raced, and my mind skittered in crazy hops.

"What do you want?" I repeated, louder this time, hoping Cassie or Mom was still awake. My heart thumped so loudly I imagined Cassie could hear it. "I don't keep much cash in the house."

"Not interested in your money. I'm just a paid messenger, making good on a promise from a mutual acquaintance. This won't take long. You right- or left-handed?"

"None of your—"

His free hand lashed out and slapped me across the face. "Right or left?"

When I didn't answer, he reached for an empty glass on the table and flipped it at me. I blocked it with my right hand.

"Thanks," he said. Still pointing the gun at me, he reached into his pocket and withdrew a folding knife. He punched a button on the handle, and a blade flipped open, glinting in the overhead light.

"Palms flat on the table."

I didn't move.

"Now! Do it now!"

Bang!

The bullet caught him in the shoulder, and he dropped the knife. I whirled to see Cassie standing in her pink nightgown at the foot of the stairs. She was holding the 9mm Beretta I'd taught her how to use after a shooter killed eleven Jews at a synagogue in Pittsburgh.

Before I could act, he fired.

Cassie staggered, and the top of her pink nightgown began to turn red.

I grabbed the knife from the floor and jammed it into his gut. He dropped his gun and wrapped both hands around mine. He shouldered me aside as he fought to pull the blade out.

A second shot rang out. The man collapsed to the floor.

I ran to Cassie and pressed my fingers against her chest to staunch the bleeding. "I called 911 from upstairs," she whispered, her voice faltering. "Here any minute." She faded out of consciousness.

I bent my head to her, fighting to calm the terror of a husband with the judgment of a physician. I felt her pulse—fast and thready; checked her breathing—rapid and shallow. "Shush, my darling. Save your strength. We'll have you in the hospital quickly." She didn't respond. Her eyes stared at the ceiling.

The piercing din of sirens jarred the night, and whirling red lights swamped the driveway as a police car, trailed by an ambulance, drove up. The front door to the house was partially ajar, and two police officers, with guns drawn, raced in, followed by two emergency medical techs. One EMT went to Cassie and prodded me aside. The other examined the masked man, but quickly joined us. They packed gauze against Cassie's chest. One started an IV, and the other left for a moment and returned, pushing a stretcher.

The officers checked on the intruder. "Dead," one of them said. "Search the house."

"No need; he was alone." I briefed them while holding Cassie's hand as the EMTs lifted her onto the stretcher. "I'm going with my wife, officers. Can one of you stay until I return? My mother and daughter are upstairs sleeping."

Incredibly, Mom had not awoken, probably deafened by the bedside white-noise machine she used to sleep.

In the ambulance, I knelt beside Cassie and stroked her face. I told her that I loved her and kissed her cold, unresponsive lips. I felt for a carotid pulse—weak and fast. She was panting for breath, frothy sputum bubbling from her nose. A bullet hole oozed red beneath her left collar bone. I adjusted the oxygen mask on her face, and the EMT increased the flow rate.

"Blood pressure?"

"Seventy systolic," the EMT said.

"She's bleeding into her lung. Have you got O-negative blood?"

"We don't carry blood, just plasma." He started a second IV and opened the stopcock to let the plasma run in at full speed.

"Did you call ahead for a surgeon and an operating room? She needs to go to surgery immediately."

He nodded. "They're waiting for us. ETA about three minutes."

The ambulance screeched to a stop in front of the emergency room entrance, where a group of white-coated people stood. They off-loaded Cassie and ran inside, pushing her stretcher.

I followed and came face-to-face with Jim McManning. "What are you doing here?"

"I'm the on-call surgeon. I could ask you the same—" He broke off when he saw Cassie. "Oh, my God. Oh, no! No!"

The ER techs rushed the stretcher to the small operating room in the emergency department. We had no time to go to the main OR.

In seconds, McManning and I dressed in caps, masks, sterile gloves, and gowns. He took over as the surgeon in charge. Larry

Finn, the scrub nurse, was already in place. Virginia Strozky helped the x-ray tech take a portable and then dashed an antiseptic solution over Cassie's chest. Another nurse infused packed red blood cells into both IVs.

McManning and I stood on opposite sides of Cassie, lying on the OR table. Larry handed McManning a scalpel. Singleton had begun anesthesia. He nodded, and McManning raised the scalpel over her chest. His hand stayed in the air and began to tremble, small shakes initially and then violently. Beads of sweat popped out on his forehead, and his eyes looked wild. He started to sway.

"I can't do this. She's my daughter, for Christ's sake. *She's my daughter!*"

I moved to the other side of the table, grabbed the scalpel from his hand, and shoved him aside.

"You may not have pulled the trigger, Jim, but you caused this. You and your anti-Semitic buddy, Dabro." I held up my gloved hands and wiggled my fingers. "The hired gun failed. These still work. Now, get the hell out of my OR so I can save my wife's life."

His face turned chalk white, and he clutched his chest. With a groan, he collapsed to the floor.

Virginia ran to him and began CPR.

CHAPTER 64

With Larry doubling as both a surgical nurse and an assistant surgeon, I opened Cassie's chest. Fortunately, the bullet was small caliber—maybe from a .22 handgun; it had collapsed Cassie's left lung but had done very little other damage. I dug it out, tied off the bleeders, and then sewed the hole in her lung closed. Singleton reinflated her lung.

"Status, Brad?"

"Three units of blood in. Pressure's one hundred systolic, oxygen sat 95 percent. She'll make it fine."

"Thank God. Lung's repaired, and I'm going to close her chest."

After I finished and saw Cassie safely off to the recovery room, I checked on McManning. He'd just come out of the catheterization lab.

"How bad?" I asked the cardiologist, Charley Harrison.

"Acute infarction caused cardiac arrest, probably from the strain of facing surgery on his daughter. Virginia resuscitated him with one shock from the defibrillator, and we rushed him to catheterization. His circumflex coronary artery is totally occluded, the left anterior descending 95 percent blocked, and his right coronary partially occluded. Left main is about 60 percent. No option for a stent. He needs immediate bypass surgery if he's going to survive."

"Did you call for surgical backup?"

Harry pointed to the clock on the wall that showed three a.m. and shook his head. "He's on his way to OR 1 to be prepped for surgery. You're it."

McManning's oft-repeated cliche, "Great surgeons would rather operate than eat," ran through my mind as I raced upstairs and began to re-scrub outside OR 1. Regardless of personal feelings, I had to operate on this anti-Semite to save his life.

CHAPTER 65

Both Cassie and McManning sailed through their post-op recoveries. Cassie went home in three days to finish recuperating, with my mom's assistance; McManning, two days after that, supported by 24-7 home nursing care.

I took several days off to be with my wife. We talked nonstop and agreed that Grandpa Jakob was right—it was safer being a Catholic—and Cassie opted for that. What to do with Zoey was the major issue.

"She's the future, Cassie," I argued. "Without Zoey and children like her, Judaism will eventually perish, and all the suffering and lives lost will have been in vain. I won't let that happen. I *can't* let that happen."

Cassie agreed we'd raise her Jewish, despite the perils. I promised that if she ever was in any danger, we could reconsider.

I brought charges against Dabro, but, smart lawyer that he was, he beat them. With the intruder dead and no provable ties to Dabro, the issue died with him.

McManning came for dinner from time to time, always with a bouquet of fresh flowers for his daughter. I was cordial but cool. He reduced his OR schedule, taking on only simple cases, and stopped operating within a year. Without the OR, he aged rapidly. The university created a search committee to select his replacement and, after screening a dozen candidates from all over the US, chose me, the youngest chief of surgery in its history. McManning died from a stroke the week after I was installed. He never spoke of Dabro or admitted complicity, but the way he treated Cassie told me all I needed to know.

I reread Jakob's memoir and relived my family's struggle against the Nazis so often that it soon became a part of me, as if I'd fought the battles and trudged the sewers alongside them. I was proud of their struggle and would do what I could to keep their memories alive so history did not repeat itself.

Becoming Jewish and facing anti-Semitism was like inheriting an old house. I didn't cause the leaks or crumbling walls, but it was mine now to try to fix. I couldn't change the past, but I could impact the future. I'd start with my daughter. For Jews to survive, the most important thing we could never forget was that we could never forget.

AUTHOR'S NOTE

Ari's Spoon is historical fiction, based on historical events and real people. It explores ethical issues of Jewish children raised by Catholics under very difficult circumstances and portrays the heroism of a group of Jews, fighting for their survival during World War II. The novel covers only a portion of the actual events that took place during the days of the Warsaw Ghetto Uprising. An outstanding day-by-day accounting is brilliantly presented in *The Bravest Battle* by Dan Kurzman.

The Holmberg/Goerner characters and exploits are fictitious, as are Rachel Glowinski, Jim McManning, the IU hospital people, and hospital events. I altered many of the scenes and incidents in Warsaw and the ghetto to include the Holmberg and Glowinski families. Most of the events took place, just without these characters. The uprising and deportations to the Umschlagplatz, Treblinka, and the other death camps were all real. The dates of the various events are correct, gleaned from multiple sources. The Ringelblum Archive is real, based on the two milk canisters unearthed in 1946 and ten metal boxes in 1950, well depicted in *Notes from the Warsaw Ghetto, from the Journal of Emanuel Ringelblum*, translated and edited by Jacob Sloan. Jakob's memoir, hidden in Torah and prayer books and buried in the Jewish cemetery, is fictitious.

Irena Sendler (1919–2008) and her accomplishments were real. She is credited with saving 2,500 children and is memorialized in Israel as Righteous Among the Nations. She was captured and imprisoned in Pawiak Prison from October 20, 1942, through January 20, 1943. She never revealed any names, despite intense torture. She was freed, not by Jakob but via a large bribe that Zegota furnished to a prison guard, who let her escape. Her life is portrayed vividly in two memorable books: *Life in a Jar* by Jack Mayer and *Irena's Children* by Tilar J. Mazzeo.

Dr. Janusz Korczak and his orphanage were real, as were the scenes describing the capture and march to the Umschlagplatz and the decorum he and his charges displayed. Jerzy Rudnicki is fictitious, though similar events happened. The Boduen's Children's Home is real and still exists, as do many of the Catholic sanctuaries, such as the Franciscan Sisters of the Mother of Mary, which provided safe haven to children of all religions during the war.

Mordechai (Angel) Anielewicz (1919–May 8, 1943) was the commander in chief of the Zydowska Organizacja Bojowa (ZOB), led the Warsaw Ghetto Uprising, and died a hero in the Mila bunker with his sweetheart, Mira Fuchrer. Shmuel Asher was the thief in charge of the bunker at 18 Mila Street and accepted the Nazis' final offer to leave but was probably sent to Treblinka. Events similar to the baptism gown and engraved spoon occurred but not by Shmuel Asher to the Holmberg family. Marek Edelman (1922–2009) took over the ZOB after Angel died and participated in the Polish Resistance. He became a noted Polish cardiologist. I "extended" his life a few years so he could interact with Gabe. He wrote *The Ghetto Fights* and gave an interview of his life, published in the book *Shielding the Flame* by Hanna Krall.

Many heart-rending nonfiction books have been written by actual survivors of the ghetto, along with notable novels, such as *The Wall* by John Hersey and *Mila 18* by Leon Uris. Sadly, those books, like mine, may chronicle reality but rarely change it.

Printed in the United States
by Baker & Taylor Publisher Services